5-14

D0896512

DRAIN YOU

DATE

BRODART, CO.

SCHLEICHER CO. PUBLIC LIBRARY
BOX 611-201 S MAIN
PH 325-853-3767
ELDORADO, TEXAS 76936-0611

DRAIN YOU

M. BETH BLOOM

SCHLEICHER CO. PUBLIC LIBRARY
BOX 611-201 S MAIN
PH 325-853-3767
ELDORADO, TEXAS 76936-0611

An imprint of HarperCollinsPublishers

HarperTeen is an imprint of HarperCollins Publishers.

Drain You

Copyright © 2012 by M. Beth Bloom

All rights reserved. Printed in the United States of America. No part
of this book may be used or reproduced in any manner whatsoever
without written permission except in the case of brief quotations
embodied in critical articles and reviews. For information address
HarperCollins Children's Books, a division of HarperCollins
Publishers, 10 East 53rd Street, New York, NY 10022.

www.epicreads.com

Library of Congress Cataloging-in-Publication
Bloom, M. B., (date)
    Drain you / M.B. Bloom. — 1st ed.
        p.   cm.
    Summary: Even after Quinn Lacey learns that the coast of
Southern California is crawling with vampires, she still tries to
keep her job at the video store, convince her parents that she is
eating well, and rescue her best friend from a fate worse than death.
    ISBN 978-0-06-203686-5 (pbk. bdg.)
    [1. Vampires—Fiction. 2. Los Angeles (Calif.)—Fiction.] I. Title.
PZ7.B816153Dr 2012   2011016551
[Fic]—dc23   CIP
                                                                  AC

Typography by Torborg Davern
12 13 14 15 16   LP/RRDH   10 9 8 7 6 5 4 3 2 1

First Edition

FOR D.B.

PART ONE

I.

SHEETS

The canyons were hot at night, even with the desert winds whipping through the hills. Everything was dry. Branches were matchsticks waiting to be lit; the leaves just brushfires that hadn't happened yet. I wished the rocks were ice cubes in a glass. Everything looked thirsty.

Through the main store window I watched a man slink sheepishly out of his car toward our video slot to return his probably overdue rental.

Sitting on the countertop with my legs dangling, I peered down into the drawer where the drop box emptied. Soft-core. *Sigh*. I had zero work to do, but I wasn't going to file it. I'd leave it there in the box to grow legs and walk itself back to the rack.

Out on the floor a woman my mother's age was staring

at the Action shelf, puzzled. She'd been in here at least an hour, maybe more. Morgan sat next to me, silently reading the *Weekly*. The overhead TV was playing a bad eighties movie with James Spader that I didn't remember picking, though I knew tonight was Wednesday, lady's choice. I looked from Spader to Morgan to our only customer to my hands. My pinkie was getting its last coat.

"Your fingernails look pretty . . . stupid," Morgan said suddenly, without moving his eyes from the paper.

I held out a hand and stared at it, tilting my head. I'd painted each nail a different color—Electric Blue, Flamingo, Vixen, Shamrock—and was seeing them now as I'd never meant them to be: sort of raver-ish. I rested them on my dirty Doc Martens to dry, noticing then that my laces were all wrong, a hole had been skipped, and the crossing pattern was a mess. I looked down at my ripped tights and baggy work shirt with the crooked Video Journeys stencil, and straightened my dad's suit vest, covered in the daily flair of band buttons and rhinestone pins. I wasn't wearing any pants, or shorts, or a skirt, just a shirt long enough to keep me decent. Underwear as outerwear, whatever. My hair was in knots, and I fingered the few strands I'd braided a week ago and considered the insult. It was accurate but hardly biting.

"Stupid," I said, my eyes flashing across my rainbow

fingernails again, "compared to what?"

It was the first week of summer vacation, and I felt compelled to be a cool slob. It was effortless, really.

"Good point," Morgan said without looking up.

The chemical stench of a counter full of Wet N Wild nail polish was starting to get to me. The heat plus the fumes plus the drone of the TV were making me feel so dazed that waving my rainbow nails back and forth in front of my eyes left color trails. I took some deep breaths, then put my elbows on the counter, held my head in my hands, and waited for more nothing to happen. Morgan started reading me a review of some new Drew Barrymore thing while I played with the nail polish bottles, stacking them, rolling them, switching their tops. When Morgan finished the review, I thought he'd turn the page and read something else, but he just closed the *Weekly* and zoned out. I peeked through my bangs to watch him watching the Spader movie. I tried to gauge his mood.

Then I said, "Hey, go help that lady. She's been here for-ev-er." I dragged the word across its three full, excruciating syllables. "I think she's lost. Or something."

He looked away from the screen but not at the paper and not at her and not at me. No one else was in the store.

"My nails are wet," I said. I blew on my fingertips and could see the paint was already smudged on every nail but the thumbs. I touched the thumbs and smudged them too, then started to seriously pick at them, chipping the polish, screwing everything up.

"Morgan," I said.

Then the action woman sighed and left without renting anything. We were alone again.

It was ten to eleven, almost closing time, and we'd rented maybe fifteen movies all night. I got up and walked aimlessly around the store, reading cop movie taglines, idly dusting shelves, rifling through the customer suggestion box. *Yr imployees are way rude*, read one. I read it out loud for Morgan. He let out a small, amused sound, but it wasn't a laugh. We didn't share jokes as much these days. I hated when he acted moody, but I still couldn't give Morgan everything he wanted, because there was just no way.

I used the pencil dangling from a string above the box to cross out and retouch a few letters. *Yr imployees are way rad*. Total improvement.

I glanced over at the counter where Morgan was still staring up into the TV screen with a tired but frustrated look in his eyes. I knew that look better than I wanted to—and I knew better to ignore it. Which was no biggie at school. There we were friends. Not *friends*-friends, not study buddies or lunch dates, just generic friends. But at work he was my *only* friend, and that disparity was what led us into so many poorly written romantic sitcom subplots.

In the past year this shared boredom and solitude and isolation had sometimes prompted me to hang on Morgan even though I had no real reason to; in most ways he barely stood out to me. I realized it was almost strange how common and unspecific I found him: blond, semi-handsome, typically Californian. It was easy to imagine Morgan on the beach, but he wasn't a beachy guy. He was serious, took himself seriously, and had once projected that onto me, unsuccessfully. So now he mainly treated me like some cute, messy pet who drank too much soda too late at night, forgot to brush her hair in the shower, and lost her keys in the laundry. When she did laundry.

Closing time was always the worst, when we'd start to shut the store down and turn off all the lights. Morgan would stand close and watch me count the money, his eyes fixed on my lips as they mouthed the amounts. But nothing ever happened, and so things were fine, better than fine even, and that was it. People talked about us like we were a secret couple, trysting around the video store after hours, and Morgan never denied the rumors, so I pretended to ignore them. I guess it made me seem unavailable, which I liked, or cool and experienced, which would help later when I was interested in seeming available again. I was at various times in our non-courtship flattered, worried, irritated, bored.

And right now I was bored. I waved my hand in front of his eyes to break his stare. "James Spader is a total jerk."

"Quinlan"—and it *was* kind of sexy when he called me by my full name—"do you need some attention?"

"No." I put my hands on my hips. I rolled my eyes. "Maybe."

Morgan huffed a short exhale through his nostrils.

"Who's cooler, Drew or me?" It was shameless and random, but I couldn't help it. We were alone, and the humpday hump was starting to feel like a mountain. I reconsidered; maybe he was *my* pet.

I tried to take it back and started to say, "Drew's a babe," but then instead, "Who cares?"

But this time he looked at me—not out into the store—and got a little too sincere. "You're, like, the coolest. You know that."

Damn. I sucked. The summer stretched out ahead of me, long and winding, and I already barely had enough deflective responses for Morgan to carry me until September. Then I'd have none left for senior year.

"Spader's the coolest, man," I said, trying to be normal. I picked up the remote and clicked off the movie. We stared at the blank screen, waiting for eleven to come and rescue us from each other.

Twenty minutes later the register was securely in the safe, the outer gates were locked, and Morgan was helping me into my holey flannel.

"Kurt's dead, dude. Surrender the fantasy," he said.

"Never fade away. Never fade away . . ." I reeled back and fell to the carpet, pretending to be badly wounded. I faked my own death, Morgan laughed.

But as I laughed with him, his expression changed. He grabbed me by the shoulder, lifted me up. "Oh my God, you gotta see this," he said, spinning me around to look out the big front window.

Naomi Sheets was crying, hysterical, out in the darkness by the side of the road.

"What is she doing?"

I squinted my eyes to see. I had no idea.

"What a freak," he said.

It wasn't the word I'd have chosen, but it wasn't far off. She looked crazy.

Naomi Sheets had never been my friend. I would almost say she'd never been anyone's friend, but that seemed too dismissive and cruel. She was rich, blandly rich, in a way that kept her safely distant and constantly busy. Naomi took horseback-riding lessons, ballet, acting classes, yoga. She crocheted, spoke three languages, played the drums, and enjoyed all her successes alone. I'd known her since our freshman year, when she transferred in from some posh Valley private school, where she was no doubt admired for her impressively golden all-over tan and eclectic skill set. That's how I thought of her and how I treated her, too: with a strange mix of reverence and confusion. Naomi was special, clearly, but she wasn't interested in being accessible. I wondered occasionally if she had hip college friends somewhere who laughed with her at the dull, forgettable high schoolers she wasted her days around.

But I knew she didn't. Naomi Sheets didn't have anyone; it was plain on her face. At school, strolling mutely through the hallways by herself, she acted like a damaged foreign exchange student, permanently lost. Some kids called her Cotton Sheets, but the nickname never fit. She was pretty and wore baby-doll dresses, Mary Jane shoes, and barrettes in her hair in a not-unstylish way. And she had these cool crooked teeth—some pointed almost like fangs and some so small they didn't touch the others—kind of like Patricia Arquette in that one movie. I imagined in an alternate universe Cotton Sheets could've been the most popular girl in school: rich, talented, skinny. But in this universe she was just a weirdo with too many teeth, too much money, too many hobbies, and too few friends. I almost liked her but hardly had a motive to. And watching her now, crying bizarrely in the shadows, I felt myself wishing we'd been friends all along.

Morgan looked at me. "What should we do?"

Suddenly it annoyed me that Naomi couldn't just pretend to hold it together so we didn't have any extra reason to gossip about her. Being a loner was one thing, but pulling a total schizo, talking-to-yourself meltdown in public was another.

"I don't know," I said. "But I'm going to go deal with it."

"Quinn, she's like possessed."

"Whatever," I said. "I'm going."

"She might get spooky on you," he said, jabbing my sides and making ghost sounds in my ear. I didn't want to laugh but did anyway, because the jabs were tickling me. Then I grabbed his wrists to stop him, and he stared into my eyes, moved one hand down to my chest, and buttoned the second button on my flannel.

"Will you let me drive you home tonight?"

"Morgan," I said, and didn't sigh.

"What?"

"Nothing." I removed his hand, unbuttoned the button, and walked toward the door.

"Fine," he said, following me.

We locked the gates, and Morgan got in his Dodge Shadow and pulled out of the Video Journeys parking lot without saying good-bye. I looked across the road and Naomi was still there, sitting on a rock, motionless.

I approached her cautiously, wondering what to say and coming up with nothing. She was facing away from the store, one hand over her face and the other by her side, balled into a fist.

"Hey, Naomi," I said, and it came out like I wanted it to—as casual as possible. "Are you, like, having a thing?"

She acted startled but stayed still. She didn't say anything for a full minute, just sat there, while I just stood there and waited for an answer. When Naomi finally said, "It's you," she didn't sound angry. "What are you doing here?"

"I work here."

"Did you see anything?"

"I saw you crying."

I don't know why, but I reached out and touched the tips of her hair. Then, I don't know why, she stood and turned and threw herself on me. But we weren't hugging, I was holding her up. If she was relieved, if she'd softened, I couldn't tell. So I just kept saying, "Hey, hey," quietly and quieter.

After a minute Naomi stepped back, and what I noticed first was that in the darkness her face didn't look sun-kissed at all, but intensely bleach-white, stern and striking, like a girl in a period piece. What I noticed second was the blood on her hands.

But there was also an eyelash on her cheek, so I focused on that instead.

"I'm okay," Naomi said.

"I know," I said back. "You've got an eyelash on your cheek."

"Where? Where?" she said frantically, and started wiping at her face.

I said, "You're supposed to make a wish, dude," but before I could finish she'd brushed the lash off and left a smear of blood beneath her right eye.

"Did I get it?"

"Yeah, but now you've got a little . . . ," I said, gesturing under my own eye.

"What?"

"Blood. I think."

Her face froze, went blank. "You better go."

"Did you fall or something?"

"I said get out of here," she said coldly. And then, emptier, "Stay away from me."

It was obvious now: Naomi Sheets didn't want friends. She didn't have any and she didn't want to make any.

I stepped back, freaked, regretting everything. I said, "Okay, it's cool, I'm leaving," realizing I should've left her alone in the first place. By now I would've been uncomfortably trapped in Morgan's passenger seat, his hand on the headrest, sneaking his fingers into my hair. Definitely preferable to this weirdness.

But Naomi was already losing it, scanning the darkness, panicked. Then she yelled out, beyond me, "Are you still here, James? Are you watching this?"

I wanted to beat it, badly, but couldn't help myself. "Who's James?"

Naomi nodded her head to indicate someone behind me. "My brother."

"I didn't know you had a brother," I said, turning around. And there he was, across the street, leaning against the wall of the video store. I thought about raising a hand to wave but didn't.

"Clean yourself up," he said to Naomi, more forcefully than I was expecting. He stepped away from the wall and took a few steps toward us, stopping in the middle of the street. Then he tilted his head in my direction, and even though it was just his profile, backlit and in shadow, I could tell he was staring at me, like we knew each other. I didn't recognize him. But I wanted to.

"Hi," I said, but he ignored it and started walking down the road, away from the video store's lights. Naomi and I didn't move until he half turned and called out over his shoulder, "Let's go." And since he meant her and him, not all of us, I still didn't move.

She seemed to have collected herself somewhat, and most of the blood was wiped off, so she looked at me and mumbled, "Sorry," then walked away, following James down the black canyon road.

"Bye," I said, but like it was a question.

The whole walk home I tried to make sense of not only what had just happened, but of Naomi as a side character in the entire context of my life. I couldn't do it, though. There were no specific memories of her at school, in the halls, in the junior/senior parking lot, during lame assemblies, gym—which we'd had together two years in a row—not so much as a single roll call stood out. She wasn't invisible; I always knew she was there. But she was like so much other background high school scenery once the summer hit—a palm tree in the library quad, teachers' notes on the dry-erase board, stickers on a locker—foggy, distant, unreal somehow.

Naomi Sheets had this whole life locked away, and however it was in actuality—full of lessons and lavishes, or strangeness and solitude—I envied her those secrets. She was thoroughly unteenage, unrevealed, and unlike me.

I thought for a second about Morgan and felt bummed, then normal. Probably just stress mixed with too many

Diet Cokes and Triscuits. My parents' cars were lined up in the driveway. The cactus garden was too manicured, the tea lights leading up the walkway to our front door an illuminated set of parallel lines. I sighed, let my shoulders slump, kicked a rock.

But the rock didn't roll.

James. He'd stopped the rock with his foot. "Nice house," he said, and bent down, tossed the rock lightly in the air, caught it, then tossed it to me. I let it fall at my feet, never lifting a hand.

"What are you doing?" I said.

"What do you mean?" He ran a hand through his hair. "Hanging out."

"Hanging out," I repeated. "Where's Naomi?"

James said nothing. He did nothing.

"Your sister's hell of weird. She never even told anyone she had a brother."

He shrugged. "Well, she does."

"Are you, like, at Cresby?" I said. Then, "Are you, like, in high school?"

"Something like that."

I nodded slowly. "Okay. Well, I'm Quinn, I live here, this is my rock." I lifted the rock. "But you know that, so . . ."

"I know who you are."

"Have we met or something?"

"No."

Then silence. Lots of silence.

"I don't get it," I said.

"I just wanted to make sure you got back safe."

"It's not the Valley, dude, it's supersafe."

"Right."

"So what happens now?"

"You go inside and I go home."

"Well, this has been a ton of fun," I said, and pulled my flannel closed, held it at the neck, then folded my arms.

"Are you cold?"

"It's eighty degrees. I'm sweating over here."

He laughed. "But you're not wearing any pants."

"Whatever," I said, rolling my eyes.

"It looks good. Your legs are . . ."

But then he stopped. And when I realized there was no adjective coming, I also realized I was holding my breath. It was like "good" meant more than "good," which it didn't. It was like "good" meant "beautiful" or "stunning" and had a capital G and was spoken in a low, smoky voice. He could have finished, *Your legs are . . . unevenly proportioned for your height and weight*, and it wouldn't have muted the chiming bells of "good."

"Cool," I said.

He shrugged. Again.

He said he was going to go but he didn't go, then he didn't say anything else, and so we just stood there. For a second I wondered if I should invite him in. We could sit on the white leather couch in the white living room that my mother had pretty much declared "off-limits" to me and my friends. We could sink our toes into the perfect white plush carpet and clink around the clear Venetian glass candies on the untouched coffee table. And under the bleached-out nouveau riche paintings with titles like *Endless Malibu Morning* and *Abstractions in Milk*, James could say "good" a hundred more times, or nothing at all.

Then I said, "You can come in if you want," but when I stretched out my arm to gesture toward the front door, the automatic porch light suddenly flashed on, and for the first time all night I saw James for real.

His hair was dirty blond and stringy, and half in his eyes. He looked like he'd been in bed all day; or else never made it to bed last night. His eyebrows were darker than the rest of his hair, and his eyelashes were too long, making his face seem almost feminine. Like a greasy pretty boy. Like a Calvin Klein model. His left ear had a diamond stud. His eyes were colorless, maybe gray, but I couldn't really tell. James was wearing an old, ripped, plain white V-neck T-shirt, a little too baggy. The collar was stretched, there was a tear on the top of the shoulder seam, and a simple gold cross on a gold chain hung around his neck. He wore jeans with the knees frayed, ringed with slight white strands of shredded thread, and he tucked them into a pair of beat-up high-top black Converses. He was not a boy like Morgan. No way he was seventeen.

"I'm not coming in," he said, putting his hands in his pockets. "It's cool, though." Then he turned, walked away, and was gone.

I lifted my arm to wave good-bye. It hung limply in space.

I dropped my keys on the counter, because it was something normal I would've done. I stomped upstairs for the benefit of my parents, and when they heard me, the amber light from under their door turned off.

I lay like a starfish on my bed, fully dressed, my Docs unlaced. First I ran through the early, normal parts of the day—breakfast, TV, the pool—but lost perspective as my night came into view: new releases, Wet N Wild, James Spader, Naomi Sheets with bloody hands and baby barrettes in her hair, some secret brother with a look collaged from my actual dreams, album covers, better than Keanu, weirder. Then a fast-forward, to future days: listless shifts at Video Journeys, new exhibits at the LACMA, double features at the New

Beverly, frozen yogurt at Penguin's, in Malibu, in the canyons, wherever. The endless summer.

But beneath my lashes, beneath the translucent lids, were silver veins and James's face. And into sleep he walked alone down the road, in silence, looking good.

2.

ICE CUBE

Through the blinds the afternoon sun burned horizontal slits onto my face. I opened one eye to spy the contents of my trashed bedroom, and it was worse than my parents ever accused, but whatever. My stuff, my mess, my problem. The edges of a Björk poster were peeling up. Some Snapple bottles were knocked over, and their paper labels—which I'd scratched off while watching MTV—were scattered on the floor in a crooked peace sign. I had a big thrift-store chair once. Like, I knew it was still there, but all I could see in its place was a mountain of clothes. Precarious stacks of V. C. Andrews and Baby-Sitter's Club books threatened to fall off my desk. Empty Starbucks to-go cups, pictures from Libby's birthday, old *Sassy* magazines, drawings I'd done of a long-haired Anthony Kiedis as a winged angel, a half-eaten box of

Girl Scout cookies, all laid out and forgotten. Seriously gross. I wanted all that junk cleaned up, but the actual ass-moving involved wasn't worth it. So instead I just cleared a path of open carpet from my bed to the door. No prob.

It was one o'clock when I made it downstairs in my Video Journeys shirt-turned-nightgown. Everyone was gone, so I ate the strawberries in the fridge right out of the carton without washing them. Then I talked to myself in a British accent, jumped on the couch, flipped through some channels, drank a Diet Coke. I grabbed a phone book and started thumbing through the *S*s. There were two Sheets residences, but I didn't have the guts.

At three Morgan called on my private line.

"If this is Matt Damon, leave a message. If it's Ben Affleck, lose my number," my recorded voice said.

"Hey it's Morgan, I'm with Matt, he says hi. Did you and Naomi make out last night? Yeah, right. Let's drive to work together tomorrow. Matt says bye. Bye, Quinn."

I stuck out my tongue.

Later, by the pool, I soaked up the last hot rays of the day. I had a few conversations with James in my head, playing both of our parts with equal intensity. I was careful not to say too much when I was acting his role, in order to keep things realistic. Weirdly, I was worse at playing myself.

I sank into the shallow end, dunked my head back, and let my hair fan out on the top of the water. I turned up Ice Cube, "It Was a Good Day," on my stereo, floated like a corpse, hit play again, listened again. Underwater, I told James he could have a free rental every night I worked. And the nights I didn't work I'd figure something out. The promise rose in bubbles to the surface. Then the song faded out. I let the CD play into the next track, and dripped dry on the concrete while swaying to the beats.

At six the sky turned purplish magenta. I'd hardly sweated and barely browned. The chlorine made my hair look like my mother's did in the seventies, so I snuck into her giant walk-in to try on some clothes. In the hidden box marked SKINNY I found kimonos, an Eagles concert T-shirt, leather Wilson's shorts, and other impossible reminders of her earlier coolness. I grabbed the silkiest thing I could find and, as an afterthought, one of my father's big cardigans.

When I was still alone at seven I noticed a note Scotch-taped to the microwave:

Quinlan: We're at the thing for Dad until midnight. Don't nuke something. Eat fresh food, please. And leave those strawberries next to the champagne. Both are off-limits. Love, Mom

But the strawberries were the only fresh food in the

fridge, so I couldn't really be blamed for eating them. For dinner I settled on tomato soup, saltines, and Diet Coke. Salt plus salt plus rat cancer. Whatever.

Nothing good was on TV, and I'd run dry on imaginary stories about Naomi and James. I hadn't crossed the pathetic line yet, but I was hovering close above it. I went from room to room, just picking up things and putting them down. I tried on a big Lakers jersey, French braided my hair, unbraided it, then collapsed on the bed, exhausted.

It was only ten, but I drifted into a light sleep anyway. An hour later I resurfaced, hazy and starving. I rolled over and grabbed the phone and laid it on my ear while I punched the number two speed dial. Morgan picked up instantly.

I said, "Hey, it's me. Got your message."

"Where were you?"

"Poolside."

"Want a ride to work tomorrow?"

"I'm gonna walk."

"Come on."

"Fine. Pick me up."

"Cool. Why didn't you call? My parents are in Maui. I called you," he said.

"I was busy doing awesome stuff. Today was a good day," I sang, not at all like Ice Cube.

"I called you," he said again.

"Morgan, what are you doing . . . right . . . now?"

"Trying to fix my cousin's old Nintendo. It sucks."

"You have to, like, blow on it, dude."

"What?"

"Like, blow on it. The cartridge."

"Why?"

"It fixes it."

The conversation died for a few seconds, and there was just breathing. Then I heard the Tetris theme song playing faintly on his end. I was starting to feel drowsy again when he said my name into the receiver.

"Mmmm?" I half asked.

"I can hold the phone up to my radio, they're playing that Cure song you like," Morgan said.

"Okay. Just, like, turn it up."

"Don't drool when you dream of me."

"What . . . ever . . ."

Then three things happened at once: Morgan said, "I love you," Robert Smith began to serenade me, and my mother spoke to my father loudly enough to wake me even if I had been asleep.

"She's in here, Elliott. Passed out in this nasty mess."

Friday at two in the afternoon, was it even possible? This time my mother had taped her note to my cheek:

Quinlan: You are un-be-lieveable. Dad's thing went great, should have seen him. Have a good shift, and let Morgan take you home tonight. No walking alone. Love you, Mom

The lingering smell of chlorine on my body was nice, so I skipped the shower. Black eyeliner, mascara, a chug of mouthwash, watermelon Lip Smacker, and I was out of the bathroom in two minutes easy. My boss, Jerry, was gone for three weeks attending some pyramid scheme seminar, so tonight I could ditch my Video Journeys shirt and go civilian. I piled my mess of long hair under a black bowler hat and put on cutoff shorts, a black bikini top, ratty Vans, a mood ring, six chain necklaces—dangling peace signs, a quartz crystal, a vintage car key—and big hoop earrings. I tied my dad's cardigan around my waist for the walk home. When I caught a glimpse of myself in the mirror on the way out the door, my eyes widened. The words "casual Friday" were a staggering understatement.

Outside it was a total scorcher, so I sat in some shade on the front lawn and listened to my Discman, waiting for Morgan and his budget Dodge Shadow. I tried to draw some band logos on the sides of my sneakers. I wrote "MADE YOU LOOK" on the back of my left hand in purple marker. On my right ankle I drew a fake rose tattoo, then licked my finger and tried to rub it off just as I noticed Morgan pulling to a stop in front of my house.

"You can't wear that to work," he said as I jumped into the front seat next to him.

I gave him a fake frown.

"And don't pretend to listen to music," he said, pulling my headphones off my ears.

"Morgan, I'll do anything you want if you just . . . chill."

"Really? Okay, then tell me everything that happened the other night with Naomi."

I slipped down in the seat and picked at my nails, imitating boredom. "Done, dude. Nothing to tell. She kind of spazzed out on me for a minute and then walked home." I shrugged.

"Right." He paused. "And there's one more thing," Morgan said, glancing over at me, "that I want you to do."

I squinted at the sun, bracing myself. "What?"

"Will you just please wear a name tag?"

"Sure. Anything you want." I turned away and watched as the palm trees, dry brush, and scattered mailboxes became the video store parking lot, too quickly.

We'd been watching *What's Eating Gilbert Grape* for what felt like two and a half hours when it finally struck me to ask, "Where . . . is . . . everybody?" I swept my arm from left to right and back again across the store, illustrating the total absence of customers, of kids, of anybody. "It's Friday night. I'm, like, beyond confused at the lack of interest in our entertainment emporium."

Morgan was eating Apple Jacks out of the box, numbly, and it all reeked of bad work ethic.

"Um, Earth to Morgan Crandall." I tapped the back of his head. "Aliens have landed, taken over the bodies of our customers, directed those bodies to who knows what Blockbusters in the city, and left us here to die of boredom."

"I'm not bored," he said. "Maybe everyone driving by saw your outfit through the window and figured we were closed for an employee beach trip." Though he'd landed a zinger, Morgan didn't gloat. He stayed glued to the TV screen.

"Ha. Ha," I said.

I slumped down to the floor and stared at the untouched racks of new releases. It was only halfway into our shift, but I already felt an overwhelming sense of déjà vu starting to wash over me. That sense that one day soon I'd have to give up and give in to the current, to the Morgan-and-me undertow. I mean, he wasn't without certain . . . attributes. But he was shameless, and he'd spent the better part of the night trying to position himself at eye level with my bikini top.

It must have been another two hours of Gilbert

dragging his feet before the store's doorbell finally rang. Usually on weekend nights I had to hole up in the break room for half my shift in order to avoid every high school weirdo, eighth-grade crush, and ex-best friend in Topanga Canyon. But the visitor was Libby, so I ran to greet her with the glee of an unleashed pug.

"Quinn, this is a really strong look for you," Libby said. She pulled on one of my bikini strings. "You're wearing a name tag on a bathing suit. Crandall must've wigged out."

"You are both just so scared of fashion."

"Whatever. He loves it. He's kind of a blond Depp, you know?" Her eyes went from the TV to Morgan and back to the actor on the screen. "Just date him already, he'd die from happiness."

"Yeah, brilliant idea, Libby."

Libbits Block had been my closest friend since the fourth grade, when she invited me to watch her dad's famous rock band play from the backstage wings at the Palladium. We ran around the greenroom stealing all the Cranberry Juice Cocktail the band had requested on their rider and then chugged until our lips were swollen and ringed with red. At midnight, once the sugar crash hit, we were in each other's arms taking best friend forever oaths, spitting into each other's palms, braiding our hair together in alliance. We learned to skateboard while holding hands, got into New Wave before anyone else, and went to the movies as each other's dates. By junior year we weren't quite as inseparable, just more realistic about the word "forever" and the significance of fluid exchange. Whereas other people *followed* Libby around, I just *was* around, and that made it easy for us to keep hanging out. Plus, neither of us was very good at making new friends. And we had history.

So I loved Libby, but in a vintage way. Like a childhood blanket, or my dad's mac and cheese. A deep love, but not one you tap into on a daily basis.

Libby lived a "charmed life"—as my mother would put it—being the daughter of a not exactly aging rock drummer and his not exactly un-hot costume-designer wife. The Blocks were totally understanding when she dyed a Manic Panic hot pink streak into her perfectly layered hair and cut her entire sneaker collection into flip-flops, or shandals, as Libby called them: half shoe, half sandal. Her parents totally bought it because they were royally hip, and Libby was their unassuming princess.

And no matter what she did to try to screw up her natural beauty—the aforementioned pink streak, ripped clothes from Barneys, occasional goth makeup—nothing ever worked. Libby was runway ready, tall and stick thin with a doe-eyed expression of world-weariness. She got more catcalls and "hey, babys" than even she cared for, leaving Libby with way too many male admirers but only one real female friend. So she hung out with her family mostly, making her seem entirely untouchable to everyone except her boyfriends. Regardless, she was still into me, and I wasn't ungrateful for it.

"Where *is* everybody?" Libby said, walking up and pirouetting a graceful 360 by the front register.

"That's what I said," I said.

"My mom's in the car having a cow about something, I totally can't hang."

Through the window I saw Stella Block calmly reading a Danielle Steel novel by the small car light. Libby was reading descriptions on the backs of movie boxes in no visible hurry.

"I heard from someone that you hung with Naomi Sheets the other night." Libby didn't look up from the videos. Morgan shoved more Apple Jacks into his mouth. A customer I hadn't noticed two aisles over loudly dropped a stack of video games.

"How is that even possible? Isn't there usually, like, a one-week delay period before the rumor mill kicks in?"

"God," Libby said. "Is it that big a secret?"

I rolled my eyes.

"Hey, I don't even care. Just thought it sounded weird. No pressure to spill."

For the second time today I dodged the same bullet.

"Whoever told you," I said, pinching Morgan's arm since Libby had gone back to reading, "was making a big deal out of nothing. Naomi was freaked about something, but it didn't even matter because her brother was there to take her home."

"Her brother who?"

"Just her brother."

"Sure," she said, holding her gaze on me for a second. Then she remembered something. "I'm actually having this party tomorrow night to celebrate. You know, a summer solstice thing. The twins are coming, and Dewey and Cooper, and Nathan, and some girls too, I think."

Of course there wouldn't be any girls but Libby. And me.

"Stiles and Sanders are coming?" I asked.

The Donnelley twins and their two best friends had graduated when we were sophomores, leaving behind a legacy of sexy sketchiness. None of them went to college—none of them went anywhere—preferring instead to continually lurk around the high school scene. The twins were both into Libby—which wasn't surprising because they were always into the same things, they were basically the same person—but in order to keep the peace, Sanders had backed out of the running last year. Stiles and Libby were on and off, sleeping together casually and then pretending not to care when they ran into each other accidentally at concerts or parties—which they did more and more often these days. She was tight-lipped about their time alone together, even to me, and I knew some house party crowded with other possible suitors and cling-ons wasn't a likely place for her to dish new heartfelt confessions. Still, it seemed unfair to make Sanders a witness. But whatever. Libby didn't approve of my holdout from Morgan, and I was in no position to challenge her motives with the twins.

"How's that going to work?" I said.

"Like butter, dude. It's cool beans."

"I'm sure."

"So you'll be there?"

"Yeah, I'm there." Party on.

"What about you, Morgan?" Libby asked.

"I've got that shift off," he said.

"Sweet. It's, like, hat themed. You have to wear a hat; it's mandatory. Crucial to your entrance."

"That's pretty weak on the theme tip," I said.

"Last minute. Live with it." She shrugged. "Just wear that thing you got that one time for my *Last of the Mohicans* party. And Morgan, you'll figure something out, right?"

"I think I can handle it."

"Cool beans," she said again, making it stick. "Well, I totally can't stay, my mom's still out there freaking."

Stella Block looked asleep, her head lolled back on the driver's-seat neck rest. I walked with Libby to the door and seized her by the elbow. She winced at my grip.

"Way to go. Now Morgan's going to take me and I'll have to be his date all night. He'll be bragging till graduation."

She tried to jerk her arm away, but I held steady. "Invite Naomi then, chill out."

I loosened in surprise at the name.

"Invite her brother too, I don't care."

I let her go.

"God, Quinn."

Then I noticed as Libby glared at me and rubbed her forearm that her wrist was covered in a stack of silver bangle bracelets, thirty, maybe forty of them. Underneath the bracelets her skin was blotched and purplish-blue, the hue of a bad bruise. She saw me staring at the jewelry and raised her arm closer.

"Stiles gave them to me. They're, like, antiques. Stella says they're Mexican silver or something. Totally eighties, but still . . ." Libby pulled her hand away as her voice trailed off.

After a pause Libby flipped her hair, smiled weakly, and said, "Well, I better go, you're at work." Then she leaned in and kissed my cheek.

I watched her through the glass as she model-walked

away. Then, remembering something, she turned around and mimed a big halo around her head and mouthed the words *Wear a hat*, slowly and deliberately. She threw up a peace sign, jumped in the car, and was gone.

Morgan was crouched over in the game aisle, reorganizing the section. I walked straight past, pretending not to hear him ask, "Need a ride to the party . . . or what?"

By ten the store was banging. I probably walked past her six times without realizing she was waiting for me to notice her. Finally, by the Disney section, I spotted the sunflower dress and my eyes focused.

"Naomi, hi."

"Which Hayley Mills movie should I get? *Pollyanna* or *The Parent Trap*?" she asked, without making eye contact. She wore lacy cream-colored socks rolled down over peach ballet slippers, and her thin, dirty-blond hair was swept to one side with a crocheted clip. She clutched a small Coach bag that looked expensive and adult-y.

"You . . . are . . . Pollyanna," I joked.

She looked up at me blankly, then back to the videos.

"Never mind," I said.

"Look," she said, "I just want to explain myself for what happened Wednesday night. James and I got in a dumb fight, and he left in the middle of it, so I ran after him and fell on some rocks and scraped my hands up.

That's it. I was just being an idiot. He felt bad about the whole thing. He didn't want you to be upset or think he'd pushed me or hurt me or anything."

"I didn't think—," I started to say, but she held up her hand, so I shut my mouth.

"Anyway. He's visiting for the summer. He's doing his own thing, he won't be around, so don't worry about it."

I was beginning to worry about it.

"And he's, like, not into dating or having friends or going out, he just sleeps late and does his own thing." She paused, fiddled with the Coach bag. "But since my parents are gonna be in Cairo for, like, two months, he's taking care of the house and watching over me. Not like watching *over* me, just like, watching out for me. You know." She exhaled and looked at me.

"So," she began again, "sorry he creeped you out and that I creeped you out. Mystery solved, whatever."

"Why did he care if I was upset about it?"

"Right . . . ," Naomi said, squinting.

"It's not like I've even thought about it really. I mean, it was sorta weird, but I don't know, maybe it wasn't." I stopped rambling, said, "It's fine."

"Cool."

"Yeah, cool. You know, everyone's wrong, I don't think you're plain at all."

"Who said I was plain?" she said sharply.

"Well, I just . . . thought that's why they called you Cotton Sheets."

She tensed her shoulders and started rummaging through the Coach purse. "They call me Cotton Sheets because they think I'm a prude." She glanced at the ceiling, irritated, like she'd had to explain this a thousand times. "Frigid," she said. The word just hung there for a minute. She zipped up the purse and it hung at her side.

"Sorry, Naomi. Seriously. I just thought it was because—"

"Yeah, I know. Stiles Donnelley made it up."

"Stiles and Sanders and those guys are jerks."

"Yep," she said.

She brushed it off, but I could tell there was more to it: a bad date, a bad kiss, worse maybe, but I could only guess. I definitely couldn't ask. I tried to think of a segue back to James, but we were too far away from him now.

All of a sudden I felt hyperaware of being half-naked in a store full of strangers. I wanted to turn off the lights and hide in the dark. I thought about walking straight past Naomi, through the front door, out into the night, down the street, home. But I didn't move.

I tried harder to think of something to say, and only one thing came to mind. "Hey, I'm actually going to this party thing tomorrow night, at Libby Block's house. It's on Mulholland. Anyway. You have to wear a lame hat, but I could totally lend you one."

She looked over at me, mystified. "What?"

"I said if you don't have a hat, then you can borrow one from me."

She laughed coldly, actually at me, and said, "Maybe."

I had about as much chance of getting Naomi Sheets to come to this party as Morgan had of getting me to go as his date.

"Well, it's totally open. You could even bring James or something if you wanted. We could all go together."

This only made her laugh more. "Not likely. Zero likeliness."

"Sure, no prob."

"If it helps"—she pointed over at Morgan behind the counter, who was staring at us shamelessly—"you can tell him I like girls and I just hit on you." She smiled, gave a small wave, and left.

During count-out, Morgan didn't ask for details. He somehow knew I wouldn't be taking his free ride either. Before we split up in the parking lot, I let him touch the bare skin on my upper back as he said good-bye. And when he left his hand there a little too long, I didn't even squirrel away from it. I knew leaning in would be wrong, but standing there feeling his rough fingers on my shoulder wasn't so bad. I put my cheek on his hand and closed my eyes.

When I couldn't pretend his hand was someone else's any longer, I told Morgan I'd find my own way to Libby's party but that I'd meet him there. He was visibly bummed but not terribly so, because he smiled when he drove past, leaning out his window, and left me with the parting words, "You looked good tonight."

It never got cold enough for my father's cardigan. After I'd been walking a few minutes, away from the glow of Video Journey's fluorescent lights, I heard faint footsteps behind me on the other side of the road. I glanced around and saw it was James but kept walking. We traveled the whole way home like this. When we got to my house, I turned and faced him.

"What's up?" I asked.

"I don't know." He crossed the street over to my side. "Nice house."

"You already said that."

"It's still nice, though."

"Okay, seriously," I said, and tried to look him in the eyes. "What's your deal? Are you training for a walkathon?"

"I thought girls loved to be walked home."

"Do you call that walking me home?"

He shrugged.

"You weren't exactly walking *with* me."

"I'm with you now." He stepped a little closer. "See?"

"Are you going to sit down?" I sat on the bottom step and patted the concrete next to me.

James hesitated for a moment, looking up at the second floor of my house. Then he sat, leaving an invisible person's body between us.

"You smell like chlorine and spearmint," he said.

"You can't smell me from over there." I scooted right over that invisible person so our knees were inches from touching. "Now you can smell me," I said.

James held his breath. Then he exhaled. The tea lights lit up parts of him: the crease in his elbow, the beds of his nails, half a jawbone, one gray eye. We were silent, and he messed with his hair.

After a while I was bored again, so I asked, "How old are you?"

"How old do I look?"

"Not seventeen."

"Correct. But I'm not much older."

"So where have you been hiding?"

"Massachusetts," he said. "Far, far away."

"Whatever. I've been there. Harvard's no biggie." I'd only been to New Hampshire, actually, but what's the diff? "Where do you hang out?" I asked.

"At your house usually."

"You know, typically when you're playing Twenty Questions, at the tenth question you get a hint."

That made him laugh, and he said, "Fine, you're right. I don't really hang out."

"I know. That's what Naomi told me. She came into the store tonight."

"Oh," he said, and looked away into the yard. "You can't tell her about this."

"Because you don't want any friends?"

"No."

"No you don't want any friends, or no you *do* want friends?"

"Right."

"But this is nice, isn't it?" It felt nice. "This is hanging out, isn't it?"

"No, it's nice," he said, nodding. Then he glanced over at me, at my knees. "I don't know if your boyfriend would be happy, but you don't seem too concerned about that."

"I'm not concerned because he's not my boyfriend." My voice came out sounding harsh, which was awesome. I was annoyed and so I was bold and so I reached out and put my hand right on his knee. I could feel the skin through the hole in his jeans.

"You're like an ice cube," he said. "Is it because you're always half-naked?"

"You just caught me on a particularly half-naked week."

"I'm into that."

I pulled at the small white threads coming from the rip in his jeans, wrapping them around my finger.

"I invited your sister to this party tomorrow night."

"Did she let you down nicely?"

"She laughed in my face," I said. "Do you want to let me down nicely too?"

"I can't go to a party."

"Because we're lame high school kids?"

"Yes," he said. Then, "No."

"Ugh. Whatever."

James stood up. My hand fell away. I stood up too and brushed myself off. Again it was like he wanted to go, but couldn't.

"Come inside," I said. "Just for a little."

"It's late. It's almost one."

I reached out and held his wrist. "You're not wearing a watch, you don't know what time it is."

"It's just a guess."

"Just come tomorrow night, it'll be stupid. Libby's parents have expensive champagne, and we can jump on the beds and listen to music. There'll be good things."

"Soon," James said, and tightened the cardigan around my waist, pulling me closer. Then he shoved his hands in his pockets and backed away from the house, still facing me.

"You're the good things," were the last words he said. I watched him go and tried to hold on to that "good" again.

Inside, the clock read 1:01, and I felt hot, not cold. I pressed an ice cube to my forehead, hoping to put out the fire before it spread.

3.

HEADDRESS

There was no getting around it: I was going to Libby's party, to meet up with Morgan, without Naomi or James, wearing a giant feather headdress. I dragged my feet all day, hoping James might magically call and offer an alternate plan. But he didn't have my number and I didn't have his. The evening heat made me itchy and too annoyed to eat. I fell asleep at six, only to wake and find myself in an empty house at eight. My mother had been so pleased to hear I was planning on leaving my bedroom for something other than work that she left her car keys under a note on my bathroom counter:

Quinlan, here are the keys. If you are in no shape to drive home, do not do so. Please sleep at Libby's, I'll know you were incapacitated. At the Getty Gala thing until past midnight. Have fun. Be safe. Don't forget to double click when you lock the Lexus.

Love, Mom

Incapacitated. Right. And sleeping at Libby's would mean I'd have to actually be there longer than an hour, which, given my cranky post-nap state of mind, seemed unlikely. I toyed with the idea of just going to Video Journeys and working a shift anyway on the slight chance that James might meet me there at eleven out of habit. I checked the TV channel guide to see if there was anything totally amazing on tonight, but summer meant all reruns, so that was no help. Morgan didn't even call to re-offer his chauffeur services, which meant he knew I was contemplating ditching out and didn't want to jinx it.

I decided to dress down since I knew I'd be topping off the outfit with a crown of giant eagle feathers, turquoise stones, and braided leather strands. Cutoffs and a loose gray tank top with lace-up sandals and a bunch of gold chains would have to do. I certainly looked like I wasn't trying too hard—which was intentional—but after a few days of bathing in the sun, the bare bronzed skin on my legs, shoulders, and arms glistened in a way that wasn't entirely uninviting—which was actually unintentional. Screw it. With the ratio of males to females that Libby's parties usually entailed, I could wear a grease-stained gas station jumpsuit and never be left alone all night.

I shoved a cherry ChapStick in my pocket, faintly

hoping James might somehow miraculously show up after all. But the pocket was a little longer than the frayed hem of my cutoffs, so the tube just hung there in the exposed white fabric at my thigh. Less than cool. I ripped out the third "Sh" page of the phone book, folded it, and stuffed it next to the ChapStick. This made my left front pocket hang even lower than the right, which looked goofy and, considering the contents, desperate. My head was already pulsing under the headdress, so I grabbed two Excedrin and downed them with Diet Coke. Whatever. This thing killed at the *Last of the Mohicans* party. I'd live.

Morgan was waiting for me on the Blocks' lawn when I pulled the Lexus up. He was wearing dirty Levi's and a clean striped T-shirt, and he slid on a Raiders football helmet as I walked over. I had to admit, Morgan looked cool. In another reality we could have been a dope couple, but in this one . . . coworkers.

"Not the least original hat I've ever seen," I said, smiling. "Not really a hat, though, is it?"

"And yours is?" he asked. "That thing looks painful. I doubt I'll last longer than an hour in this." He tapped the side of his helmet.

"Me too. I think the headdress is cutting off circulation. Thinking hurts."

We walked up the driveway toward the Blocks' house.

Music was blasting. Libby greeted us with a deep curtsy at the door. Though I'd expected nothing less than spectacular, Libby's attire was still an impressive testament to her dedication. She had on an abnormally tall, fitted top hat, and she'd ringed the brim with a single sparkly silver ribbon and half a dozen silk flowers. Her ivory dress was fancy and floor-length, with tiers that wrapped around her body at diagonal angles. Morgan and I broke into applause. She curtsied again and, after admiring our headdress/helmet combo, gave us a small volley of dainty opera claps for successfully following instructions. We hadn't let Libby down, and I felt better for it.

It was only then that we turned our attentions to the actual party, which was in full swing, and much less mild than I had hoped. What was I thinking, that I could just sneak in, nod along to some live Germs bootleg, sip a Snapple, snack on some hummus, and peace out? I hesitated in Libby's long hallway, listening to the bumpy bass of muffled music over voices too indistinct to identify. Libby pushed past, waving us to follow, but when I didn't move, Morgan grabbed my hand and led the way.

The huge living room was darkly lit with dim purple lights and filled to capacity with dancing teens. Thankfully, it didn't seem like there'd be drama tonight; everyone had gotten the official "wear a hat" memo, and all heads were covered. Caps, berets, turbans, beanies: A universe of hats floated above the dance floor, accompanied by random fashions and red plastic cups. The Blocks' retro concert posters and vintage photographs were being ogled everywhere, while Libby drifted through like a celeb, dropping wild anecdotes and explanations for her eternal coolness. It had been a long time since I'd been freshly impressed by the lifestyle of Libby's parents—it's easy to feel blasé after your ninth sit-in at the KROQ studios—but seeing it all in this light, through the eyes of strangers, I couldn't help but feel that purely L.A. magic again.

And they were strangers. All of them. I recognized some of the faces—I'd been at my high school for three semi-social years—but couldn't match any of them with names. What was popularity anyway? Being known? Knowing? I could claim neither, but scenes like these made me feel like that Pavement song: an extra in the movie adaptation of the sequel to my life.

"Who are all these people?" I shouted in Libby's ear over the music, while she tried to dance with me to some Dr. Dre song.

"Frosh, sophs, who knows?" she shouted back.

"And you're listening to rap now?"

"*We're* listening to rap now."

I'd always been listening to rap, and Libby'd always been sighing and making a puke face about it.

"You look pretty," I said.

"Me? Yuck, whatever," she said back, actually checking herself out in some reflection behind me. "Now you, you look crucial."

I loved when Libby said stuff like that to me, and for someone so totally into herself, she said stuff like that all the time.

"This was so us when we were freshmen," I said, looking around. "Only we were dorks."

"We were terrified." She fixed my bangs.

"Yeah, but I'm still terrified."

"Stop pretending you're a loser."

It was true; I did do that. But I wasn't a loser, I was Libbits Block's best friend, and when everyone had decided that counted for something, I started to think so too.

"Well, I didn't come with one of them," I said, pointing at the giant archway to the kitchen where Stiles and Sanders stood drinking with their posse. "Or two of them."

I'd meant it as a joke, but Libby didn't smile.

"Kidding. I know you're just with Stiles."

"He's cool, right?" she asked, and it was hard to tell, but maybe she really did want my opinion.

So I told her, "He's so cool."

"He's kind of intense, though. Sometimes."

"So what? He's like post-senior, he's like grade thirteen. That's hot. They're all pretty hot," I said, my eyes wandering over to them again.

"You don't want any of them."

I said, "I know," but that hadn't always been the case.

"I'm serious, Quinn."

"I know, Libby, it's cool."

"I think I might, like, love him. Is that weird?"

"It's not that weird."

"Not like I love *you*, of course," Libby said, and made a face, then pushed me.

"I love you too, you know that." I said it because it was true, or at least it was mainly true, and that was close enough.

"Oh God, we're being so stupid right now." She took a drink of her champagne.

"Yeah," I said, but I felt like this was so much less stupid than how we usually acted. Libby was already distracted, though, and only getting more so. Her eyes kept roving over to peer at the twins.

Beyond them, the kitchen was packed. It was wall-to-wall, all strangers, crowded together in a throng sprawling from the refrigerator all the way to the breakfast table. People were even smoking inside, which was gross and a total Libby rule violation. My empty stomach was growling, and I saw several bowls of nondescript snacks on the kitchen counter. I looked down in my cup at the small amount of Libby's secret champagne—I imagined most kids here were drinking some combination of Stella's Listerine, orange juice, Mountain Dew, and five-dollar Russian vodka—and knew I needed to get to those Doritos before I found myself pressed up against some smoky-smelling freshman feeling barfy.

"Libby, I need food. . . ."

"So go get some." She winked in Stiles's direction, wobbling tipsily. Her silver bracelets jangled with the music.

"Fine, I will."

Libby shrugged and danced away, her off-white layers shimmying in unison.

"Look away," someone whispered low in my ear. "It's like staring into the sun." I didn't have to turn around to know it was Nathan Visser, Libby's former part-time boyfriend for years.

"Deal with it, Nathan. She looks like a goddess with a cocktail."

"She looks . . . like a vanilla soft serve."

"You're not even wearing a hat," I said disapprovingly. But I felt for him. I knew what it was like to orbit around planet Libby.

My mind was locked on food, though, so I kept

moving. I had to eat if I was going to survive this rager. Even if the twins were guarding the chips.

Stiles was the first to see me coming, and he looked as arrogant as always. He wore his black hair cut short on the sides and long on top so it dripped down his forehead, plastered in place by a yacht captain's hat. He looked like a carefully styled millionaire, a classic James Spader villain. I never remembered his eyes being so light, like they were glass. Like I could see inside him and there was nothing there. And if his eyes were translucent glass, then his skin was opaque glass, smooth and white. He was an eerie, hollow dude.

Sanders was the same, cocky and uncomfortably handsome. His black hair was parted on the side, and the longest piece reached his chin. Slick, manicured, he was nearly identical to Stiles: the creepy crystal eyes, the immaculate skin and posture, the starched chinos. Sanders held a matching captain's hat in one hand and a plastic cup in the other. I tried to shove through them, but they stood arm to arm, forming a wall.

"Move, you guys," I said.

"Already hammered and it's only ten thirty." Sanders clicked his tongue. His jaw was angular, harsh, a mirror reflection of his twin's. He stared me down and up and down again. I tugged on my shorts for something to do.

"Shouldn't you have a skipper hat, Sanders? You can't

both be captain, so I'm guessing you're first mate?" I still had some spit left in me before I puked on his Sperry loafers.

"Libby said you'd be good for a laugh," Stiles said.

The party spun around me: disorienting fuzzy bass, sweaty shapes throbbing to the beat, strangers surrounding, Spaders encroaching. I struggled to get my headdress off before I collapsed. It was screwed on tight, the rusted lid on an empty jar.

I tried to remember where I'd set the keys to the Lexus. I tried to summon Morgan with whatever witchy will I could muster. I sensed two bodies come up behind me, trapping me against the evil S.S. Donnelley. I turned around.

Dewey Kaplan stood rigid and clean in crisp white jeans and a white button-down, nothing like the slacker he used to be. He too had lost all his sweet round features, the cherubic ones that a couple years ago made him seem friendly. Those were gone, replaced by a frozen mask, by a pod-person void. I remembered how he'd worn a dirty Metallica shirt in his senior yearbook photo, and I'd admitted to Libby that I thought he looked totally sick. I guess I used to sort of be into Dewey back then, when he was a hesher and had hair like Dave Grohl used to have—before he became Stiles's and Sanders's clone. I hadn't really noticed their features all melting together, becoming the same vacant disguise.

Cooper Richards was at Dewey's side, even more expressionless, even more clone-y. He'd also thrown away his whole high school deal—basketball shorts, Air Jordans, backward Stüssy hat—for pleated pants, a tailored dress shirt, the same numbed-out vibe. How long ago had I stopped paying attention? When had they all become so similar? I barely knew Cooper when he was varsity royalty, but I could tell I didn't want to know him now.

He licked his lips at me and held up a brown-bagged bottle. "Thirsty? We brought our own."

Dewey nudged him and grabbed the bottle. "That's not for her, man." Then he poured for Stiles and Sanders, the red wine thick and dark in their cups. They drank deeply, gorging on it.

"Gross, what did you spike that with? Corn syrup? It looks like pudding." I tried to push past them again. "You're all mental."

"Whoo . . . ooops," Stiles said, spilling wine from his cup onto my tank top. Sanders and Dewey cracked up but Cooper went stiff, twitching slightly, then lunged down and grabbed the hem of my shirt and started licking the stain.

Then I heard, "What's your problem, Richards?" and there was Morgan, reaching in and pulling me out. His helmet was gone and his breath smelled like stale beer.

"Quinn, are you cool?"

I nodded, shaking. Morgan's soft, blemished complexion was a guiding light, completely out of place among these chiseled faces. I wanted to wrap my arms around him but couldn't.

"Yeah, cool as can be," I said, straightening myself. "It's just getting a little cult-y around here."

They opened up the ring and let us leave, then huddled back together, ignoring us. We moved back toward the dance area. There were twice as many people as before, and the music was twice as loud. I looked around for Libby. For Naomi. For James. Hopeless, I grabbed the beer out of Morgan's hand and chugged.

"Whoa, settle down there, chief," Morgan said, but I'd already nearly emptied the can. It tasted awful.

"I hate beer," I moaned. "I hate this party."

"I thought Cooper was going to eat you."

"I know. I was almost to the kitchen. I just . . . wanted . . . some . . ." I didn't finish. The floor scooped me up where I stood, and I blinked as it hit me. I felt my hot cheek against the shag carpet.

"Oh, no way. I'm taking you to the bathroom."

"Where's Libby?" I mumbled.

"Nuh-uh. Bathroom, now." Morgan hoisted me off the floor and onto his back, somehow hauling my rag-doll body up the roped-off staircase and into the quiet master bedroom. He shut the door behind us and laid me on the bed. "Seriously, Quinn, you're wiggy."

"I've got to eat something."

"Savory or sweet?"

"Savory, sir."

And then he was gone, bounding down the stairs to hunt and gather.

I stumbled into the bathroom and splashed water on my face. Then I splashed water on the wine stain, but it was no use; the shirt was ruined. I stared at myself in the mirror above the sink. My face looked green. The feather headdress made it all an even more garish, cruel, crazy joke, but I was afraid if I took it off my head would come with it. Was it two in the morning?

The bathroom clock read 10:52.

Yeah, I was a real party animal. Whatever hopes I had of exiting Libby's house with dignity intact were dwindling fast. But I couldn't leave before Morgan came back with the food because, well, I needed the food so I could drive without totaling the Lexus. But if I stayed, that'd add one more point to the long-running Morgan Crandall scoreboard for undying loyalty to a girl who didn't deserve it. My selfishness was pathetic, second only to my low alcohol tolerance and right above my socializing skills—or lack thereof. People shouldn't even look in the mirror when they're drunk. These kinds of self-realizations are never helpful. This wasn't supposed to be some dark-night-of-the-soul thing. I came to . . . party.

Next thing I knew I was lying on the carpet again, dialing a number on the phone by my head. The folded piece of phone-book paper had somehow unfolded, come out of my pocket, and attached itself to my left hand.

"Hello?" Naomi sounded confused, either because she'd never given anyone her phone number—which was a real possibility—or because it was actually closer to three a.m. I looked at the clock to check that I hadn't read it wrong. 10:57. It wasn't too late to call on a weekend night.

"Hey, it's Quinn, I'm at the party. You never showed, you know?" I tried to keep it light. I tried not to sound like the worst, most out-of-it person ever.

"When I said zero likeliness—"

"Right." I acted like I was brushing it off, like it totally didn't matter if Naomi came or anyone she was related to. "I said you could borrow a hat."

She laughed at that. I relaxed a little.

"So you're not having a good time then? If you're calling me."

"No, I'm having a sucky time. Whatever you're doing has got to be a million times better. What *are* you doing?"

"Watching a movie."

"I *love* movies," I said, hitting my head against the carpet.

"You can come over. It's cool." Maybe it was optimism on my part, but Naomi didn't sound annoyed or put out. For a moment I imagined she might actually want someone to hang out with on a Saturday night. I felt a sudden victory; I was turning this night around. I could see myself in less than an hour sandwiched between James and Naomi on the couch with a movie, sharing popcorn in the dark, chatting idly through the boring parts. My body went limp just picturing it: popcorn. . . .

"I'm alone, though," she added. "Like, it'd just be you and me."

"Where's your brother?" It came out like a dying girl's last wish.

"Out doing whatever he does. I don't even want to know."

I didn't have time to think about what that could mean, because I heard Morgan's voice at the bottom of the stairs telling someone he left his coat in the bedroom. I had maybe thirty more seconds.

"Can I sleep over too?" The cool performance was over. Maybe there'd be another show at midnight.

"It's pretty boring here." But it wasn't a no.

"Naomi, I am so there." I found a pen and scribbled down her address on the phone-book page. The Sheets lived ten minutes from Libby, less than seven from me, and for a second I felt weird for never having known that. Then I felt another sharp pang of hunger. I hung up the phone just as Morgan opened the door.

"Still starvin', Marvin?" He reached down around me with both arms, a bag of honey mustard sourdough pretzels in one hand and a glistening, cold Diet Coke in the other. He knew me so well it was impossible to resist. If I could've asked God for anything in the world to eat at that moment, I would've asked for exactly that. It was hard to keep fighting it when all the other cute boys were cult members or unsolved mysteries.

"Pretty much ready to black out," I said, and let him hug me into his chest. He sniffed my hair behind the feathers.

"Want to take this stupid thing off?" he asked, but since he was looking at all of me—all over me—I couldn't tell if he was talking about the stained shirt or the headdress.

"I'll keep it on. I'm leaving in a minute anyway. It's like a bad Jason movie down there." I opened the pretzels and ate a handful, in heaven. "All that underage drinking and foreplay, heads are bound to roll. Stabbings are a major concern."

"I found the keys to the Lexus," he said, dropping them next to me. "But you don't have to drive home if you feel sick. I can take you, then tomorrow we could drive back here and pick it up."

No way was I agreeing to two more rides. I wished I'd asked for that stupid run-down Toyota when I turned sixteen instead of a trip to Hawaii with Libby. I'd traded five decent days on the beach for an eternity in the passenger seat of Morgan's sedan.

"My mom would flip. She told me to stay here if I couldn't drive."

"Whatever. Just sleep in my sister's room. She lets older girls have the top bunk all the time." He smiled and fingered my tank top strap. I was almost beyond rescue. The time to escape was now. Thankfully, I was sobering up fast with the pretzels and the soda, plus the hunch that I'd have to dodge a kiss in less than a minute.

But when he slowly leaned in for it, I stayed a solid mass and gripped the bag of pretzels in one hand and held the Diet Coke for dear life in the other. My eyes were wide blue marbles staring into an advancing blur. I was plywood, immovable. And yet somehow my lips parted to mold against the shape of his.

"Morgan. Dude." It was all I could say.

"I'm thinking about . . . us . . . evolving," he whispered.

And I was thinking about dissolving. I had my keys and Naomi's address; I was as good as gone. This was going to be one of my top five worst departures ever, and I had once walked right into the forest scenery while exiting stage left during a production of *A Midsummer Night's Dream*. I played Mustardseed the fairy and had about seven lines, but I still managed to knock down half the set. For a whole semester they called me Shakes. It was only a coincidence Shakespeare had written the play.

And that paled in comparison to this.

He said, "Quinn," but I was up and out the door and in the hallway before Morgan could say my name again. I wasn't turning around for anything. I was on a mission to find Libby and end this part of the evening. I'd see James's face before I closed my eyes tonight—I'd make it happen.

The scene downstairs hadn't thinned out at all. It was like a riot. Hats were off, so were most of the lights, and I had to fight to squeeze myself through the sea of teenagers. The twins were nowhere to be seen, but their doubles were lurking in the laundry room with some burnout kid. Dewey was sort of holding him up, sniffing his hair, it looked like. Inspecting his fingernails. Cooper had the door to the garage propped open, and beyond them was blackness. Not my problem. My eyes searched only for the prize: vanilla soft serve. Vanilla soft serve. The goddess with the cocktail.

I found Nathan by the stereo. He raised his beer can to toast my Diet Coke.

"Designated driver?" Nathan asked.

"Designated hitter, actually."

"Vicious. You girls are way cruel."

"Whatever. Where's Libby?"

He shrugged. "I think I saw her go into her dad's studio, like, ten minutes ago."

"Alone?"

"Like you care."

Nathan's face was Morgan's; I couldn't deal.

I wedged my way through the mob and down the dark hallway leading to Nigel Block's music studio. The door was closed.

"Libby," I shouted. "Libby, I have to go, so I'm saying good-bye." I opened the door a crack, keeping my eyes on the floor. "I'm coming in now. . . ."

But Nathan was wrong. The room was empty.

I went out the side door onto the patio. The night air was a total relief. I passed a girl in a sombrero vomiting onto Stella's Japanese rock garden. Empty red cups littered the ground. Halfway to the Lexus, discarded by the side of the house, I saw Libby's ornamented top hat in the dirt. Behind an overgrowth of ivy I thought I spied a ripple of cream-colored fabric and so began walking quickly to the car, wanting to leave a tender moment alone. I fumbled at the door with my mother's keys and, without turning my head, caught a glimpse of them.

Libby was leaning with her whole body against the side of the house. Her long, bony arm was extended gracefully, the palm upturned like a poised ballerina. Stiles stood beside her, holding her palm to his mouth, kissing it. In the darkness the silver bangle bracelets shone as Stiles slid them up her forearm. Libby rolled her head around in ecstasy as his lips locked on her wrist. When the low moan of Libby's voice changed from gasps of pleasure to higher sounds of almost-pain, I scrambled into the car. Once inside I glanced back again and tried to remember that she wanted him, that she didn't need saving. Then Libby went limp in his arms, still with her delicate wrist to Stiles's mouth. His body heaved; her eyes closed.

I drove to Naomi's in silence. I'd memorized the directions.

My whole being guided me there.

I walked down the curved path to the Sheetses' residence. The front door was at street level, but the rest of the house behind it was lower, nestled into the side of the mountain. A separate walkway led down to a detached garage with a narrow staircase up to a private studio. Above it the view was incredible; I could see the whole city laid out, twinkling and calm. I exhaled deeply, draining my entire self, down to my toes, and finally felt a little peace.

Naomi looked tired when she opened the door. I imagined my appearance. Somewhere between hot mess and Sunset street urchin.

She didn't say hello, just asked, "Where'd you get that feather headdress?"

My head had been numb for so long I'd forgotten that I was still wearing the damn thing. I slid it off, untangling my hair, and held it out for her. My forehead throbbed, my head itched.

"You want it?" I said. "It's yours."

Naomi took it, and when she held out her arm, gesturing for me to come in, the warm, dark house spread before me like an open invitation.

4.

SLEEPOVER

Naomi didn't offer the grand tour and I didn't ask for it, just tried to sneak in glances when she wasn't looking. The house was classic canyons—rustic, woodsy with a big stone fireplace and cabin motif—but with flourishes of exotic travel. Clay pots painted in rich reds, warm oranges, and yellows; ritual masks made of straw and animal hair; ethnic musical instruments. I'd seen worse replicas in the Adventureland section of Disneyland. None of the furniture matched. Every piece of art functioned in a totally clashing color scheme. My mother would've had a heart attack.

My eyes went everywhere at once. I felt like I was in an expensive, private chalet retreat in the Sudan. I half expected Naomi to launch into a wistful tale about her expeditions with Mowgli and Simba, but she just lounged back on a mudcloth-covered settee, twirling her hair. This was all just the same old, same old for her. In this way I saw Naomi as the jungle princess version of Libby, relishing rooibos tea rather than Asti sparkling wine, preferring sitars to Fenders, benefits over house parties; accepting the extraordinary as the ordinary.

Suddenly I realized: There was no TV in the living room. Whoa. Bold.

"Are your parents, like, explorers?" It wasn't the first idiotic thing I'd said all night.

"Not even. They teach at UCLA. My father's an art historian, and my mother is an ethnomusicologist." That all seemed awesome, so I didn't know why she rolled her eyes and stared at her nails.

"Are you kidding?"

My mother, Bonnie, was a real estate agent; my father, Elliott, a freelance food critic for the *L.A. Times* and a full-time trust-fund inheritor, whose only degree was the art of time wastage.

"They met in South America on a seminar tour. Daniel and Charlotte."

Naomi grabbed a picture from the mantel and tossed it in my lap. They were stuffy, sure, but like famously stuffy. In the photograph Daniel had on tortoiseshell glasses and a cashmere turtleneck under a beige safari jacket—think Gregory Peck as Indiana Jones—and Charlotte looked like Sissy Spacek in a dashiki.

"James kind of looks like your father. I mean, from what I could see of him that night at the video store." It seemed unassuming enough, but I couldn't tell how it sounded to her.

She stared at the picture, her back to me. "I guess so." Then she turned around and walked past me. "Let's go downstairs."

Downstairs was just as rustic and woodsy, with built-in shelves lined with antique books and small statues and trinkets. Naomi opened a door and led me into her room, which was full of all the things you'd ever dream possible for the life of a Topanga Canyon horse girl: riding crops, multicolored prize ribbons, framed photos of Naomi on horseback leaping over obstacles, horse figurines stuck in the poses of numerous trots and gaits. Scattered in the far corner was evidence of other part-time pastimes: a tennis racket, a cello case covered in glittery stickers, crochet hooks hanging on half-finished scarves attached to balls of rainbow yarn, sketch pads and tracing paper, karate blocks, some tarot cards. I would've felt an almost perfect kinship with Naomi and her bedroom—just two messy ladies holed up with our respective precious junk—but there was one major difference: Her trash was actually useful. And her Tori Amos poster wasn't peeling off the wall. And she had trophies, loads of them, for things like cross-country running and fencing and competitive tofu cook-offs. They gave trophies for tofu cook-offs, and Naomi was winning them.

I tried to keep telling myself that she had zero friends, was a social outcast, and had sacrificed every stupid wonderful high school experience for a chaotic collection of props that made her seem well-rounded. But it didn't work, and I had to be honest: This girl was rad. I liked her. My life was now divided between every day before and up to last Wednesday—starting at that moment on the road outside the video store—and each day since.

We set up on her futon and picked out *Jurassic Park* and dimmed the lights. Through the movie I noticed Naomi softening in small ways: She laughed easier, her eyebrows pressed together less, her vibe mellowed. I didn't have to work at bonding with her; it came naturally. And I wasn't using her to get to James—though he was always vaguely on my mind, even during the suspenseful *T. rex* chase scene climax—I wanted to be closer to both of them equally. Or semi-equally.

The last swells of the movie's theme song coincided with the clock turning two. Naomi was yawning. But my earlier nap and those Diet Cokes had me feeling wired even after a high-drama night like tonight. And I was in the mood to roam. Snoop. Whatever.

"Just grab anything out of that drawer if you want

something to sleep in," she said, stretching and yawning again, signaling the end of our hang-out. "I'm gonna do bathroom stuff."

Then she disappeared down the hall.

I stood up and went out into the hallway, passing by a door on my left that gurgled with the sound of water splashing into a sink. I leaned closer and heard Naomi brushing her teeth and humming the *Jurassic Park* score. I said her name, loudly. No response. She couldn't hear me.

I stepped farther down the hall, toward a door that was halfway cracked. I gently pushed on it, and it swung open silently. It was another bedroom, and hanging above the bed was a giant subway-size poster of a 1970s William Claxton photograph that I recognized from my father's LACMA members' calendar. I'd found it in less than thirty seconds: James's room.

The bookshelf spilled over with classics and comics and a hundred plays. There were wooden crates of jazz and soul records against one wall, all dusty, and on top sat an even dustier seventies turntable. Above a small desk was another huge vintage poster, this one of Woody Allen and Diane Keaton having drinks on a rooftop in *Annie Hall*. Postcards of Edward Hopper paintings and Groucho Marx were arranged alongside it. Everywhere were more clues, more details to absorb: literary quotes scribbled on notecards thumbtacked to a cork bulletin board, cups filled with pens and scissors, an old typewriter, a bouncy ball, a squishy stress ball, a mason jar of loose change.

My eyes focused on a framed picture of James on a beach, lying in the sun, holding a paperback. I held it closer to my face. The boy in the picture was James, but wasn't. His hair was different, a little darker and a little shorter. His skin was tanner, and his face wasn't as sculpted around the cheekbones and jawline. His eyes weren't the same strange gray. This James wore glasses with black rims, had freckles on his face and arms and a wider smile. He was more like Morgan, or Nathan: definitely cute but definitely no grunge Calvin Klein model.

I set the picture down and sat on his bed. Had I imagined him some way he wasn't? I tried to remember his face from last night, but I couldn't picture it and got distracted by a pair of beat-up, drawn-on, old Converses lying by the side of the bed. The canvas on both shoes was threadbare by the big toe. I slipped my feet inside, wanting an immediate connection with his things, his body.

"What the hell are you doing?" Naomi was standing in the doorway.

I kicked off the shoes, startled, and stood up. "Naomi," I said.

She turned around and stalked down the hallway to

her room, where I followed with my shoulders slumped.

"You can't go in there. *I* can't even go in there, okay?"

The smell of toothpaste on her breath made me go blank.

"Okay, Quinn?"

But I wanted to be in there.

"Yeah, of course. I'm, like, the sorriest, I swear. I'm having the best time. I really am."

Naomi nodded and shut off the light and got into bed. I crawled into the sleeping bag she'd laid out for me on the floor. We lay quietly in the darkness for a few minutes, and I listened to her steady breathing.

"Sorry I didn't come to the party tonight. You sounded like you could've used some backup," Naomi said.

"No, I needed a forklift. And a harpoon gun. And a buffet table. But your company would've been cool."

"Next time I'll come. Unless your boyfriend doesn't want a third wheel."

"He's not my boyfriend!" I said, sitting up so fast I hit my head on the corner of the dresser. I lay down again, embarrassed and dizzy. "He's *not* my boyfriend."

"Does he know that? Because you might want to tell him."

"I'm getting around to it."

We were silent for a while, and then Naomi stirred in her sheets and said my name: "Quinn?" She paused, and the pause was heavier than her asking, "Are you afraid of dying?"

"Are you about to kill me?" I said. It was a joke, but something about Naomi had scared me ever since I saw her that night outside Video Journeys.

"Probably not." I could tell she was smiling.

I started to smile too until a flash of Libby pressed up against her house, moaning, slipped into my head and stuck there.

"So . . ." Naomi hesitated, and I remembered the question.

"No," I told her. "I'm not afraid of dying. What's the point?"

"Good. That's good." It wasn't her brother's "good," but it made me feel better. She rolled over, and the blanket mountain became a smooth quilt river. Less than five minutes later, at the start of a snore and the sound of a car pulling up, I snuck up the stairs.

Through the living room window I saw him. James was walking down to the Sheetses' detached garage. I made for the front door, but by the time I'd undone the locks and gotten outside, he was gone. It was silent. The wind gently stirred my hair, filling my nose with the scent of hydrangeas and basil plants. This place was sensory overload inside and out.

I went down the dirt steps and then I saw him, leaning up against the garage, holding his face in one hand.

"Hey," I said.

He looked up. He looked sort of sad. "What are you doing here?"

"Stalking you." I smiled. He didn't. "I was just hanging out with Naomi."

He nodded. "Oh."

"You didn't come. To the party. I wore a feather headdress."

"Does that count as a hat?"

"Yes. It's a Native American's hat. They wore them all the time when they settled the West."

I looked out at the Los Angeles lights, glittering, spread out beneath us. I could see downtown and the 101 curving up into the Valley.

"I would've liked to have seen you in that," he said.

"Well, I gave it to your sister. She's going to add it to your natural history museum in the living room."

His eyebrows touched together with worry. "Where's she now?"

"Passed out. I bored her to sleep with anecdotes of my dull evening," I said. I looked up the stairs to the room above the garage. "What's going on up there?"

"It's two thirty. Don't you want to go to sleep?"

"You always think you know what time it is. And I'm

not sleepy," I said, because it was true. I couldn't sleep: adrenaline, Diet Coke, and curiosity coursed through me.

"Come up to my room then."

He led the way up the narrow staircase. If he was leading me to his room, then whose stinky Converses had I slipped my feet into less than an hour ago?

As we reached the doorway he opened the door, then abruptly stopped, fumbling for the light switch inside, and I bumped into him from behind. He turned around and at first was smiling, but then his face went cold. He started backing away, his eyes wide, frozen, full of dread, until he was up against the far wall.

"What? What's wrong?"

"What happened to you?" He pointed at the stain on my shirt.

"This? Nothing, just some jerks spilled their wine on me."

"What jerks?" James was still frozen.

"I don't know. Guys who used to go to my school. Nobody important." I was backpedaling, trying to remember the moment.

Then he turned his nose down into his shoulder. He breathed in the cotton. "You have to take your shirt off," he said, closing his eyes.

"What?" I touched the tank top. "Why?" I sniffed at the stain, but it smelled like nothing. It smelled like clothes. Maybe a hint of chlorine.

Still holding his nose into his shoulder, James bent over and grabbed a blue wadded-up ball of fabric off the floor and tossed it at me. "Here. You have to take your shirt off," he repeated.

I didn't understand what was happening, and then what was happening was I was taking my shirt off, even forgetting to turn around to cover myself. This courtship was retarded, backward, moving in zigzags instead of a straight line. We hadn't ever kissed, or hugged, or even held hands; five minutes of knee touching was the extent of our intimacy so far. But now here I was in his bedroom, stripping, topless, past two in the morning, getting scolded for having a stain on my tank top.

Then I was wearing his blue T-shirt and smoothing it out. It was too big and so soft. I said, "Okay, done."

James opened his eyes cautiously, then relaxed.

I stepped to the door and dropped my shirt off the stairs. It landed on a dark pile of dirt.

"Thanks," he said.

"Sure."

"I didn't mean to be rude."

"It's okay."

"I'm sorry. For real." He came and wrapped his arms around me, his cheek against my dirty hair.

He sighed. "That was a close one, though."

"Was it?" I didn't get it. Mega clean freak?

"I know that wasn't normal."

"I don't care about normal," I said, looking around the room for the first time. You couldn't technically call it a bedroom, because there was no bed. There wasn't really any furniture at all except for a small desk covered in clothes, trash, *Spin* magazines, and a broken Walkman with headphones. A crooked lamp stood in one corner, one of the bulbs burned out. There was a black electric guitar—missing most of its strings—propped up against a tiny amp. A big faded rug covered most of the floor. An old brown mini-fridge huddled against another wall, where a pile of books was stacked on top. Okay, so James definitely wasn't a clean freak. I knew that he didn't live here year-round, I knew he was away at school most of the time, so he probably kept his important possessions and other furniture there, but still—not a single photo or poster on the walls?

I stared at the bareness, wondering. Something was so wrong, but I couldn't place it. The walls were off-white and old-looking and totally barren, but that wasn't the problem. I wobbled a bit and it hit me: no windows. There were no windows anywhere. It was a face without eyebrows, too weird.

"Sorry there's nowhere to sit. I'm not here often."

"Where do you sleep?" I had to know where I would

sleep if I slept over. If I slept over tonight, for instance.

"On the floor, in the walk-in." He pointed to a sliding closet door over on the far wall. "I like confined spaces when I sleep. Creature comforts."

I sat down on the rug and patted the spot in front of me. James sat too, stretching his long, thin legs out. He messed with his hair, and then he reached around me and tucked in the tag of his blue shirt, under the neck. I felt his touch, and it was awesome.

"Thanks for coming over," he said.

"Thanks for . . . inviting me?"

"Yeah, sorry. I'm like an island."

"Like Aruba?"

"More like Cape Fear."

I gestured to the room, to the empty walls. "So, what? You hate fresh air?"

"L.A.'s too bright. And I sleep too late."

"I sleep till dinner and I still have windows. There're these things called blinds. Ask Naomi about them."

"Thanks for the tip," he said. "So, how were the hats?"

"The party was a total stain. Pun intended. Libby looked great, but she's dating one of those jerks who spilled their wine on me, so I know she's a mess." I rolled my eyes and said, "And now Morgan's pissed at me for—" and then I stopped myself, realizing I didn't want to talk about this in front of James. "So, whatever. It was lame I even went. I should've come here."

"No, I should've come with you. Or at least made Naomi go. We suck at going to parties."

"Me too. I never want to go out, but when Libby says 'party jump' you just say 'how high?' and pull it together." I noticed I was tapping my foot, which I only did when I was nervous. "She's, like, my best friend."

"Sure," he said, and then to stop the tapping he started stroking my foot. "Well, next time I'll come for protection."

"Just from Morgan, please." Then I nodded and said, "Or *for* Morgan. *From* me."

And that was it, the conversation about my night was over. I could tell James had zero intention of offering up his own evening's activities, but for some reason I felt okay about it. Things seemed somehow simplified up in this little glowing box.

I leaned back and lay flat on the floor, using a sweatshirt hoodie for a pillow. "What's boarding school like?"

He moved over and lay alongside me, both of us facing up. There was a cobwebbed ceiling fan, but it wasn't on.

"It's like . . . nonboarding school," he said.

"Duh. But is it weird living there? Don't you miss being home?"

"Sometimes, but school's pretty cool. I mean, I get along with everybody."

"Do you have a roommate or something?"

James leaned up on his side, on his elbow, facing me. "Luke."

"Do you let him have the bed?"

"No, he has his own closet to sleep in."

"Right." I didn't know if I'd ever know when James was kidding. Never? Always?

I realized it was way too hot: My shirt was damp, my skin glistened with sweat. "Can you turn that fan on?"

"It's broken."

"Great."

I propped my knees up to let them air out. I was dripping.

"Hey," he said. "Give me your arm."

"What arm? I've melted into the rug. I'm a puddle resembling a girl."

"Just give it to me."

I held out my arm for him and James took it, his left hand at my elbow, his right around my wrist. "Stay still," he said, and then, "Don't move," as he lowered his face to the crease where my arm folded. He kissed the crease with his open mouth. I felt his tongue, maybe his teeth, the soft wet inside of his lips. Then he pulled his face away.

"Now close your eyes," James said, "and tell me when my finger gets to the kiss."

I closed my eyes. He moved his finger up my arm, slowly, and sometimes it felt like he moved it backward too, down my arm again, toward my wrist.

"Now," I said, my eyes still closed, my voice nothing but breath.

"Not even close, dude."

I opened my eyes and saw he wasn't even halfway up my forearm. He was closer to my palm than my elbow. "Damn," I said. I dropped my arm a little in his hands. I could still feel the sticky wetness on my skin.

"James," I said.

"Yes?"

"I might never leave this house. It's my favorite house ever."

"That's okay," he said.

"Really?"

He nodded. "All I need is the closet."

"James," I said.

He nodded.

"Don't sleep in the closet."

He laughed. "I don't tell you what to do."

"Yes, you do. You told me to stay still."

"Oh yeah. Sorry about that."

"No, it's awesome you did."

We didn't say anything for a while, and then he said, "You should go back to Naomi."

"Why?"

"The sun will be up in less than an hour."

It was a weird way of putting it, but he was right, it was so late it was early.

"And I can't tell Naomi about this?"

"Negative."

"But I'll see you at breakfast in a few hours?"

"Double negative."

"That means a positive, right?"

"I was told there'd be no math on this exam."

"I won't even look at you," I said, knowing that'd be the hardest part.

"I'm a late sleeper."

"Yeah, I heard."

"I'll be awake tomorrow night."

"I have a shift."

"I'll be awake after your shift."

"It's a date, dude," I said, obviously flirting. So obviously.

He gave me a "Don't get ahead of yourself, dude" look, and then he said, "We'll take a walk."

"Now?" I said, and stood up.

"Tomorrow night, Quinn. Now, you go."

I knew I wouldn't be getting any good-night kiss. His

affection was too random. A future goal: Next time I took my shirt off in front of him, he wouldn't be looking away.

I walked down the narrow staircase and heard James shut the door behind me. The sky was purple and red, getting lighter, making room for the sun. I grabbed my gray tank top out of the dirt and shoved it in my pocket. Hadn't needed that cherry ChapStick after all.

When I slipped back into Naomi's room, she barely stirred. I took off my shorts and squeezed into the sleeping bag, zipping it up over my head. I thought of James on the floor of his tiny walk-in closet. I touched his T-shirt to my underwear. Before I fell asleep, I sniffed the fabric again, but the smell of my sweat covered up his scent. *Blues for a blue T-shirt*, I thought, and closed my eyes on the weirdest day.

5.

SUNDAY

During the few short hours I did sleep, I dreamed of Libby. Somehow she had slipped her way into a subconscious overflowing with images of James's mouth, hair, eyes, voice, hands. But the dreams I had of her weren't just collages and cobwebs of the previous night's events, and they didn't seem like premonitions of events to come. They were just echoes of real-life Libby. Me and Libby lying on beach towels by my pool, her in an American flag print two-piece. Libby at Video Journeys, renting a video, asking my opinion of it, but I don't recognize the title. Libby just floating around places I always am, doing things we always do, with no particular agenda. One final image lingered with me—it was the one swimming beneath my eyelids as I opened them to Naomi's empty room. In it, Libby's in front of my house, in the street, dancing like a spirit, or a ghost, a see-through memory. She's there, but she's not. I lay on the floor in my sleeping bag for a few minutes, not moving. Somehow I knew Libby wanted to be thought of, she wanted to be remembered, just like she had since we were nine years old. And just like since we were nine, not only in dreams, I gave in to her.

At noon I got up. Upstairs Naomi was sitting by herself at the kitchen counter, reading. "Hey," she said. "You missed the morning." She gave me breakfast anyway: a bowl of Kashi with soymilk and a cup of loose-leaf Darjeeling tea with agave nectar. Even the meals here were exotic. I'd never be able to wake up to a Diet Coke and plain rice cake again without feeling deprived.

Later, after breakfast, Naomi walked me to the door to say good-bye.

"Stop by the video store sometime," I said. "I know someone who works there, and I hear she practically *gives* videos away."

Then I waved and walked toward the car, and she leaned against the door frame, waving back.

With her eyes on me, I couldn't sneak back up those narrow stairs. I felt self-conscious about even glancing up at his room. I got to the Lexus and reached for the door handle, and it opened instantly. I groaned at my irresponsibility: I'd forgotten to double-click the thingy, so the car had sat unlocked all night long. And someone had taken advantage and set a small folded note on the driver's seat.

Naomi was still at the door watching me, so I just sat on the piece of paper, started the car, and drove away slowly, past the house, the hydrangea bushes, the basil plants, the garage, that tiny white box that sat on top of it.

When I'd driven a couple of blocks and was turning onto the main canyon road, I reached under myself and pulled out the folded page. *quinlan*, it said on the outside, in the simplest lowercase letters.

> *quinlan,*
> *the shirt isn't a gift, it's a trade. i want something of*
> *yours.*
> *james*

I'd read it thirteen times by the time I parked the Lexus in our driveway and turned off the car.

Until this moment my life's plans had been: graduate from high school, go to Paris, marry Leonardo DiCaprio, die in my sleep. But to have James want me was even better. Take away Leo; burn me alive. My chest hurt.

I didn't wait outside my house that night for anyone to pick me up for work, because no one was coming.

My walk to Video Journeys was relatively peaceful.

I tried to prepare suitable responses to every possible scenario with Morgan, even one that ended in the video store exploding. I tried to expect anger, sadness, sarcasm. Mostly I expected him to ignore me, so as not to incur any anger, sadness, or sarcasm. I didn't, however, expect him to ask Jerry's son Alex to cover for him, making me more anxious with anticipation for our next shift together. So I'd forgotten to expect torture.

Alex was fine, but he did everything for me before I could even think to do it. He answered the phone on the first ring, greeted each customer at the first sound of the front bell, and restocked all the videos the moment they dropped in the return slot. Without even dumb busywork to distract myself, I could already tell this shift was going to drive me nuts. I tried to just zone out and straighten boxes and wait for that occasional customer who actually asked a question to my face.

Normally when I worked with Morgan I never took a break, because the whole thing was a break. But with Morgan gone I racked my brain for a legit excuse to take fifteen in Jerry's office.

I went to the counter where Alex was standing and said, "Hey, can I check the calendar in the back for second? I might need to move a shift."

Alex waved me to go ahead without even paying attention. Whatever. Morgan had to come back to work at some point. He couldn't call in sick for a month. If I had to spend the rest of my summer stuck alone here with Alex—or worse, Jerry—I'd quit. I'd take that temp job at the *Times* my parents were always encouraging me to consider. I'd wear panty hose and sensible work apparel. I'd get rides to the office with my father.

Hold it. No way. Not in this reality.

I dialed Morgan's number.

"Hello?" He sounded annoyed already.

"Hi, dude."

"Why are you calling me? Aren't you at work?"

"Yes. Without *you*. You know, you totally could've worked today, nothing happened. It's like, not even a thing, I promise."

"Oh, you're *kidding*, right?"

I was making it worse, and about to make it the worst: "Morgan, you know you're amazing."

"I don't have to listen to this."

"But think about if you even really like me. I mean, in your mind you could have just created this spark that you don't even feel. Like maybe it's just that I'm always around, sometimes half-naked, super needy, and you just . . . sort of . . . made the wrong connection. Out of boredom. Totally normal."

"You're unreal," he said, as if amused.

"Morgan, listen. We have this unspoken thing. So, it's

like you can't speak it. You can't say it out loud. It's an undercurrent. It's not understandable to us."

"I do *not* have to listen to this."

"Morgan, let's just forgive each other. Please."

"You're the one who's bored."

"I know." I knew.

"You're the one who can't understand it." He was raising his voice. "You'll end up kissing me one night during count-out just to have something to do. Then I'll have to forgive you for using me and you can forgive me for taking advantage of you."

Silence.

I wanted to deny it but couldn't. I wiped my eyes with the back of my hands. Morgan mattered to me; he always had. I couldn't lose him. It was my most selfish and darkest secret. I never wanted to hear him say he loved me, but I had to believe he felt it. My breathing was ragged, my crying audible, but he said nothing.

"I'll quit," I said. "You'll never have to be alone with me again."

"No, you won't," Morgan said, and sighed, but he wasn't saying it to cheer me up. He was reasoning with himself.

"Can't everything just be the same? If you think maybe I'll come around one day, then can't you just come back to work so we can hang out and go back to normal?"

I didn't know what I was saying. I was scum, the lowest, and no one was there to slap me or smack the phone out of my hand.

"You're a brat."

And then, guided by nothing, prompted by no one, I became the lamest person alive: "You know who's really cute, and cooler than me, and has a better body and would be totally into you?"

Total, awful silence.

"Naomi Sheets," I said.

"Quinn. You're a psycho."

More tears fell out of my eyes. "I know. I know."

"I'm hanging up now."

"You should."

He did.

Whatever real love I had for Morgan—no matter how skewed and small and mostly self-serving—I had to force myself to let it go. And even though it made no sense, I had to cry a little longer for Morgan. Right then Alex opened the office door and saw my face, puffy and wet.

"Go home. I can close out alone tonight." He looked away from me, at the schedule on the wall.

"Why?"

"It's not a request."

I couldn't call James to change our plans, because he had no phone. I'd just have to go home for a few hours and walk back here at eleven, meeting him out front as if I'd worked a full regular shift.

So I collected my stuff, collected myself, and wandered outside, feeling ridiculous for being sent home after two hours of uselessness. But I deserved punishment. Even if it didn't fit the crime.

When I reached my house and saw three unfamiliar cars parked in our driveway, I put two and two together and guessed that my parents were having guests over tonight. I also guessed that my mother would probably kill me if I crashed her party looking this way: splotchy, post-sobbing, like an extra from *Les Miz*.

Fortunately, the eight adults in the dining room were too busy with appetizers and Riesling to notice me sneak past them up the stairs. I climbed into bed and hugged a pillow over my face and crashed. Later, when I willed myself awake, I was covered in sweat. I looked over at my clock and panicked: 10:56.

I sprang out of bed and started searching for a shoe I hadn't seen in weeks but that somehow seemed crucial for my meeting up with James. In my rational mind I knew James wouldn't just leave if he didn't see me outside the video store at exactly ten past eleven. He'd probably wait a while, or even start walking to my house, and then we'd meet in the middle. That'd be the best-case scenario.

Almost romantic, really. Worst-case scenario: James goes home. If that happened, I'd have to sneak out after my parents were asleep, take the Lexus without permission, and deal with the consequences tomorrow. Worst, worst-case scenario: James bails to do whatever weird stuff Naomi alluded to last night and I can't find him. Then I'd have to call her again, invite myself over for the second night in a row, lure her to fall deeply asleep, and sneak off to the garage studio to wait for him, thereby confirming Morgan's theory that I was both a brat *and* a psycho. What a drag.

Seriously, I needed that damn shoe.

I only had half a minute to give myself a once-over in the mirror. I was wearing a short, ripped, white cotton button-down dress with the first three buttons missing, but it came across less as scandalous and steamy than it did just sloppy. My earrings were tangled up in my hair, and all my chain necklaces had somehow coiled together into one fat knot. I gave up on finding the cute shoes and so settled on my dirty flower-print ankle-high Docs, unlaced, with no socks. The sweat from my nap plus basic summer night body heat had smeared my black eyeliner into raccoon chic and my cheeks into crazy flushed rouge pots. My skin felt like damp flypaper. The fabric of my dress was so thin I could see my black underwear and bra in the mirror but now it was 10:59, so I had no time to change.

I noticed a half-empty Diet Coke on my bedside table and chugged it. The taste was warm and flat and syrupy and reinforcing. I was ready to sprint for my life. Instead I tripped down most of the stairs, dropping my keys and bag onto the tile foyer floor.

"Quinny?"

My father's voice.

I pivoted, calmly, in his direction. Eight adult-y adults were sitting in the den, in silence, staring at me. My father stood up from the white leather couch.

"Where are you going?"

"It's cool, Dad." I tried to smooth out my dress, wondering just how transparent it might look under the chandelier.

"So, you're leaving then?" He raised his eyebrows inquisitively. A very well-dressed woman in a pashmina sweaterdress sitting next to my mother took a sip from a glass of white wine.

"I'm . . . not even here. I'm, like, at work right now anyway."

The couples looked from me to each other to my parents, then down at their wineglasses. Beverages in the white room? My mother was probably beyond edgy. I could detect serious vibes being thrown my way: *Do not cause a scene. Do not cause a scene.*

"Morgan's here to pick me up," I said, super casual.

My mother relaxed visibly at the sound of his name.

"That's her little boyfriend," she explained, and the couples nodded in understanding.

"Grab a long-sleeve, sweetie," she said, standing up and guiding the guests out the sliding door to the backyard patio.

"Be back whenever," my father said, following her.

Would it always be this easy?

"Right . . .," I said, suddenly alone.

I dashed down the stone steps, my mind racing, trying to calculate the odds of James's whereabouts. I was past the tea lights and nearly to the street before I noticed Libby lying on the hood of her car, parked across the road, in front of our neighbors' house. I froze. Libby didn't typically come to my house. And right now I really didn't have time for her visit. I looked down the long, dark canyon road to my left: Video Journeys. Somewhere, James. And then I looked to my right: Libby, in a nightgown, sprawled across her hood, barely visible under a streetlamp, at eleven on a Sunday night. Damn it.

"Libby, this better be so good. You better be a pregnant runaway with diabetes right now," I said, walking toward her. "Drive me to Video Journeys." I went to the passenger side and opened the door. "Get in."

"Why?" she asked, sounding dazed, or drunk. "Why aren't you there now?"

"Dumb reasons," I said. "Don't worry about it."

"Then why do you have to go back?" She leaned over on her side, facing away from me, and curled her long legs up under her.

"Libby, what are you doing here? I'm sure whatever it is we can totally talk about it later. I just have to go meet someone at the video store. Like, right now. So, either take me or don't, but I gotta go." Time was not on my side. I pictured James loitering in the Video Journeys parking lot, checking where his watch would be.

"Whatever, Quinn," she said. And then, "You know Morgan can wait." She laughed in a drugged, distant way. "He'll wait foreeeeever for you, you know. . . ."

"Seriously, dude? Are you on planet Earth?" But when she finally rolled over to face me, I could see that she wasn't. She was not on planet Earth.

Libby was white, translucent. I could see the blue veins running along her forehead and under her eyes, more pronounced than usual. She drifted her limbs in a weird pendulum motion, like she was keeping time with an inaudible song. Her wrists were frailer, and the one she'd worn the silver bracelets on was now wrapped in a bulky white bandage. She looked drained, wild-eyed, sick. Her perfectly straight, flat hair was kinked like a bad home perm.

"Okay. So what'd you take? Stella's prescriptions?"

She shook her head. She didn't blink.

"All right. So what, you're stoned? Tripping? Alien invasion? Poltergeist?" I pointed to her nightgown. "Help me out here, Lib."

"Let's just sit here, okay? Let's just enjoy the night." She closed her eyes and smiled up at the starless sky. "It's best at night," she said, reaching out to hold my hand. Her palm was warm, but her fingers were cold.

"Come on, you're scaring me."

She laughed a light, empty laugh. Then Libby slid off the hood and started to twirl slowly in the street, humming something foggy and quiet.

Then it hit me, and I said it out loud: "I dreamed this."

"Did you have fun at my party?" Libby asked.

"No. It sucked."

Libby smiled a vacant smile to herself, said nothing.

"And thanks a lot for protecting me from those guys. I thought they were going to wear my skin over their skin. Cooper especially."

"You lived."

"Whatever, dude. Not cool."

Nothing about this was cool.

She danced over in my direction, her arms out, eyes still closed. "You know, you used to like hanging out with me. Aren't you happy to see your best friend?" She stopped in front of me and stroked under my chin, holding my face in her hand.

"Yeah, this is great." My voice was trembling. I prayed for James to come later, because if he came now, there'd be no way to explain what he was seeing. I couldn't understand it myself. Libby was the living dead. She wasn't there. I felt like if I reached out my hand it would pass right through her skin.

"Do you want to talk about the bandage on your wrist, or what? I've seen this episode. *Dateline* calls them 'cutters,' you know."

More twirling.

"What's with the melodrama? You came here in a nightgown?"

"I never got dressed today. Long night."

"Right. You're high, and it's bad stuff. I'll go inside and get you a Diet Coke or something. Triscuits. Whatever. You need a nap and a bag of chips, pronto." I started for the house, but she danced over and blocked me from the steps.

"I'm meeting Stiles at midnight, so you can go find Morgan and—"

"Look," I interrupted, finally pissed. "You've gone crazy, obviously, which would normally only sort of be my problem except for the fact that you're not here to visit me, you're here to drive *me* crazy. What the hell is wrong with you?"

I was panting, livid. Libby and I had only been in one

fight ever, in the eighth grade. She'd promised to go with me to the culmination dance. We'd agreed together: no dates, no matter what. Then two nights before the dance she called and pretended to be too sick, claiming Stella wouldn't let her go because she might be contagious. Then five minutes later, Jordan Justman called to invite me to the dance as his date. He'd bribed Libby to bail on me so he could swoop in. Then when I wasn't into him groping me behind the gym, Jordan admitted to the whole scheme, swearing Libby had given him the green light. She and I didn't speak for that entire summer before high school. But eventually I had to forgive her. I still remembered her crying over the phone to me, "We'll go to a dance together next year."

But by next year she was with Nathan. So whatever.

Then Libby's face changed. Suddenly she looked sad, puzzled, like she didn't know where she was or how she'd gotten here. She fingered her nightgown like it was the first time she'd seen it. My anger gave way to sadness. My eyes welled up for the second time tonight.

I reached out my hand to Libby, but she just sat on the ground and began humming again softly to herself. I could see her bare feet, dirty and cut up. She started to hum a little louder, and then I could make out some of the words.

"'One baby to another says I'm lucky to have met you,'" she sang.

I knew the song. Libby and I knew all the same songs.

"I'm worried about your wrist. You don't look good. Talk to me. I won't tell Stella, I swear." A few tears ran down my cheeks, but she didn't notice. I wanted her to cry with me. I had that sick feeling again. It was that top hat in the dirt. I didn't want to ask, but I did: "Did you do it to yourself, or did . . . someone . . . do it to you?"

She ignored me, sang more. "'It is now my duty to completely drain you . . .'"

Nirvana.

I got on the ground too and hugged her and held on tightly, pushing her face in my shoulder. She felt light and breakable. I felt like I could break her bones if I hugged hard enough.

But Libby'd never broken a bone, and I knew that. I knew everything about Libby, but everything I knew about Libby was about some other Libby, a younger, different version that didn't exist anymore. Up until now our friendship had been slowly dissolving in a totally normal, undramatic way, because of time and distance and the general growing-up-ness and growing-apart-ness that happens in high school. But losing her like that wasn't the same as having her ripped away. It wasn't at all the same as having her just taken from me.

At some point Libby chose boys over best friends, but I never held it against her because I would've done the same thing—if I'd had a boy. I'd never wanted to be a loner, never wanted to be alone, but I realized I was except for Libby, and holding her was like holding the last person on earth who really knew me. I wanted to tell Libby that I couldn't keep letting her drift away, and that I had to do the opposite now: I had to reclaim her. To protect the only real relationship in my life, I had to revive the bond we had back when we were fragile fourth graders who loved each other more than candy.

But first I'd have to stop this craziness. And that meant stopping Stiles.

"I'll kill him," I said. "I'll get Morgan to run him over in his Dodge Shadow."

"Won't do any good," she whispered. She looked up at the moon. "It'll be midnight soon. I've got to go . . . home."

"I want to come with you." I shouted, "I'm coming with you!"

"You can't go with her."

The voice was behind me: James.

"Is she okay?" I asked.

"She can drive."

"How do you know?"

"I just do."

"But she's been hurt," I said.

"Quinn. Believe me." Then, "You want your parents' friends to see this?"

I imagined the woman in the pashmina sweaterdress walking out arm in arm with her husband and discovering this teenage meltdown so close to their Infiniti.

Together we lifted Libby up and walked her to her car. She paid no attention to James, didn't ask who he was, didn't even look at him.

"James," I said, not wanting Libby to go, not wanting Libby to stay. Not knowing what to want. And when he opened the driver's-side door and helped Libby climb into her Mustang, I still didn't know.

Libby turned on the engine, and James reached in and flipped the headlights on. Then, finally—and for the first time—she noticed him. Her eyes fixed on his face. She reached out a hand, put it on his cheek. James gently removed it and placed it back inside the car and leaned in to say something I couldn't hear. Libby nodded and drove away, never looking back.

James turned to me. "Are you crying?"

"No." Not anymore.

"I went to the video store."

"Why did you even come here?"

"Didn't you get my note?"

"Yeah."

"So don't be like this."

"Whatever you want, James."

Everyone's hopeless tragedies just bled into one another. In an easy world I'd be with Morgan, James would fade away into the Valley, the hills, to Massachusetts or wherever he came from, and Libby would tell Stiles to chill on the drugs and violent stuff. But in a perfect world all the Spaders would disappear, so would Morgan's feelings for me, and James would love me.

"This is what I want," he said as he reached out a hand for my neck.

I didn't collapse into him, or wrap my arms around his waist, or press my face against his chest. I didn't know how to get the things I wanted now that I knew to want them. I didn't move as he stroked my hair.

"But I want something more," James said.

I wanted something more too, so badly, but he didn't mean that, or anything like that. He was talking about our trade.

"I can't give you my dress," I said, looking down at it. "I don't have anything else." I thought of my body, what there was to give. A fingernail. An eyelash. A lock of hair. But James wasn't a forensic scientist. He was my date. Sort of.

So I unclasped one of the knotted gold chains from

my neck and held it up for him. He fastened it around his own neck. It hung just slightly lower than the small gold cross shining against his pale white chest. I never wanted it back.

6.

STUFF

James didn't ask questions because he didn't want
to answer questions, but he did give me small, warm looks
as we walked quietly through the canyons. I noticed it
most when we passed under one streetlight, then another.
Everything was better in the dark, cooler, like in a black–
and-white photograph.

Sometimes James's shoulder brushed against mine as
we walked, but mostly it didn't. Mostly we just paced on,
staring ahead at the curving black road. My body felt
exhausted, but I couldn't relax. James wasn't Morgan, he
wasn't just a dude, some guy I could joke with, then flirt
with, then leave.

"Do you like living in Cambridge?" I asked finally.

"I guess. I like the seasons, the leaves changing colors."

I said, "We have colors and seasons here, too," but

then stopped myself. No, we didn't.

"The color of money at the Four Seasons doesn't count."

"Ha, ha." I fake-smiled.

"But here's cool too."

"When do you go back? I mean, when do your parents get back to L.A.?"

James looked up like he was counting weeks or days in his head, but he took too long so I interrupted, "You know, my parents think I'm with that guy Morgan right now. It's the only way they'd let me go out. I don't know what they'd do if they found out I was with you."

"No MTV for a week?"

I rolled my eyes. "Maybe. Maybe they don't care."

"I'm sure they care if you lie."

"Probably. I don't know. I mean, I'm seventeen. Pretty hard to deal with."

"Sure. I remember seventeen."

"Spare me. You turned twenty and your life's so great?"

"Not at all. I used to rock out. I used to shred."

"You were in a band?" I said it like it was dreamy. I said it in the dreamy way a dumb groupie at the Roxy would.

"Yeah. I played, like, two chords, just through pedals. We sucked."

"Artsy, huh?"

"Thurston Moore came to one of our shows. Pretty artsy."

"I don't believe you."

"Ask him about it," he said. "Ask him about Malcolm Hex."

"Ew."

"Told you we sucked."

"Well, now I believe you."

"We covered 'Stairway.' Or part of it. More like a deconstruction really."

"Disgusting. When's that from? The sixties?"

He pretended to be offended.

"So," I asked, "what's the deal with your parents?"

"Daniel and Charlotte are fine. They let me do my thing."

"I wasn't aware you had a thing."

"Sure. Stalking, sixties culture-jamming, other hideous stuff."

"Reading?"

"I shuffle between *Green Eggs and Ham* and *Ham on Rye*."

"Sports?"

"Please."

"Dating?"

"Less so."

"Bummer. Anything else of note?"

"Not really. I'm kind of in a 'me' phase."

"You're preaching to the preacher with that one."

"What about your parents, are they so bad?"

"No," I said. "They're neutral."

"They're neutral but they side with Morgan?"

"He's just really safe."

"Oh. Safe." James thought about that for a minute. "Makes sense."

"It's stupid. Everyone's safe. It's high school."

He said, "Well, I'm not safe."

"Yeah, you're a total heartbreaker. Obviously." I waved my hand at him.

He didn't say anything to that, just motioned to a small patch of grass on the side of the canyon, where we sat down.

"Morgan totally doesn't matter," I said. It felt weird saying it.

"It's okay. He can matter. I only met you less than a week ago."

"Still," I said, reaching for his hand. I held it in mine and traced the veins between his knuckles and his wrist bone. In the dark it looked like he had no lines or wrinkles. My fingers stroked his fingers, then moved down again to his palm.

"That was your best friend Libby back there?" James lifted his free hand to my face, pushing my bangs to the side.

"'Was' being the crucial word. I don't know what she is now."

"You should stay away from her."

I pushed his hand, then backed away from him and folded my arms across my chest. "That's, like, the exact opposite of what I'm going to do."

"She's messed up. You know I'm right."

"I don't know anything."

"You're going to get hurt."

"Yeah, when the twins run me over in their Mazda."

"This is serious."

"Then help me," I said. "If you don't want me to get hurt, then help me help Libby."

"I am helping you. Some advice: Libby's on her own trip now."

"It's not her, it's her boyfriend, Stiles. We have to threaten him or something."

James shook his head.

"What?"

"No."

"You know something, don't you?" I squinted my eyes to read him. Mostly James was a mood ring and I just had to guess what the different colors meant, but right now he was a decoder ring and I had to guess the hidden message. "What do you know?"

"I know she's toast."

"She's not toast. She's a warm Pop-Tart—she's not crispy yet."

"She's in trouble. And if she's in trouble and you're around her, then you're in trouble. I know guys like Stiles. Not safe."

"You know guys like Stiles?" I asked.

"The not safe"—James tapped his chest—"can spot the not safe."

"What did you say to Libby? When you leaned into the window, before she drove away."

"I told her to leave you alone."

"Why? She needs me."

"You can't do anything."

"Shut up." I pulled my knees up to hide my face and turned away from him.

"Quinn."

"I don't understand. I don't understand." I felt James up against my back, cradling me. He pressed his lips to the back of my head, then kissed across my neck, to my earlobe, and held his mouth there.

"It's not the end of the world."

"Yes, it is." I braced my arms over his, locking them into position around me.

"It's not. Trust me."

I lifted one hand behind me and interlocked my fingers with his messy hair. I noticed his eyes were down, lined up exactly with the bare skin on my collarbone, watching my black cotton bra rise and fall. After a second it felt like I was holding his head there. Like if I let go he'd pull away.

"What's wrong?"

"Just give me a second." James turned his head and faced away, down the hill.

"I'm mad at *you*. You give *me* a second." We sat in silence.

Then he said, "Second's up," and he was back.

I moved my body around so we were facing each other again.

"You're pretty pissed at me."

It was weird; I could be pissed and totally not pissed at the same time. "Listen," I said, touching my chain around his neck, "if I tell you to go away, like, if I shout at you to go, will you?"

"Not if you don't mean it," he said.

"I probably won't ever mean it."

"You're tired," he said.

"*You're* tired."

He didn't look tired, though.

Then my eyes closed again and he said, "I'm boring you."

I would have fake-yawned to be cute, but if it turned into a real one it'd be too soon. "So tell me a secret."

"I have one, but it's pretty weird."

I waved my hand, like, *Lay it on me.*

"Last Wednesday, in front of the video store, that wasn't the first time I'd seen you."

"What do you mean?"

In my worn-out haze, I tried to think back. I had no recollection of ever seeing Naomi outside of school. I'd never seen her at a party, renting a movie, at the mall, at the grocery store. And of course I'd never seen her with him. I would've noticed.

"It was around Christmas. Like, a year and a half ago."

"Was it at Libby's party?" Dudes, dudes, and more faceless dudes.

"No."

"Were you a mall Santa? Did I sit on your lap?"

"At least you're not freaking out."

"James, just tell me."

"I was walking on Laurel Pass. I saw you skateboarding."

"And?"

"And you wiped out. It was late."

Casually I said, "I remember that," but it wasn't casual; it was bizarre. That night I'd actually been skateboarding home from the Blocks' Christmas cocktail party. Libby was supposed to drive me home, but she and Nathan got into a huge fight over something very unhuge. Whatever. My board slipped out from under me and I did a serious face-plant on the concrete. I got a crazy bloody nose and a split lip, but I was alone. I knew I was alone because I called out for help for ten straight minutes and no one came. Not even a car drove by.

"I didn't want to creep you out," he said. "Some weirdo coming out of the darkness."

"Yeah, real horrifying." Remembering the pain and embarrassment annoyed me. And then to realize he'd been watching me the whole time, yelling and bleeding and cussing at myself, annoyed me even more.

"But you were cool, remember? You got up and skated home."

"And you were where? Hiding in the bushes?"

"Sort of."

"Doing what?"

"I was just out."

"Just out checking for bloody asphalt?"

His voice laughed a short, "Yeah."

"What am I missing here?"

"Look, I saw you and didn't want to bother you."

"Well, I'm officially creeped out."

"Good. Be creeped out."

"I wish you'd just . . . hung out with me." This was the most aggravating point of all. James had been there, and if he'd just said hey, we could have met, spent two amazing weeks together, started a correspondence, had a long-distance thing. Then I would've already been friends with Naomi and not had to deal with Morgan's weirdness for all of junior year because I'd be making out at this exact moment on the grass, on a date, with my sexy older boyfriend.

Then I said, kind of angry, "Doesn't matter if you'd scared me. Who wouldn't help a bleeding, limping girl in a Christmas dress all alone on a dark, cold night?"

"I wasn't in any condition to be helping anyone."

"What the hell does that mean?"

"It doesn't mean anything. That's why you like me anyway, right? Because I'm mysterious?" Then he looked up and met my eyes for the first time all night, and I didn't like it.

In a very small voice I said, "That's not why."

"Sorry. Sometimes I'm rude to girls I think are sexy."

"You're confusing."

"I described you to Naomi afterward. She told me to leave you alone."

"Why? What's wrong with me?"

James stopped to think about the question for too long.

"Wait," I said, "you think I'm sexy?"

His eyes drifted across my face, down my neck, to my unbuttoned dress. He left them there and nodded, slowly, yes.

"With a bloody nose? You think bloody noses are sexy?"

He squinted. "That's a harder question to answer."

"Is it?"

Then he cupped my face in his hands and pressed his lips to my forehead, leaving them on my skin. I closed my eyes to enjoy the moment, but it was impossible to open them again once he pulled away. The rest of my body screamed at me: *BED*. I shook my head to fight off the feeling, but it must've looked like slow motion to James, because he started lifting me off the grass.

"Home, dude?"

"Home, dude," I said, and yawned for real. I hung my arms around his waist and let him half carry me, half shuffle me along.

"So are you going to put my picture in your locker?"

"It's summer. I can't get to my locker."

"How about your diary?"

I stuck out my tongue. "That's private."

And then we were quiet for a while.

Then, because there was nothing to say, I started saying everything. I confessed my random crushes on young Springsteen and Will Smith, stuck up for television, citing the many ways it'd shaped my once vulnerable mind, bashed baseball, admitted to having a retainer I never wore. I told him I wanted to learn how to play, in no particular order of importance, the upright bass, the tenor saxophone, and the drums, but I'd settle for a drum machine. I recited Tennessee Williams lines, *Seinfeld* quotes, Smashing Pumpkins lyrics, told my only good joke, performed my only celebrity impression, badly. Strong beliefs on eighties Lakers versus nineties Bulls, Diet Coke versus Coca-Cola Classic, Kurt versus Courtney, West Coast rap versus East Coast rap, Converse versus Vans.

At times James looked at me like I was an alien, and other times he looked at me like I was his kind of alien. Most of the time he just pulled me in tighter to hug his body and smelled my hair and kissed the top of my head.

Soon we were on my block. When I could see the tea lights outside of my house, James interrupted me.

He was like, "First crush?"

If it counted: "Aladdin."

"First kiss?"

Skip that. "Boring."

He asked about my first . . . anything else.

Skip that one too. "Nothing to tell."

He wanted to know had I ever had my heart broken.

Easy: no.

Had I ever broken anyone's heart?

Simple: one person's, every day for a year.

But he didn't ask the most obvious question in this line of questioning: Had I ever been in love?

Not before now. Not even close.

When we reached my stone steps, I said, "Come upstairs. Please." I smiled at him, wobbly. The yawns were coming on strong. I was almost asleep on my feet.

He said, "You can't even open your eyes." But it wasn't a no.

I pulled him through the front door and up the stairs. He hesitated in my doorway and raised his eyebrows at the janky state of my room.

"Don't judge me, Mr. No Windows No Phone No Bed No Furniture," I said between yawns. "Bless this mess." I jumped on the bed once and then flopped down on it.

James stood over me, his expression soft but preoccupied.

I pulled on his arm a little. "Lie down with me, please."

"Saying please doesn't work on me. What about mom and dad?"

I pointed at the pillow next to me, at the small folded white piece of paper lying on it.

James picked up the note and read aloud: "'Quinlan, great dinner party, wish you had stayed for dessert. Next time invite Morgan in. If we're gone when you wake up, don't forget to eat a proper meal. No soda, please, although the odds of us paying your college tuition with money from recycled cans are increasing. This room has gone beyond a mother's reproach. Love you, Mom.'"

James set the note on my nightstand next to a Diet Coke can.

"Told you she thinks I'm with Morgan. Libby *saw* you and she still probably thinks I'm with Morgan."

Libby. Where was she now?

James knelt down next to the bed and touched my flushed cheek with the back of his hand. I faded in and out of sleep while he said things I couldn't really understand about Libby and Stiles. Then he took off my Docs and put my Garfield stuffed animal under my arm and laid a light blanket over me.

"Obviously we're supposed to kiss now," I mumbled.

"We already kissed. You're delirious."

"Not on the lips."

"You're asleep."

"You're not taking advantage. I want you to do it." I reached my hand to touch just below his neck, that area of exposed skin above his shirt's V where our necklaces hung together.

"Maybe I don't want to kiss a sleeping pill." He flashed a slanted smile and said, "Maybe I want a little proactive contact sport," but I knew that wasn't it. Some other reason kept his mouth so specifically off mine, but I wasn't going to find out tonight.

I thought I fell asleep again, but when I opened my eyes he was still there, holding my hand, and it was in this hallucinating state that I offered up the only real secret I had.

"James, I think I love"—but something stopped me—"stuff. I love stuff."

I *was* delirious. It wasn't much of a secret anyway.

Then James pulled away from me and followed the path back to my door. "Stuff . . . is cool, Quinn. I'm really, really into stuff too."

It was the best.

But if it was the best, then why wasn't it easier, as I floated into dreams, to pretend not to hear the doubt in his voice?

7.

INVITATION

Woke up at four thirty in the afternoon feeling steam-rolled. Bulldozed. Yeah, I loved the nightlife. Apparently being with James meant trading all my lazy sunny days by the pool for midnight walks and five a.m. long good-byes. Which would've been fine except that the bags under my eyes were becoming deep dark pools of their own. I was learning that bodies didn't like the sleep-all-day, hang-out-all-night schedule. And yet James seemed to be pulling it off, so who knows.

I only had an hour to get ready for work, and I wanted to make it count. First of all, after yesterday's humiliating dismissal, I knew I'd have some serious butt-kissing to do. That meant dressing like a semi-sane girl and a respon-sible employee, having all emotional meltdowns before six, and volunteering to handle even the most menial tasks, like calling customers with late fees and rewriting the entire New Releases dry-erase board. Also I had to prepare for the potentially worst coworker ever, which for different reasons entirely might be either a judgmental version of Alex or a pissed-off version of Morgan. I preferred the pissed-off Morgan, but bratty, selfish beggars can't be choosers. Secondly, I needed to call Naomi and accidentally mention I had a shift tonight in hopes that she'd then happen to mention it to James, whom I'd forgotten to tell last night when I was trying to lure him into my bed. Third, I had to find Libby somehow, even if that meant tracking her down by phone at the Spader sanctuary and then commanding her to come visit me at the store. Finally, had to feed myself real food. And sneak out a Diet Coke for emergencies. Which, after last night, I was pretty much banking on.

I set about my tasks in order. My loveliest look was a vintage rayon forties dress that my mother had bought me at Aardvarks on Melrose. I paired it with a ripped, too-small denim jacket and some scuffed lace-up boots, because I could only stand to look so precious. With all the gold jewelry, the black eyeliner, and the knotted bird's-nest hair that I tried to comb to no avail, I appeared exactly the same as I did on other who-cares workdays, except that somewhere beneath all the junk was a dainty rose print instead of a dirty Beat Happening shirt. So much for put together.

I skipped ahead to my mother's request and ate some

fruit. This would please her and prove to both of us that I could survive without being hand-fed. I wasn't sure if a tangerine and seven raspberries sufficed as a full meal, considering I'd slept straight through breakfast and lunch, so I rounded it out with seven Saltines and guacamole and a stick of string cheese. I scribbled her a note of my own on the kitchen counter:

> *Mom, no immediate plans to clean aforementioned bedroom/tornado site, BUT am totally full and well fed. After work tonight might be out late with someone special. Don't worry, I'll be good.*
>
> *Love, Me*

I had about fifteen minutes left to make my calls. I climbed on a bar stool at the counter and grabbed the phone. Naomi first. I knew I needed to seem like a cool cucumber, like, keep it smooth. I let the dial tone drone for a full fifteen seconds while I fixed my hair, straightened myself, and swiveled around a few revolutions. Then I practiced saying, "Hi, Naomi," into the mouthpiece a half-dozen times. I dialed and exhaled a long sigh before she answered.

"Hello?"

I said, "Hey, lady," but the "Hey, lady" wasn't me, it was Tom Jones.

"Quinn?"

"Yeah, hi. What's up?"

"Um, nothing. Just got back from riding, about to take a shower."

"Cool, shower." I yelled at myself: *Get to it. Get to it.* I tapped the top of the phone against my forehead. Screw the cucumber; I was a zucchini.

Naomi drew out the word, "Ohhh-kay," and it made me feel crazy. Crazier. "What's up with you?"

"About to go to work. You know, got a shift at the store like always. I'll be there all night. Until eleven. Then I'm just going to walk home. No plans."

"You can come over . . . if you want." Naomi sounded sort of disappointed, like she thought we were already done with the "awkward acquaintances" phase. And we were. Sort of. But she'd misunderstood my nervousness and overly specific outline of the evening, and now things were worse. I couldn't say no to her because I was basically begging her, but if God made miracles and James showed up to walk me home, I couldn't actually say yes to her either.

So I said, "Maybe?"

"Whatever, okay."

"So . . . I'll just be at the store."

"Right. And I'll be here if you want to hang out."

"Okay, well, I get off at eleven. Like always." This was a mess.

"Like you said." I heard Naomi turn the shower on.

Now my inner monologue ordered: *Hang up the phone, Quinn. Hang it. Up.*

"And Morgan's not taking me home either."

Wow.

"Be safe then?" The sound of running water was getting louder.

Something was seriously wrong with me, because I literally said, "Safe isn't always the best way to be."

"What?"

"Bye, Naomi. Bye."

Surprisingly painful, actually.

This second phone call would be easy breezy as long as I didn't start crying. But then again, if I was going to cry, I'd better do it now.

Stella answered on the third ring, sounding totally out of it. She said Libby wasn't home, that she'd spent the night at Stiles's and was probably still there now. Okay, no big deal, I'd just call Stiles . . . at his underground lair, where he most likely had Libby chained to a radiator and she was loving it. Stella gave me the number, which contained not even one six, let alone the three in a row I'd expected. His answering machine beeped a single beep with no outgoing message.

"Oh. Okay. Hi, this is Quinn Lacey, I'm looking for Libby. I know she's with you, so just go get her." I waited a second. "Libby, listen, sorry about last night.

Whatever my friend James told you, it's not how I feel. I still want to see you, so please come by the store tonight and we'll talk about whatever's going on. Or we can talk about other stuff, doesn't matter. I just want to see you and make sure you're okay. I'm going to guess for both of our sakes you were just having a rough night. Okay, so come by. Love you, bye."

The phone beeped back at me while I rushed to get the last words out. I contemplated calling again, just to make sure my message hadn't gotten erased or cut off, but I could only stand to be so much of a weirdo. Even if Stiles ignored me, Stella knew I was looking for Libby. I'd covered my bases and done my best. Psychic powers were out, meal was in, best dress was on, and I'd gotten more done in one hour than I had in three days.

I ran to Morgan when I saw him behind the front counter. He wanted to be moody and dismissive, I could tell, but once I was bounding toward him he opened his arms for me with only the smallest reluctance. I babbled about whatever, not allowing for a single moment of awkwardness or self-reflection from either of us. We put *The Basketball Diaries* on. During one particularly intimate scene, Morgan turned to me and yanked on one of my tiny braids.

"Hey, aren't you going to marry Leo? Once you get to Paris?"

"Oh, Morgan, you're so smart." I wasn't being sarcastic either; he remembered everything.

We were back in full swing. Okay, maybe more like semi-swing, but it felt great. I didn't care if it was denial or repression or just teenage madness, but pretending like he didn't love me and I didn't not love him was a refreshing change. We weren't talking about anything that wasn't directly in front of us: an annoying customer trying to return a busted copy of *Beetlejuice*, how the Jim Carroll book was way more disturbing than the movie, my new silver nail polish, licorice whips. Morgan even mentioned the recent heat wave; we were talking weather! I waited for things to turn, braced myself for the total bitch-out I deserved, but Morgan kept it light and pleasant. Until a certain point.

"Hey, so you remember at Libby's party the other night?" He sounded composed, but I still pretended to stare at a copy of *Terminator 2* like it was a Dead Sea Scroll.

"Uh-huh."

"Yeah, well, after you left," he said, and I tensed up, digging my fingernails into the small cardboard box, "this freshman girl kind of hit on me. I thought you'd think that was . . . funny, or something."

I peered over at him, and his face was normal.

"Nice," I said, and high-fived him. "Fresh meat."

Morgan laughed, and I felt my whole body relax. He wasn't trying to make me jealous or pivot the conversation into some lecture about how he was lovable and better than my repeated rejection. That's of course how I would've played it, but Morgan was better than that.

"Just a stupid turn of events. You lose some, you win some. Kind of." He laughed to himself again, but maybe this time there was a little edge.

"What kind of hat did she have on?"

"Bride's veil."

"She came looking for love. Did you get her number?"

"Yeah, I did, and she seemed really into it. But when I left, I saw her standing outside, talking to Sanders. Fresh meat? He was probably thinking the same thing."

Somebody had to take those dudes down, stat.

"Speak of the devil . . . ," Morgan said, and his voice trailed off as the store's doorbell rang.

Please be Sanders. Please be Sanders, I prayed.

But Morgan had mistaken Stiles for his twin. Damn it. Stiles was devilish—no doubt about that—but not in a predictable way. He'd literally fallen into the Gap and come out a netherworld poster boy. He was wearing a tucked-in, plain white button-down shirt with the top three buttons undone and the sleeves rolled up to his elbows. His khaki chinos were formfitting but casually wrinkled in the total "Who, me?" kind of way that usually worked on teenage, crush-having suckers like myself. Loafers with no socks. A silver Seiko watch. A fifties straw fedora pushed back on his head. He was a pale, preppy nightmare, and he was coming right at me.

"Quinlan," he said, wrapping one hand around my wrist and flashing a nasty sweet smile, "come over here and help me choose something."

I stared at Morgan, who was clearly freaked, and tried to curve my lips into something resembling a smile. Then I turned back to Stiles and pointed over to the side wall, and my smile was gone.

"Those are the Employee Picks. You don't need any help."

"Oh, but I do," he said, leading me to the corner of the store where Morgan and I had displayed our personal faves.

"Fine. How about *Sleeping with the Enemy*? Or have you seen that too many times?"

He ignored me and eyed me up and down. "You look delicious tonight."

"You look like a psychotic yachtsman. Where's Libby?"

"Oh no, did I forget to give her your message? I know I wrote it down but . . . I don't remember where I put the paper." He reached out and felt my dress's rayon fabric between two long, bony fingers.

"You can't keep her from me forever. And whatever it is you're doing to make her act like a bad acid casualty, you better stop."

"I can't tell Libby what to do." He spoke slowly and methodically, never blinking. If someone could be totally empty, he was totally empty.

I imagined James's voice telling me to run.

"Well, I can, and I will. And you'll be old news. Rent a movie and leave."

I started to turn away, but he grabbed my arm, harder.

"Libby wants to be with me. Just ask her." Then he leaned in and breathed the words in my ear: "She likes it."

"I don't care if she likes it, she's not a person anymore. She's just some cult chick." I was petrified, shaking.

Stiles was thrilled. "Don't be such a drama queen. She's still a *person*," he said, then added, "With banging legs." Then he traced along my jawbone, devouring me with his eyes. "Not that I wouldn't mind breaking off a little piece of you . . ."

I wrenched my arm free and stepped back and glared at him.

"Besides," he said, lightening his tone and surveying his manicured nails, "Libby's not your 'bestie' anymore. Things change. If you love someone, set them free." Stiles didn't sing it like Sting, he said it like Satan, and he laughed.

"Listen, you Dahmer," I seethed, balling my fists, "I will set you on fire."

"How adorable, the feisty thing really works for you." Then he cocked his head and shot me an icy look. I could handle the look, but I couldn't handle the question: "Do you put up this much of a fight with James?" Stiles raised his dark eyebrows, hoping he'd hit a nerve.

He'd hit one, ripped it open, and left it thrashing around like a live wire.

"You . . . do . . . *not* . . . know James."

"Not personally, no." His lips curled up around his straight white teeth. "But Libby mentioned him. Said he was a lot like me, actually." His smile grew meaner, and there was nothing left to do but hate him with all my strength—and that was draining my strength.

I was out of things to say, so I said, "You're a terrible person."

It must've sounded hilarious, because Stiles just laughed. I stared at him, dumbfounded. So dumbfounded I didn't even move when he stepped closer and placed a hand on my shoulder.

"Oh, this is good, priceless," he said. "You're a little pet now, I see the fun in it, I really do. But if you don't like what Libby's become, then you'd better find yourself another boyfriend, pumpkin." His lips popped on the *P*s.

It was either the word "boyfriend," the word "pump-kin," or Stiles's long fingers twisting a strand of my hair that suddenly summoned Morgan to my side before I could even respond.

"Whoa, whoa, whoa, Body Snatcher," Morgan said, shoving his hand against Stiles's chest to back him up. "What are you, freebasing? Take a walk and a chill. We're out of videos."

Morgan pointed to the front door, tapped his foot on the carpet, and waited. Thank God my head was buried in my hands so I didn't have to see Stiles's last horrifying leer in my direction. The bell rang with his exit. Morgan had rescued me again. For now.

"Quinn," he said, putting his arms around my shoulders.

"Don't worry about it."

"Quinlan," Morgan said, more serious this time.

I dropped my hands and faced him. His eyes were sad; he looked sorry for me. I couldn't take it. I panicked and pointed a shaky finger in his face.

"I said . . . don't . . . worry about it! Just, just . . . go watch a movie!"

I stomped away to Jerry's office and slammed the door. Behind me I heard Morgan mutter "Fine" like I'd punched him in the stomach and poured Diet Coke in his gas tank.

I sat in the office and stared into space until the motivational posters on the walls were just rectangular splotches of hazy color. If I hadn't been wearing my nicest dress when Stiles touched me, I would've burned it.

It was nine. I had two hours until James came to pick me up—hopefully—so I just had to pull my tweaked-out mess together, go beg Morgan to forgive me *again*, and finish this shift like a lady, not a bag of rattled-up bones.

"Okay," I said, sighing, walking up to Morgan, "was I being more of a brat or a psycho just then?"

"Fifty-fifty, Lacey." He smiled. It was okay.

Appreciation filled my body; it could be so easy with Morgan.

"Sorry. Just an average reaction to a run-in with a serial killer, I guess." I shrugged, breathed slowly, but couldn't really get back to normal.

"Serial killer? More like an Abercrombie zombie with a charge card and a Mazda RX-7."

"You noticed that too, huh?"

"Yeah, does he have to be so suave?"

"Told you. Total Spader."

"Nailed it," Morgan said, raising his hand for a high five. When our palms slapped, he locked his fingers with mine and gave them a gentle squeeze. "Won't always be around to deliver you from evil."

"I know. You're a good friend." I rested my head

lightly on his shoulder and closed my eyes. "I'm going to work on being a good friend back."

Morgan said, "What should we watch next?" and he gestured widely to the empty store filled with hundreds of picture boxes.

"Nothing scary, please."

James, if you can hear me, get your beautiful body over here.

"*Fantasia*?"

Because you've got some serious explaining to do.

"Sounds awesome."

The sinking, suspicious feeling started around ten to eleven. I was beginning to chew the inside of my lip raw, pacing in front of the huge front window, scanning outside for James's arrival and Stiles's departure, but I sensed a definite absence and presence—in that order. My stomach was so jumpy I could hardly get the licorice and Diet Coke down, and I was doing a poor job of hiding my anxiety from Morgan. When he offered to close down ten minutes early, I almost bit his head off. I needed those last ten minutes. The problem with psychic powers is that they come with a vicious case of the hunches. James wasn't on his way and Stiles was out there in the shadows, lurking, waiting. I was certain of both.

How fast could I run? Not that I could in a million

years imagine Stiles daring to scuff his polished loafers just to scare some video store girl. Of course, knowing him, he'd probably be like one of those horror movie villains that moved painfully slow, barely breaking a sweat. Unless Stiles brought his posse to pitch in—or Libby, dear God, as bait—I doubted he could catch me.

On the other, *other* hand, there was Morgan. And his Dodge Shadow. And that shame spiral.

I pressed my forehead to the glass and mumbled, "You suck, you suck, you suck."

Then the ten minutes were up and we were bolting the front door and dropping the outside gates. Count-out commenced. We shut the main lights off, left the neon overnight ones on. We double-checked the safe's lock, gathered our bag of junk-food trash, set the alarm, and headed out the back door. I wasn't farther than two inches from Morgan the entire time.

"You're going to give me a panic attack," he said as I followed him to the Dumpster.

"Sorry, too many Diet Cokes. Got me edgy."

"It's cool. You'll walk it off." He knew better than to offer a ride.

So it was time to beg.

I started to say, "Morgan, would you mind . . ." and leaned my body against his car, hoping he'd catch my drift.

"Is that a good idea?" He looked genuinely concerned. For both of us.

There was a breeze coming down the canyons, and it shook the trees with a whispery sound. I looked into the dark and felt someone out there watching. I was outside my body, seeing the color in my face run out, but I was inside my body too, feeling my stomach tense with dread.

"Quinn, hey, you look . . . green. You're, like, not a color in nature."

"Green's a color in nature."

Morgan petted my hair and I tried to smile.

"C'mon, get in," he said.

We drove to my house in silence. I leaned my head against the window and looked away into the trees, the alleys, the front yards, all passing by in a dark blur. But there was nothing, no one, no dirty-blond wanderers, no black-haired pursuers, pale angels, or paler devils. The hills were hot and empty and quiet.

I considered asking him to escort me to the door, but Morgan misread the hesitation on my face.

He said, "You don't have to thank me or get weird. You can always have a ride. It's not a big deal."

"Morgan, what can I say?"

"Don't try to kiss me, I'm not in the mood."

We laughed very small laughs together at a joke neither of us should've found particularly funny.

"Did you ever call your bride? After Libby's party?"

"Yeah. She didn't answer, and never called back. Whatever."

But Morgan wasn't crushed enough. I wanted him to care, to keep calling, to keep trying.

"You're some cool, older senior guy. She'll call."

"Don't get your hopes up."

I got out of the car and shut the door and pressed my hand against the window. It was a serious high five for a serious bail-out.

I thought I heard twigs snapping in the woods across the street, so I made a straight line for the front door, almost running. When I got to the porch, I turned around and waved to Morgan, who was watching, waiting for me to get inside, and then he drove away.

Once inside I locked the door and stared out the small window into the yard, looking for movement. The canyon winds ruffled the grass, some leaves fell, but otherwise it was still and dark. The house was silent. I turned on the porch light, then the chandelier light, and then, because the switch was next to those, the garage light too. I said "Hello" to no one, just to hear my own voice. Then I slid down my back to the ground.

It was 11:13. I would wait exactly forty-seven minutes for James. And if he hadn't magically arrived here by midnight, I'd confirm myself as the lamest, most desperate girl ever by going to his house to look for him.

At 11:42 I stripped to my underwear, snuck into the backyard, and sank to the bottom of my pool. No one was waiting for me in the darkness of the deep end. The water felt good, bracing; it woke me up, got me focused back on my current tasks: find Libby, save Libby, find James, kiss James, maul James, press James for details on Stiles, find Stiles, fight Stiles, find Morgan, find his bride, make them fall in love, make Naomi understand, make Libby normal again, kiss James again, eat a few pieces of fruit. Total order.

At 11:50 I walked through the side door to our downstairs bathroom, dripping wet. I flicked the switch for the red heat lamp and soaked in the warmth, toweling off, feeling new. The chlorine made my hair extra wild and wavy. My makeup hadn't bled too badly, just blurred, giving me those exaggerated black eyes I usually got from heavy summertime naps. I stared in the mirror, frowning. I looked fine but not awesome, which would only matter if Naomi wasn't alone at the Sheets's house.

At midnight I wrote the smallest note in the scratchiest legible handwriting.

Mom and Dad, took the Lexus to Libby's. Be back before you know it's gone. Sorry, Quinn

Could've been true. I had every reason to go pound down the Blocks' door looking for Libby. And I might've even been back before my parents woke to discover the note and the Lexus missing. But I was on a hunt for James, and striking out was not an option. I wanted to be out all night, all morning, until tomorrow, tomorrow night. So actually none of the note was true. Except maybe the sorry part. And I was getting sorrier every second.

8.

REVEAL

The moment she opened the door, I could tell Naomi wasn't surprised to see me. I could also tell she wasn't exactly happy to see me.

"Hey," she muttered, then led me into the African sitting room and lay back on the settee and stared at me. We sat in silence while Naomi twisted small strands of her hair, tapped her feet together, and drummed her fingers on the mudcloth cushions. She was clearly waiting for someone, and she just as clearly had no intention of telling me who that might be. Watching her ignore me, I started to wonder, more and more, if maybe Naomi simply didn't like me.

And if she didn't like me, then bummer for me, but bummer for her too, because I was feeling defiant. I wasn't going anywhere; I could play the waiting game.

Naomi broke the silence first. She said, "Look, I know I said you could come over, but I think maybe you should go. I'm exhausted, and you look . . . exhausted too."

"I don't have to sleep over or anything, but couldn't we just hang out a little longer? I had a bad night."

"So now I'm the one you call after a bad night?" She paused and peered sideways at me. "I thought that was Morgan's job."

It sucked. And it kind of hurt, too. But she didn't say it like she was trying to be mean, just like she wanted to get the point across.

"Well, I don't want it to be Morgan's job."

"Well, you should. Because he's a hell of a lot better for you than some people."

"'Better' doesn't mean anything," I said. "Some people are the ones I want, some aren't." I folded my arms across my chest.

"Doesn't matter what you want, you don't know everything." Naomi reconsidered her words. "You don't know anything."

"What are you talking about?"

"This conversation is over. Would you mind going home?"

"What don't I know?" I said, standing up, arms still folded.

"I'm not going to talk about this, and you should

thank me for that." Naomi stood up too. "You should thank me for this, and you should thank me for sending you home before he gets back." Then she turned away and started walking toward the kitchen.

"Yeah, mondo thanks."

She turned back to me, more pissed. "I'm saving your life."

"I like my life fine the way it is."

"I did too, so get *out* of it."

This had gone from numb to cold to hostile too fast. But then something broke in Naomi, and when she said, "Please, Quinn," the sadness was scarier than the anger.

I couldn't think of what to say. I reached a hand for her shoulder, warmly, and when I touched her skin, it was nice to feel we were both warm.

"I'm not trying to *marry* him, Naomi. God. I just want him to . . . be my boyfriend, you know?"

Naomi's eyes bulged, her jaw dropped. She flung my hand off her shoulder.

"Marry him?"

She grabbed both my wrists, tightly, and started dragging me to the front door. I tried to struggle free, but my shoes slid on the hardwood floor.

"Naomi," I said.

"Oh, I'm sorry, you just want him to be your boyfriend." She was seething, still dragging me. Her hands were like a trap, and the trap had fingernails.

"It's not that big a deal!"

And the fingernails were digging in.

"Naomi!"

She was going to rip my arms out of their sockets.

Then we were outside, on the porch, Naomi forcibly wrenching me closer to the Lexus. Her face was red, livid. I was in literal shock. Tears were en route.

I couldn't fight anymore, so I just sank my body to the ground, to the dirt driveway, but she didn't stop pulling me. I was weak, limp, trying to understand this and failing, failing, failing.

"Naomi!" I screamed, starting to sob, grabbing onto bits of gravel, giving up.

Then I heard, "Naomi."

She heard it too. She let go.

James was halfway down the driveway, hobbling toward the house in the dark, hunched over. I squinted to make sure I was seeing it right. I was. He was covered in blood, the front of his shirt splattered, his hands stained.

"James," I said, getting up and moving toward him. "What's wrong? What happened?"

He didn't respond, just held up a hand. His eyes lolled back in his head every few blinks. I glanced at Naomi, but she wasn't by the car anymore. She was backed against the doorway to her house, repulsed and terrified.

I said to James, "You didn't come to the store, you didn't meet me." But I could see James didn't want me tonight. His face told me I shouldn't have come.

Naomi cut in. "I asked her to go, but she wouldn't listen. So if you're going to tell her, tell her now."

I couldn't keep up.

James told Naomi, "She can stay if she wants."

"I'm staying," I said. "You're hurt."

Naomi screamed and beat a fist against the stucco wall behind her. "He's not hurt, you idiot, someone else is!"

Right then James's knees buckled, and he fainted to the pavement. Naomi screamed again, and her face turned so white it wasn't even green.

"James!" I crouched down and rolled him onto his back. He was clutching his stomach, moaning in a muffled, distant way.

Naomi shoved me backward and scooped James up so his whole weight was propped against her. "Get the hell out of here," she said without turning around.

"Stop, Naomi," James said hazily. Then he managed to raise his head slightly. "Quinn, go home."

I said the only word I knew to say: "No."

He closed his eyes and said, "Fine. Just wait outside for a while at least."

A thought hit me: "Did Stiles do this to you?"

He opened his mouth to answer, but Naomi interrupted. "I told you, you don't know *anything*."

She was right.

James allowed Naomi to turn him around, and they went inside and closed the door.

I cried to myself and let the tears dry on my cheeks. Get a grip, Lacey.

I crept around the yard to the garden. During my breakfast with Naomi yesterday morning, I'd noticed a small side door inside the pantry that led out onto the terrace. I tried not to step on Charlotte's flowers but it was dark, so whatever, and if there were cacti, then whatever too. I had to be in there. I couldn't *not* be in there. I got to the door. I tried the handle. Unlocked.

Then I held my breath and slowly opened it. I slipped in and silently shut the door behind me and tiptoed farther into the pantry, into a nook rimmed with teas and organic snacks stamped with fancy fonts. I peered through the slats on the cupboard and could see James and Naomi in the kitchen. He was on the ground facing away from me, curled against some cabinets, while she crouched over him, stroking his forehead with a damp towel.

They were already talking. I could hear every word.

". . . doesn't make sense. You never get sick."

"I know. . . . It's . . . something in the blood."

"Who was it?" Naomi said it very quietly.

No answer.

"James." She stopped petting his head. "Who was it?"

"No one. It's never anyone, really."

Then he slumped over, facing toward the pantry, and I could see him for real.

His thin, V-neck T-shirt was splattered with a dirty brownish maroon dye, and the dye had to be blood, but I'd never seen blood dried and dark like that. He still had my necklace on. My eyes froze on the small gold chain.

But his hands were caked with a weird rust coloring, and his hair was too wet with sweat. He was still clutching his stomach and groaning lightly, but I couldn't see any visible cuts on his body.

Naomi stood and leaned against the counter. "So you were drugged?"

I could've fallen straight through the floor. Drugs. Mystery solved.

"She was out partying or something. I don't know. She was alone." James held his head in his hands. "There was no one else there."

He could've been describing that night he saw me: a girl all alone, wandering in the darkness, some empty part of the canyons where no cars drive. So this girl was drunk? Lost? Then she gave him drugs?

Naomi broke into louder sobs. They were erratic, out of control.

I was crying too—at her crying, at the blood, at this whole scene. Because I knew if Naomi was this freaked, then James was in real danger.

"I have to . . . throw this up somehow. Get it out of me . . ."

She crouched down next to him again.

"Will it kill you?"

I couldn't breathe. Was that what I was witnessing, an overdose? Why weren't they calling the police?

"No," James said. He pressed his cheek against hers. "You know it'd take more than that."

She said, "Okay. Okay, okay, okay." Naomi's words were my own.

James felt at his throat, held a hand to his chest.

"How'd you even get home?" she asked.

"I started crawling." He put his hand in her lap. "Then I managed to walk somehow."

"But . . . why were you feeding again so soon?"

James bowed his head. I scrolled through every word I'd ever heard referring to drug use. Every weird verb or phrase any cool kid had ever said about some party pill or pot or whatever. Never ever the word *feeding*. James said nothing. He squeezed around his middle again.

Naomi began to shake her head. At first it was slight and slow, but gradually her head moved faster, more frantic.

"No. No. Because of *her*?"

"I had to."

Every new sentence multiplied my confusion. Her who? This canyon girl who fed him pills and left him to die?

Naomi said, "Why?" and then she whispered the word sadly into her hands a hundred times.

James tried to prop himself up against the cabinet. "This way I don't get the urge."

"Just shut up." Naomi pushed James away, then straightened her dress to stand.

"She matters to me."

"You can't do this to people!" She flung a cup of pens off the counter onto the floor.

"Give me a break, Naomi."

"*You* give *me* a break. She already knows Stiles, she knows something's wrong with him." Naomi glared down at James. "She'll see it in you. She'll tell everyone."

"No, she won't."

"We'll have to move."

"No, we won't. I promise."

"Well, what are you going to say to her?"

Then James started to gag, loudly. He grabbed onto the kitchen counter and pulled himself to his feet, leaning his whole body over the sink, coughing violently. I closed my eyes, heard the sounds of more coughing, liquid, gurgling. Finally I peeked again through the slats and saw the sink splashed with blood, parts of the countertop, some of it dripping onto the white tile floor. This blood was fresher, brighter red.

My stomach turned. I covered my mouth.

Naomi screamed noise. Then she screamed, "James!"

He twitched and sank back to the floor.

"What's happening?" Naomi cried, bending down and wiping at his mouth and face where blood had splattered.

"It's okay, I'll be okay. . . ."

"Go back to Cambridge. You can leave tonight. I'll call Whit."

James nodded, pained. His hair covered his eyes as he hung his head, then nodded again.

Naomi got up, went to the phone by the microwave, and dialed. A few seconds later she said, "It's Naomi. Come home now, he's leaving." Then she hung up.

I was close to passing out. Nothing held my body up but habit and a bulk crate of goji berry granola bars.

James coughed again and said, "I want someone to be close to. You can understand that."

But she couldn't. Naomi's tears were gone, her empathy was all dried up. She stared down at him in pure judgment. "Yeah, I get it. You want to ruin Quinn's life just like you ruined ours." There was a cold pause. "That girl's dead, James." Then, even colder, the words: "You killed her."

"Naomi."

"And Quinn's either going to end up in a straitjacket or a body bag. This is your mess, you clean it up."

"Naomi," James said again.

And that's when it happened: I fell. Hard. The shelf I was leaning against dislodged from its wall-hanging, and I fell into everything. Tin cans, cylinders of tea, boxes of cereal, couscous, a full spice rack, bags of dried fruit; all of it came crashing down in a heap on top of me.

I scrambled to get to my feet, my heart flipping out. There'd be no need to sneak back out through the garden now. I knew I should just walk into the kitchen, give my regards to the horror scene in progress, and keep walking right out the front door. Except for the fact that I had no legs.

And no one came to expose me. No one moved at all. A part of me prayed that Naomi would swing open the pantry door and reveal they'd only been rehearsing for a summer-school play, that this was actually just a low-budget cable TV candid home video prank show, and wow, what a hilarious comedy of errors this had all been. *But Quinn, that's just fake blood made from corn syrup!* Anything. But a larger part of me knew that this was all for real. James puked blood and did drugs, and Naomi hated both of us.

The silence from the kitchen was horrible. They were waiting for me.

I pushed the door open. Light flooded into the pantry.

"Of course. Aren't you *so* happy now?"

My eyes were on the ground, so I wasn't sure if Naomi was talking to me or James. But then she said, "Quinn," sharply. "Are. You. Happy. Now? Now that you know?"

"I'm not happy." I mouthed the words: *I don't know anything.*

James's eyes were closed; he didn't even look at me.

I started to walk to James, but Naomi shouted, "You're pathetic"—to me—"and you're disgusting"—to him—"and I'm leaving." She turned and left. Seconds later a door slammed.

I looked over at James. He looked dead.

But then he spoke. "Hit the light," he said, gesturing at the wall switch. I went over and flicked it.

The kitchen was dark now except for some weak moonlight coming in through a window above the sink. My eyes slowly adjusted, and the terror reasserted itself. Blood was splattered everywhere, James was groaning, and I was in a strange family's house when I should have been in my own. This night was a nightmare.

I tried to focus on James to calm myself because, despite everything, he seemed calm. He looked gruesome, but he looked calm. I went and knelt by him.

"How long were you in there?"

"Too long."

"You heard everything?"

"I don't know." I paused. "I think so."

"Why are you still here?"

"I don't know." I wanted to touch him but was scared to.

"I'm not going to hurt you."

"I know that."

"But I do hurt people."

"Like tonight?"

He was quiet. Then, "Yes."

"Is that girl really dead?"

Again a pause. Again, "Yes."

"And you killed her for . . . pills?"

"No." He sighed and reached for my hand, but I held it away.

"But you're into drugs?" Everything was a guess.

"No . . . no." His voice was rasping. He shook his head. "I can't say it like this. Let's not say anything."

But we'd done that. We'd been doing that.

James slid over, laid his head in my lap, and curled his legs up under him. Cautiously I fingered his hair, touched along the side of his jaw. I tried to steady his breathing but couldn't, because he didn't seem to be exhaling.

"So. You kill people." My head swam. "Is there . . . a reason?"

"I need them." His voice swirled.

"Need them how?"

"Quinn." He put his hand over my hand and guided it down to his shirt. "This isn't my blood."

"I . . . know," I whispered.

"I need the blood. . . ."

"For what?"

"To go on."

"Like a vampire?"

I didn't say the word to mean anything. Vampires needed blood. Like in the movies. Books. Whatever.

James placed my hand inside his thin white T-shirt, over his chest, his heart. I felt nothing. I pressed my hand harder, felt around. Nothing. Stillness. He moved my other hand to the veins on his wrist. More nothing, more stillness. I reached my hand up to his throat, put two fingers there. The same. The same impossible thing.

"Her blood was dirty. I didn't know."

But his words didn't register with me. Nothing did. "You're not real." I touched his face once more and then pushed myself out from under him. I said it again, "You aren't real."

He leaned to look at me. "I am."

"So, what? You never age? You live forever, you drink blood? That room is your coffin?" I pointed to nowhere, some white room in the distance I'd never see again. I backed away farther, sliding myself across the kitchen floor.

He just nodded, his head on the tile.

"And Naomi?"

"She's like you."

"How? How long?" Everything was shaking: the floor, the room, my body, my voice.

"Not that long."

"No way."

"I was coming to see you tonight." He reached for me. "But then this . . ."

"No." No.

I was floating now, up over our bodies, over the blood, over our mess.

"You weren't ever supposed to know."

I floated over the Sheetses' house, the detached garage, the dead end, the Lexus, the street.

"The girl was me," I said to the cloudless night sky above the canyons. "I was her. You were going to kill me that night on the road. It was so easy. I bled for you."

I rose higher above Los Angeles, the Hollywood Hills, the 101.

"I didn't go near you." His voice was far away from me.

"You're dead. You're not here. I'm not here."

Below me, a hundred miles down, James coughed more blood, and the shape of a girl rose to her feet.

"Libby's in trouble," he told me. "She'll be worse off than me soon."

"I'm not here."

Floating keys floated into my floating hands. When I dropped down, I was inches from my mother's car door, unlocking it, climbing in, starting the engine.

Go home, I told myself. I looked over at the house, dark and quiet.

Go home now. I saw James's old note on the passenger seat, a folded reminder of an earlier life. My face was still wet. I wiped at it. Tears, not blood.

Go home now. Go.

I turned the keys and went.

Miraculously, I made it to my bed. I pulled blankets over my head until everything went black. Soon I was sweating and suffocating. And remembering. I had to recalculate every tiny hint and obscure detail into this new wretched equation. Every joke, every smile, every touch, was now a different thing, something unreal and dead. My memories were all corrupted, in pieces.

I waited for the fear to take hold and disfigure every sweet vision I had of James's face into something awful and evil. But the fear didn't flood my mind as much as the loneliness. I felt lonely for James, for Naomi, for Libby, for myself. Loving James was seriously not okay, and I knew it. His whole life—existence, whatever—wasn't real. My taste in guys had gone from lame to dystopian.

But I still wanted him any small way I could have him. I tossed and turned under the covers but couldn't shake it. He'd kill and drink blood instead of Diet Cokes. He'd sleep all day and never see the sun with me. He'd stay twenty forever and I'd age beyond him every year. Weirdly, I almost didn't care. I felt lonely because after tonight I didn't know if James would forgive *me*.

I understood Libby plainly for the first time in weeks. If she thought she loved Stiles—a shiver at the thought—I could imagine her letting him do anything, forgiving him everything. If Stiles was the same . . . species . . . as James, then I guess I'd have no right to interfere. But it wasn't like that. Stiles was twisted, perverted, and I didn't need James to tell me he was slowly killing my best friend. He was sucking her dry. He was keeping her alive—for now.

Naomi knew all this too.

Stiles and Sanders and Dewey and Cooper. And James. They lived among us. Mythical movie creatures came to my video store, went to parties with me, kissed my neck and tasted the salty sweat there. They threatened me. They protected me. So I had to suspend my disbelief now. Everything was real—angel devils and devil devils—and I had to love and fight them both.

Somehow sleep came easily for me. I left behind the

land of the living—Morgan, my parents, bosses and customers, high school freshmen in party hats—and joined
Libby in the world of the undead, where heaven was hell
and hell held the immortal boyfriend of my dreams.

Libby spread across the hood of an old Mustang. She
sang me Nirvana.

9.

GAMES

Unfortunately, the new day meant a new deal—and I could barely deal. Last night's shock and numbness faded fast as I finally crawled out of bed deep into the afternoon, obliterated, still wearing that stupid vintage rayon dress, looking like the leftovers of the girl formerly known as Quinlan Lacey. Every part of my body ached, but my eyes were the worst. Two bleary, blurry, rubbed-out wells with black rings around them and faint tearstain trails.

I put on whatever—literally, who even knew, my mother's silk kimono over a tube top and cutoff shorts maybe?—and hunted down the darkest sunglasses in the house: my dad's Ray-Bans, hidden away in a desk drawer in his office. I was in threads. I would've sobbed at a car insurance commercial or screamed at the ding of a microwave timer.

There was my night life, which was my real life—despite being a wrecked life—but there was also this. And this I had to fake.

My parents were both downstairs reading the *Times* when I finally descended the stairs from my crypt.

"Well, well, Wells," my father said, looking up over his paper. An H. G. Wells joke. Classic Dad.

"Oh, hi, guys." I grabbed my mother's coffee mug out of her hand and swigged.

"We're not guys, we're Mom and Dad." My mother took the mug back, threw me a sideways disapproving glance, and turned her attention back to the article she was reading.

"Right, sorry." I crashed on the couch next to my father and toyed with the fabric on the elbow of his linen sports coat. "Hey, why aren't you guys at work?"

"There's been a blackout all night and morning because they're doing construction. Remember?" My dad knocked on my head to see if anyone was in there. Nope.

"Don't panic. We won't be in your way." My mother pointed to a spread on the kitchen counter: bagels, doughnuts, muffins, fresh fruit, yogurt, all in organized to-go containers. "Impromptu late lunch in Griffith Park with a few friends. Grab what you want before we take off."

"Not hungry, Mom."

The food looked alien. I felt ill. I imagined James

having to eat it. I imagined having to eat blood. I swallowed long and hard.

"Quinn, you're looking a little pasty," my mother said, frowning.

"So eat a pastry!" My father laughed.

Really, you guys? Not today.

"Oh, Morgan called this morning. Do you have a shift tonight?"

As I stood up at the sound of his name, my mother handed me the phone. When I wouldn't take it from her, she shoved it at me.

"Don't play games. You're a strong woman. He'll appreciate you for it."

"Mom, you're, like, not even in the ballpark with that."

I knew I should've let it go, because then my mother noticed my clothes. "What are you wearing?"

Suddenly both of them focused on my outfit at the same time, an expression of total confusion on their faces.

"Uh, this," I mumbled.

"Call Morgan."

"Fine." I took the phone and walked out the back door into the sunshine. I dialed Morgan's number. He picked up on the first ring.

"Morgan, I can't go to work tonight. I'm bailing—can you cover for me?"

"What's wrong?"

"I'm, like, toaster-caked. Out of it. Cadaverous."

"Okay, but you might get fired. In Alex's eyes you're, like, approaching *Bell Jar* status."

Fired? Nope, didn't care. "Whatever."

"Whatever. Call me when you're making sense." He hung up.

Inside my parents were gathering together all the food into canvas bags, getting ready to go.

"Are you driving Dad's car?" I asked.

"Is there something you want, Quinn?" My mother took her hands off the bagels so she could put them on her hips.

"I was going to go to Libby's."

"Fine, take the Lex. Don't forget to—"

"Double-click the lock. Got it. Love you."

We blew kisses in the air. My father waved.

I grabbed the keys.

Off to the Blocks' house to not find Libby, press Stella for info, and make the most of the sunlight hours before eight o'clock hit and the rest of the canyons woke up.

I knocked four times on the front door before I heard Stella Block's voice shouting at me from the backyard to come find her. I walked around through the side gate into the large Japanese garden, where she was sprawled out on a hammock. In one hand she was holding an airport-style gothic romance novel and in the other a tall glass of something on ice. She smiled when she saw me, waved, took off her big sunglasses, and lifted the brim of her huge wide-brimmed hat.

"Look at you, Miss Diva." She tugged on my silk kimono and winked. Stella spoke slowly, the sun in her voice, a real L.A. babe. She was more than twice my age and looked better in a one-piece bathing suit than I could ever hope to. When she was Libby's and my age, she was a glam queen who drew lightning bolts on her face with eyeliner and wore ripped-up leotards with military boots.

"Hey, Stella. Is Libby here?"

"Libby who?" She smiled and leaned back into the hammock, closing her eyes against the bright sun. "Oh, my teenage daughter who doesn't love me enough to come home from her boyfriend's house for dinner every once in awhile? That Libby?"

"I think that's her."

"Nope, not home. Sorry, sister." Stella reached out and squeezed my hand. "But stay awhile, pretend I gave birth to you." She patted a big stone next to her for me to sit on.

My list was still in order, and Libby was high on that list. But I felt bad for Stella because she didn't know that her only daughter was some zombie squeeze-toy. And I knew Libby would comfort my mom if the tables were turned. Of course, in a certain way the tables already were turned, since I was semi-in-love with my own Stoker. What a mess. Whatever, my plans could spare half an hour with Stella Block.

Besides, the sun was still out. I wouldn't find anyone I was looking for until sunset anyway. And after dusk I probably wouldn't be the only one looking.

"So. Have you met Stiles?" I hid behind the dark sunglasses.

"He seems fine. He's polite." Stella sounded bored. "Well dressed. I think he irons his shoes." She laughed at her joke.

"You should see his brother."

"Really?"

"You have no idea."

"Do you like Stiles?" Stella said, sipping her beverage.

"I don't know. No. I think he's weird." Right now the faking felt real, and it wasn't so hard to act calm about it. "Doesn't his and Libby's relationship seem . . . intense to you?"

"Well, of course it does, Quinlan, but they're seventeen-year-olds. It's normal to be too intense at that age. I'd prefer her to come home *once* in a while, but Stiles and her like to stay up late, doing their thing. Which is fine. It's summer!" She toasted her glass up in the air. "To staying young."

"Yeah."

I tried to remember my list: *Save Libby. Save her and bring her back.*

Finally Stella noticed my mood. "People change when they're in love." She paused and gave me a soft look, and I worried maybe Stella was faking too. "You know?"

"I guess."

"Is everything okay?"

"No, not really." I turned away from her gaze. "But I'm going to fix it. I'll fix it and it'll be fine."

Stella reached her arms up in the air for a big stretch and yawned. Then she curled back on to the swaying hammock. "Good. I can't have my girls fighting." She smiled at the sun and closed her eyes.

Later on Stella made me a small snack—crackers, peanut butter, a cup of tea—and we gossiped about more mundane topics than best friends and their captors. We tanned out together and she told me some A-list rumors she'd heard while wardrobing a recent *Vanity Fair* shoot. Finally, at about seven thirty, the sun started to slip behind the house and the L.A. smog turned the skyline to purple haze.

Stella kept chatting, wandering lazily around the garden to water a few extra-parched plants and sip slowly at a Pellegrino she'd grabbed from the fridge. I nodded and smiled but only half listened because my brain was in Libby mode, and since I knew where to find her now, I had to go save her. Because I loved her. It was the only love I could focus on.

During a pause in one of Stella's stories, I stood up and interrupted. "This has been really great."

"Do you need to leave?"

"Yeah. Dinner with the parents." I fake-frowned.

Stella put down the watering can and came over and took my hands in hers and held them tightly for a second. "When you see Libby, tell her to give her old mom a call. Okay?"

"Sure."

"And hey . . . don't worry about Stiles. He's just a high school boyfriend." She swatted her hand toward me like she was shooing a fly. "You know those don't last."

"Right." I turned and waved good-bye and headed for the gate.

"Oh, and Quinn," Stella called out. "I didn't even ask. How's *your* boyfriend?"

He's totally dead, just like Libby's. Thanks for asking.

"You mean Morgan?"

Stella nodded.

"Right," I said, smiling like everything was normal. "He's killer." Then I waved my keys over my shoulder and went to go find my best friend.

I realized while on the way to Stiles and Sanders's guest-house slash evil lair that I actually had no plan. This morning it'd seemed so clear—go there, throw Libby in a duffel bag, drive home—but as dusk settled and the streetlights turned on, it hit me that this was going to be a lot, lot harder.

I turned down Topanga Canyon and scanned for the side street they lived on. All the houses looked the same in the shadows. Maybe everyone in this whole canyon was evil and eighteen and drank blood.

Then I came to the street and cruised along it and saw the narrow driveway on the side of the property that led back to the guesthouse. There were two cars parked in front. I thought about slashing the tires or opening up the hoods and banging on stuff or even just ripping off all the stereo knobs. They'd probably be more pissed about that than losing Libby.

The guesthouse was totally dark except for a single light in the front room facing the yard. I knocked on the door and one of the twins cracked it open half an inch, stared at me with one narrowed eye, then swung it all the way open. Sanders. A huge, cold, satisfied smile lit up his face. He leaned against the door frame suavely, one arm up. His skin was porcelain—ridiculously white and smooth and waiting for a good smashing.

"It's my lucky night," he said.

I tried to look past him into the living room. "Libby!" I shouted over his shoulder. "Libby, it's Quinn. I'm here!"

Sanders exhaled with fake exhaustion and waved his hand as if to let me go on screaming all night.

"Libby!" I shifted to meet his eyes. "Where's Libby? I'm not kidding, Sanders."

"You don't look like you're kidding."

I pushed past him into the house, feeling his eyes on my back.

"Libby," I called out again, and again, "Libby, where are you?"

"Please keep it down." He held a finger up to his magenta lips, then moved it to mine like, *Shhh.* "People are sleeping."

"Look," I said, turning around. "I know what you are."

"A Sagittarius?"

"*Right.* And I know what your brother's doing to Libby. So why don't you tell him to get some other girl for his pacifier? It's L.A. Shouldn't be too hard."

"Nothing's too hard anymore," Sanders said, stepping closer. "If Stiles wanted someone else he'd take someone else, wouldn't he?"

Then he stepped even closer, only inches away, and slipped a hand beneath my mother's kimono, touching a finger to my bare leg. He traced an S shape along the side of my thigh. "She's way into it. And honestly," he said, dripping more evil, "you would be too."

"Wildest dreams, you freak."

"I'm sure your boyfriend's sleeping well these days."

He wasn't talking about Morgan.

"But if he doesn't suck your blood, then what"—Sanders stopped, breaking into light laughter before composing himself—"*does* he suck?"

"You're a perv." I swung a clumsy fist at him, but he caught it and leaned in all the way.

He pushed my hair to one side and slowly put his tongue to my earlobe.

He was sucking my earlobe.

Then I heard, "Quinny?" Libby's voice floated out from down the hall. At the sound of it Sanders stepped back, crossed the room, and slouched down on the couch like he'd been there all along.

"Quinny!" Libby said again, skipping toward me. She was still in the same nightgown I'd seen her in . . . how many days ago? And she was still barefoot, paler even than before, her hair frizzy and dry, sticking out in every direction.

"Well, hello." Stiles was right behind her, grinning.

I ignored him. "Libby!" I cried back, reaching out my arms for her and hugging her tightly. "We have to go, okay? Please?"

"I'm soooo haaappy you're heeeere." She stretched out each word, singing them to me.

I pulled Libby off, squeezed her hard around the wrists. "Get lucid for me, we're leaving."

"But you just got here." Her eyes clouded. Then she slipped her hands free and began gliding around the floor like the ghost of Ginger Rogers.

Stiles and Sanders shared a gross smile.

"Sorry, Quinny," Stiles said, stepping casually in my direction. "But we're in the middle of something. You should stay"—he paused, reaching out a hand to brush my bangs—"and watch."

My will was weakening. They were too calm, too collected, spoke softly, had good manners, good haircuts, perfect skin; these were smooth criminals. The seduction felt so natural it was like it wasn't even happening.

Then Stiles and Sanders went tense.

"Someone's here," Sanders said. He tilted his head as if listening to some impossibly quiet sound.

Stiles looked at me. "Are you alone?"

"Of course I'm alone. You think I brought my mom?"

Sanders went to the window and peered through the blinds into the yard. "I know I heard something."

Someone said, "You did," and we all turned to the front door. It was James.

"Followed you," he said to me.

I gave him a small smile but he looked exhausted, like he hadn't recovered from last night.

"Thanks for stopping by." Stiles.

"I'm not here to fight." James.

"How diplomatic of you."

Sanders moved next to his brother.

Libby was still swaying to her dream-musical over in the corner.

"If you're here for her," Stiles said, wrapping his arm around Libby and pulling her into his side, "then you *are* here for a fight." He licked the side of her face slowly, from chin to temple. She moaned with pleasure, then laughed. It was the worst, worst thing ever.

"Look, I get it," James said. "But you don't need this particular girl, you can have your pick."

"So I picked."

"I told you, I'm not going to fight."

Fight. Fight, fight, fight, I thought. *Rip them apart. Kick their asses.*

Sanders leered at me, down to the frayed edge of my cutoff shorts. "Lucky for you. Because you wouldn't win."

"You only live once," Stiles said, looking James in the eyes. "And after that . . . you can take what you want."

James said, "Not exactly, man."

"So it's settled," Sanders interrupted. "You're leaving," he said, pointing to James, "and the ladies are staying."

"I'll leave," he said. "But Quinn's coming too."

"Not yet," I snapped. I got up in Stiles's face. "We're taking Libby. She's not yours!"

I reached for Libby's hand, but Stiles slapped it away, hard. My forearm stung.

James froze. He didn't do anything.

"This is over," Stiles hissed through his teeth. "Now I'm just annoyed. Listen." He stopped, turned to Libby, and spoke hypnotically: "Do you want to leave with your friend or stay here with us?"

When Libby realized that an actual reply was expected of her, and that the whole room was waiting, her face changed expression, from vacant to panicked, and she retreated to the corner of the living room and crouched on the ground. I couldn't watch her like this. Then she mumbled, "I'll just see you later, okay?"

Stiles adjusted his collar. "From the mouth of a babe."

I lunged and grabbed a fistful of Stiles's shirt and pounded against his chest until the pocket tore off in my hand.

Then it was chaos. A cold hand covered my mouth, twisted my body, and slammed me down to the floor. Suddenly James was ripping, clawing, at Sanders. I scrambled on all fours to the edge of the kitchen and covered my head. There was loud grunting, some fierce growls, the sound of swift movements, a body thrown into a chair.

Then everything went quiet except for heavy breathing. I peeked up and James, Sanders, and Stiles were standing in a tight circle in the middle of the room, staring each other down, panting. Sanders's shirt was shredded on one side and James's arm had some long scrapes on it and a chair was on its back, broken in half, but otherwise the scene was the same. No motion; just three dead bodies in a staring contest.

"Do you want this to get worse?" Sanders asked James.

Stiles touched his lower lip, which looked bruised.

James said, "You don't own the canyons."

Then Stiles relaxed. His eyes sparkled like he'd thought of something. He said to James, "Why are you even here?"

"What are you talking about?"

"In this part of the city. Do you know someone here?" Stiles paused, thinking. "Do you live here?"

James didn't flinch. "No."

"He's lying," Sanders said.

Stiles held up a hand to silence his brother. "*Obviously* he's lying."

Then he turned to Libby, who was still huddled in the corner of the room, her eyes riveted by something invisible in the air.

"Libby, pay attention. I need to ask you something."

Stiles knelt down in front of her. "How does your friend know this guy?" He pointed at James.

Libby didn't even look where Stiles was pointing, just sang, "I don't know. . . ."

Sanders huffed, said, "Useless," and rolled his eyes.

Stiles stood up and walked over to James. "We're going to make you wish you'd never come—" He hesitated, searched James's face, and somehow found the answer. Then he finished, "To see your family."

The Sheets family. Naomi. Daniel and Charlotte. The stranger named Whit.

"No," I said to myself, my hot cheek still against the cool linoleum kitchen floor.

"Or"—Stiles held up a single finger in front of him—"you could leave now and never come back."

No one moved. No one said anything. I kept breathing; I was the only one.

"Those are your two options."

Both choices sucked impossibly. Either throw Libby into the fiery pit of this guesthouse hell and let her die a little every day over and over until her last breath, or else . . .

I wanted to throw up. I already knew James's decision.

James stepped back, lowered his eyes. Like he was defeated.

"Well?" Sanders yelled, impatient.

"We're going," James said. "We're going now." He looked over at me for the first time since the fight and held out a hand, gesturing for me to join him. I got up and ran to him. I wrapped my arms around his arm.

"Wise," Stiles said. "I can't have you and your screeching little girlfriend staging rescue missions every night."

"You won't see us again," James said, too sincere.

"I'll keep Libby, you can keep . . . her." Stiles nodded in my direction.

James shrugged when he looked at me. His face said, *This is it*, then he pressed the top of his forehead to mine. He was finished, I could tell.

But even now, with the battle lost and my friend halfway to a padded cell, I prayed. I prayed the roof would crumble and night would be day and the sunlight would roast these goth creeps to cigarette ash. I prayed I'd join the SWAT team and come back and blow them to bits. I prayed to make things any way but how they were.

"When this ends," Sanders said to me, "you and I could always double-date. I'm sure Libby would like that. Look at her, she's in heaven."

Libby was splayed out on the ground on her back like a cat, her bare feet up against one wall. Her hands played lightly with the air.

"She's in a K-hole, you maniac."

Stiles pretended to yawn.

"Quinn." James started pulling my body toward the door.

I had to accept it: I wasn't Libby's savior. I had to accept that I had to leave Libby here, in this nightmare, for Stiles to do as he pleased, for however long it pleased him.

"Libby, I love you!" I yelled out to her from the doorway. "And Stella says to call her!" James was pulling me outside, but I kept my eyes on Libby, hoping for a glimmer of recognition at the sound of her own mother's name. But her eyes were static; gray, unfocused, snow.

"That's not Libby," James whispered.

It wasn't. She was a goner.

James pressed my body against him and led me down the driveway.

"Ta-ta," Stiles called out behind us.

Then he closed the door and we were alone in the night. It was quiet out. Warmish.

When we were at my car, I turned to James. "We can't give up."

"These aren't games. This isn't fiction." He looked seriously broken. "This isn't some Anne Rice joke."

"Yeah, you're more Stephen King, I get it."

He didn't argue with me, just put a hand over his face and shook his head. He leaned back against the Lexus.

I stood in front of him and grabbed his shoulders. "James, I know they're dangerous, I know they're not playing around, I do get it." I reached for his waist, but he stopped me.

"Quinn, please. If I try to fight them, I might not die but Libby *will*." He said it like a fact.

I stared at the ground.

"Not gonna happen," he said.

"Fine."

"It's too complicated."

"Whatever," I said. Saving Libby simply was not up for debate.

James was petting my hair and saying comforting things, but my brain was elsewhere. I started hatching a new plan, one in which I stole Libby back in the daylight, at the brightest hour, their weakest moment. I'd kidnap her and hide her where no one in this zip code—dead or alive—would know to go. I'd nurse Libby back to health, deprogram her, give her all my extra blood, and remind her of all our favorite things, our favorite hunks, our favorite bands—all our times together.

I tried again. "I'll get her during the day."

James stared at me, waited.

"They'll be asleep, hibernating, whatever. This way you can totally stay out of it."

He shook his head. "When Libby's gone, they'll know what happened."

"What if we stock up, like in the movies? Wooden stakes. Holy water."

He looked at me like I was the biggest idiot. Like he was sad for me.

"Crucifixes?"

He turned away, annoyed. "Only sunlight and fire work."

I was unfazed. I didn't have superpowers, but I had tricks. My witchy will. I could do this. I ran a hand along his chest, then slipped it underneath his T-shirt's fabric and felt his flesh. I wanted him on my side again.

James held me away. "How are you not scared of me? After last night."

A flashback of him writhing on the kitchen floor, puking the drugged-up blood of a girl he'd just killed.

"Definitely wasn't one of your top ten sexiest moments."

"Definitely not." He smiled, then caught himself smiling and stopped. "I don't want you to be afraid of me. But you need to be. At least a little bit."

I closed my eyes and nodded. What James lived on, what he needed, was an evil thing. But he didn't choose to be at the top of this bizarro dark fantasy food chain, so I couldn't condemn him for it. I had a choice, though.

And I chose to forgive him, to side against every human I knew and didn't know. A B-minus in tenth-grade ethics class becomes an F in real life too easily. Accepting all the blood spilled would torment me for as long as I chose to love James. But afraid of him? I just didn't feel that way inside.

"I'll live with it."

"Okay," he said. "You've been briefed."

Our eyes locked.

Then our lips locked, and we were making out. Majorly. He licked my teeth, my tongue, the shape of my mouth. I ran my hands through his messy hair. I threw the last bit of strength I had into it. I crushed his body against the Lexus, only slightly worried that it might leave a dent.

Could it get better than this?

"Come home with me, will you?" James asked between kisses.

It could get better for sure.

"Hell yes," I said, one hand already on the keys, and those keys flying to the ignition.

10.

HISTORY

I followed James's car through the winding canyons. I wasn't tired or hungry or bored or weird. I was wholly focused on this night. I was here, now. I tucked Libby away. I gave Morgan a rest. I let Naomi go.

We parked, and James led me up the stairs to his room. Inside we weren't kissing, but I was waiting for us to. When I went in for his lips, he gently restrained me. James wanted to talk. For the first time ever.

"Ask me anything," he said, sitting down on the big faded rug.

"Are we boyfriend and girlfriend?"

"That's your question?"

"That's my first question."

"I'm going to grant you one do-over."

"How's this: Are we going to talk all night?"

He squinted at me. "You love to talk."

"I know. But you don't."

"Well that's the give-and-take of dating."

"Wait, so we *are* dating?"

"Settle down."

I could tell he really wanted this to happen, so I stopped teasing. I sat Indian-style with my elbows on my knees and rested my head in my upturned palms.

He gave me a Serious James face before beginning. "I have a universe of weirdness on my chest, and I need to get some of it off. Starting with that night after the party, when you showed up here with blood on your shirt—"

I could've gagged. Of course it wasn't a wine stain.

"I flipped out," he said. "I don't always flip out around blood, but you caught me off guard."

"Sorry."

"So am I."

"But the blood was from a bottle. How'd they get it in there?"

"A few plastic tubes and a bicycle pump. Home Depot on Sunset. Pretty basic."

I tried to picture it. The twins and Dewey and Cooper: Spader surgeons in linen and khaki scrubs. Budget horror hospital. Too gruesome.

I asked, "Do you do that?" even though I didn't want to know.

"Well, it's like . . . flat Diet Coke."

I raised a hand to stop him. "Say no more."

"I know how it sounds, but we do it to stay low-profile. It's not cool to cause a scene. We have to try to fit in. Trust me, you'd rather see that than . . ." His voice trailed off.

"Maybe." I thought about it and said, "But none of you fit in. You're all *obviously* scene-stealers."

"Really? Seemed like breaking news to you."

"Huh."

"Look. You wake up late, skip dinner, act aloof, people think you're a jerk, not a monster."

I did all those things. Was I a jerk? A little monster?

James scooted closer. "Quinn. I don't want you in a room like that, like tonight. You shouldn't be in that world."

"But I'm in your world. I mean, we're all in the same world, right?"

"To know one is enough."

I didn't say anything.

"To know one is, like, too much."

"You can't drag me into all this and then tell me to forget it."

"I know. That's my fault. I got you involved despite strong advice not to."

I thought of Naomi. I turned away. If there'd been

a window, I would've looked out of it. "It's just like in those bogus movies. The vampire never falls for another vampire. Why do they always go for regular people and then feel tortured by it? That's so lame."

"Don't get all your insights from Hollywood."

"And don't talk to me like I'm seven. I'm seventeen. And you're only twenty."

"Twenty-two, technically."

"Fine. You win," I said.

"No, it's just that you have to believe me when I say . . . this is the least awesome, last thing anyone should have to be dealing with." He paused, putting a hand under my chin and turning my face back to look at him. "I don't want to be dealing with it. I'm glad I don't even know how it happened. I don't want that memory."

He tugged on the stud in his earlobe. "Ryan Hunter pierced this in the seventh grade with a safety pin off his Misfits hoodie. I prefer remembering that as the most physical pain I've ever felt in my entire life."

"So you didn't feel any of it?"

"I mean I was trashed, like blackout trashed. That might've numbed some of the pain."

"Ya think?" I rolled my eyes.

"But it was just some bar. Somewhere my band had played a dozen times."

"That's it? What about 'it was a dark and stormy night'?"

"It was a dark and . . . smoggy night."

"That's the vaguest thing I've ever heard."

"It's just text for your next D.A.R.E. newsletter."

"Like a regular bar, like some Eastside bar? Like I could go there?"

"You're underage."

"You know what I mean."

"Yeah, you could go there. But don't."

"Just a regular cool-kid bar."

"Quinn, there aren't underground bat caves."

"So why you?"

"No reason."

"Then why aren't you dead?"

"I am dead."

"Get real, James."

"I don't know. Some of us want to convert, not kill."

"Which are you more into?"

"Well, I'm definitely not *into* killing, but you can't drink just a little . . . you have to go all the way or they become one too. That's so much worse."

"Is it?" I pictured Libby.

He didn't hesitate: "It is."

"The twins seem to be having an awesome time."

He shrugged and said in a quieter voice, "Not me."

There was nothing to say to that, so I asked, "How many are there?"

"It's a big city."

"It's not a big high school." I thought of Stiles and Sanders and Dewey and Cooper. "So you got drunk and that's it?"

"Kind of. It was a normal night otherwise." He paused, then shrugged, then said, "Well it felt like one at the time."

"How could you not feel the bite?"

"The thing is, even if I felt it, even if it hurt, you wake up and all you can think about . . . is blood."

I could only say, "Oh."

"The other memories, of before, when I was living at home and taking lame community college classes, and playing music, hanging out, whatever, are so foggy it's like they didn't even happen. This part is so vivid it's like the real stuff was never real."

"Well, what was the real James like?"

"Like this. Only . . . you know."

"So then what?"

"I woke up on the floor of our bassist's place. Hungover. Hungry. The band went out for breakfast, but I couldn't get up. Later I tried to drink everything in the fridge, but it all tasted rotten, like, wrong. Even the tap water made me nauseous." He almost smiled. "And not just 'cause it's L.A."

"Weird."

"First you think you'll sleep it off. Then all you do is sleep. Parts of my body would go numb, or get supersensitive. I thought for sure I'd been drugged, but ten days in a mini coma? That's no drug I've heard of."

"You didn't go to the doctor?"

"I tried to. Got dropped off by my drummer at the ER one night, when I was still out of it. Before I even got inside, though, this EMT stopped me, said he'd give me something right out of the ambulance, that I didn't have to wait. And he already knew what was wrong with me, symptom for symptom, like he was reading it off a list. Then he diagnosed me: dead. He said I'd died. And now I was becoming something else."

"Heavy."

"Beyond heavy. But he was already handing me an IV bag of blood from his coat pocket—he knew I wanted it before even I did. No time for denial."

"So this guy . . . helps vampires?"

"You're not understanding. I'm telling you, we're everywhere."

Goose bumps.

"I'm just one of the ones who's not very good at hiding it."

I gave him an "Oh, please" look. "You do fine."

"Couldn't hide it from Naomi for long." Then he said out loud, but more to himself, "Sucked."

"Were your parents pissed?" Mine would lose it.

"They don't know."

"I can't believe your sister accepted it. Doesn't seem like her style."

"Well, obviously she doesn't really want me around."

I always wanted James around.

"And these days I'm barely that hungry anymore. And it's not like I'd go after my family." He shook his head, then nodded his head. "Also, I don't live here."

I said, "Oh yeah," and looked around the empty room. "So what's the deal in Cambridge?"

"I'd heard a rumor around L.A. of this fake college on the East Coast. I took a red-eye out. Total long shot; they never admit anyone new. And they didn't want me either, until they found out who my parents were. The guy who runs it, Luke, is really into anthropology. Worships my mom and dad. It's the only reason I got in. They probably think I'm secretly brilliant or something. Luke's cool, though. Rides a Vespa."

"Like a scooter?" I made a face.

"I mean, people think we're trust-fund kids, but no one bothers us. We're stuck in a stuck-up college town, but whatever. And it keeps up the illusion for my parents that I'm there working, saving up money to study music at Berklee."

I tried to imagine it: a bunch of equally hot versions of James living together, sleeping all day, hunting for coeds and postgrads at night. Whoa.

"Are there schools like that here?" I crossed my fingers tightly in my lap.

"Not any that I've heard of."

"You could start one in L.A."

"No. It's different on the West Coast. Everyone's roaming. Sometimes I can go days, weeks, without seeing one, and when I do, they're usually alone."

"But sometimes you bump into one around the city, just doing their thing?"

"Ever seen a good-looking dude wearing a leather jacket and dark sunglasses on an August night?"

"Hello, Sunset Strip."

"Well."

"No way."

"Yes way."

Leave it to L.A. vampires to be the most badass of them all.

"But you still like it here. You come back every once in a while to see your family, right?"

I was up to speed. We were using the present tense.

"No."

"No?"

"Not really. They only needed me to take care of Naomi."

"If anyone can take care of themselves, it's Naomi."

"Whitley was supposed to come, but he's avoiding our parents."

"Whitley."

"Whit. Middle child."

Oh. Whit. Whose room I'd ogled and whose shoes I'd invaded.

"How many of you is Naomi hiding?"

"She's really only hiding me. Wouldn't you?"

"Yeah, hide you all for myself."

I put out the vibe, but he didn't go for it, just said, "I've kind of ruined her life."

"And now I'm partying on those ruins. Right?"

"Maybe." James touched my cheek.

"Harsh."

"I'm not trying to make you feel worse." A pause. "How *do* you feel?"

"I feel . . . everything. How do you feel?"

"Still weird. You look . . . unsatisfied."

I was unsatisfied, and the words rushed out: "Have you ever turned someone? Have you ever killed another one?"

"Neither."

"Cool." I settled back on my folded legs. "Or bummer?"

"No bummer."

"Now can I have my do-over question?" I yanked

lightly on his sleeve while James waited patiently for me to continue. In my smallest voice: "Can you still have sex?"

It wasn't the exact question I'd wanted to ask, but it was close enough.

"Um . . ."

"This is so embarrassing."

"No, it's totally fine."

"Okay, question mark?"

"Honestly," he said, trying to act casual, "haven't tried it yet."

"Don't you get . . . randy?" I was already laughing. My vocab was laughable.

He was laughing too. "Come here."

I crawled into his lap, straddling him, and kissed his neck and ears, moving one hand over his leg, from his calf to the exposed skin at the rip in the knee of his jeans to his thigh. I gripped him there.

"I thought you'd ask the most epic question," he said between breaths.

"Which one?"

"What happened when I met you."

"Oh, I know the answer to that one. High jinks ensued."

"No. I, like, fell in love."

"With a human?" I touched his lips and he kissed and sucked my finger.

"I know."

"Disgusting."

"Dangerous."

"Whatever."

Then I kissed him, hard at first, then very, very soft. His fingers traced lines up my legs, making me tremble.

"I want to go in there," I said, pointing to the walk-in closet.

He kissed my mouth and stood up with me still in his lap. I wrapped my legs around him, never breaking our long, steady kiss. Still entangled, he carried me across the room into the closet. Once inside I slid down his body to the mattress on the floor. There was a single blanket, a couple of pillows, and four walls, nothing more. Then he closed the closet. Total darkness.

We rolled around awkwardly, knees and elbows bumping into walls and body parts while we stripped each other's clothes off. It was amazing; not the suave seduction like I'd daydreamed but the very human fore-play between a girl and a boy. James was shaking, just as nervous as I was, trying to please and give pleasure. I moaned for him and didn't have to fake it, because every touch was surreal, sublime. Everything was how I wanted it, every way was right.

Suddenly, with less pain than I'd expected, he was inside. James let out a few gasps and hit his fist against the wall behind my head. He tucked his face into his shoulder, careful to keep his mouth away from the veins on my neck.

"It's okay," I whispered. "It's okay."

It was okay, good, great.

Unbelievable.

At some point I woke up, but I didn't remember falling asleep. I lay there in the pitch black for a while. It could've been three in the morning, noon, six thirty at night. Eventually I realized there wasn't a familiar body lying next to me. I called out for James. No answer.

I slid the closet doors open. His room was the same emptiness, my mother's silk kimono the only sign that anyone had even been here last night. I crawled out on my hands and knees, adjusting my eyes from complete darkness to slightly amber darkness, and called his name again. Nothing.

I tried to stay calm, react rationally. James loved me. He'd told me so over and over last night, whispering it into my ears and hair as I drifted. It was the last thing I'd heard and the last thing I'd forget. So it was okay. He was in the main house with Naomi. He was getting some fresh air. He was . . . feeding. But he was around.

I stood up slowly, dizzily, my body stiff and achy from sleeping cramped in a weird coffin room. I stretched out my muscles and cracked my joints and yawned groggily. I looked down at my naked body and reached for underwear and the kimono. I cinched the tie around my waist and walked toward the door, pulling the silky fabric around me.

"James . . .," I said, my voice trailing off as I walked outside. The sun was high in the sky, the brightest time of the day. Twelve-ish, one, two in the afternoon.

I went back inside, and that's when I saw it. I dropped to my knees, began to cry quietly. There, peeking out of the front pocket of my cutoff shorts, was the corner of a folded piece of white paper.

Quinn, I know this seems like good-bye, but it isn't.
I can make everything better, I just have to go. I
hope that makes sense. I said I wouldn't hurt you,
and I meant it. I do love you. I'll be back, okay?
James

My heart stopped. Even my tears stopped. He was gone.

PART TWO

II.

LIVING

Empty windows of nothingness punctuated by meaningless details involving totally mundane nonevents.

Morgan left me a message. I got fired from Video Journeys.

Of course I couldn't claim getting sacked came as any sort of surprise. I'd abandoned the number one rule of the prescheduled work shift: showing up. And just to seal the deal and make it absolutely obvious that Jerry was justified in laying me off, I somehow lost the keys to the store's front door, dead bolt, and outer gates. And I ignored his messages to please return my stupid work shirt.

I spent hours numbly watching the pool sweep silently cruising the bottom of the pool. I imagined swimming down and letting my long knotted hair get sucked into one of its vents. I lay out on our deck chairs for hours, days, praying the sun would burn my skin, erase me. I tried to substitute heavy sweating for tears; I swam laps for escape; I slept and slept and slept just for something to do.

The idea of boundaries slowly sunk in, became crucial. It worked like this: I left everyone alone, they left me alone.

It had been only five days since I'd drifted away from that tiny upstairs room and transformed into my current state as a pathetic speck of dust. But five days feels like five years to a speck of dust. And to a particularly sad, brokenhearted speck of dust like me, five days felt like forever. It felt like a really, really, like, long time.

But when five days feels like infinity, it's amazing how much your life can change. It was amazing how all of a sudden I could sit through the NBA finals start to finish, every game, the preshow warm-ups, the play-by-plays, the elaborate halftime shows, the locker room follow-up interviews. I even amazed myself by eating entire sit-down dinners with my parents. Multiple nights in a row.

Also amazing: I cleaned my room. I thought my parents would see it as a testament to my fine-ness, but my mother knew me too well. She saw straight through the semicleanliness and recognized it for what it was: a small, twisted cry for help. This was when my mother realized for the first time that I was in the throes of some greater tragedy. Of course, in her classically clueless Mom way, she assigned the blame to typical teenage dramarama between me and Libby. But it was such darkness to even hear her name spoken that I dissolved immediately from tight-lipped to wet-eyed to broke-down, thus validating my mother's theory and making everything worse, worse, worse.

In my attempt to stay grounded, my parents literally grounded me. They had a solid laundry list of reasons: for getting fired from my job, for lying about being at that one place when I was actually at another place, for casual auto theft, and for looting through my parents' closets to steal clothes that they finally noticed were missing. Like I cared. I didn't even put up a fight, which I think bummed them out at first and then sort of scared them. But I was a different Quinn now. I was Speck of Dust Quinn. So ground me the entire summer, lock me in the house, handcuff me to a wicker chair. Whatever. Specks of dust can live on Diet Coke alone.

Without an excuse to put on my Video Journeys shirt, pajamas became my new uniform. Well, pajamas meaning a leopard-print bikini top and a pair of old athletic gray sweat shorts. I didn't shower, was incapable of concentrating for more than five minutes at a time, wouldn't read, wouldn't listen to music, stared at magazine ads like I thought they might come to life, unfolded my origami collection, threw away pictures of myself, compulsively cut pieces of paper into tiny strips of confetti.

All of this—the pretending that my life actually had to continue forward even if not in the same way or in any recognizable way to the previous Quinlan Lacey—was at least better than thinking about *them*. Anything was better than thinking about Naomi or Morgan. Torture was better than thinking about Libby.

James.

It was one p.m. My father was home, for whatever random reason, working on the crossword puzzle in an old *LA Weekly*. His Jaguar was in the garage, which meant he wasn't stranded at the house. We didn't have any food in the fridge, which usually factored into his daily afternoon plans. There wasn't anything special on the Western channel—I checked. So why then was my father cussing at a musty, yellowing, half-finished word search?

"You're here to babysit me, aren't you?" I yelled from the top of the stairs. "Go away. I know I'm grounded. I'm not going anywhere."

"You know, the world doesn't revolve around you, Quinny," my father recited from some ancient text my mother had written on parental platitudes.

"Dad, the world doesn't, like, revolve at all. Don't worry about it."

"Morgan called while you were sleeping. He wants to talk to you."

"Um, obviously not, because if he wanted to talk to me he'd have called on my personal line. When he calls on your line, it means he wants to annoy me by turning my family against me. Now you love him and you're on his side. It's a plot. So I'm not calling him." I exhaled.

"Honey, am I supposed to understand any of that?"

"Like you care, seriously. I'm fine, stop babysitting me."

"If I leave and you jump out a window, your mother will kill me."

"Hilarious, Dad. What's a six-letter word for jail keeper?"

"Warden."

"Parent."

"Actually, you're not grounded anymore," he said, walking up the stairs toward me.

"I want to be grounded," I said. "I like it."

"You don't like anything."

The truth was ruthless. So my parents had been paying attention.

"And as much as I'm proud to have a daughter totally unimpressed by material things," my father said, guiding me by the shoulders into my bedroom, "it's time for you to put on a new outfit and some makeup."

The sweat shorts were affecting my whole family.

"Go outside and do something, Quinn. Pretend to have fun. No one wants to be around a miserable teenager."

"Cool, Dad. I'll just go hang out with none of my no friends. Beauty idea."

"Do you want to run some errands?"

"Obviously."

Then my father sat on my bed for the first time ever in the entirety of my bed-having life. Like at least twelve or thirteen years. He patted the spot next to him on my worn-out bedspread and looked at me with the sappiest fake frown on his face. I hated when my dad got cute. I hated more when he walked in on me watching television during a tampon commercial and nodded at me knowingly, like he understood the feeling of an inserted foreign object into a bleeding body part he didn't have. That sucked. But nothing could be worse than my father trying to heart-to-heart it out with me on the subject of boys. Oh my God, un-bear-able.

"I forgot what the floor looked like in here," he said, looking down at the carpet.

"Yeah I know, I'm so disgusting."

"I love you, you're my daughter, but you're driving us crazy."

"I cleaned up." I glanced around the room. "A little bit."

My father blinked and then raised the corners of his

mouth into an apologetic smile. My defenses were failing. I couldn't drive everyone crazy.

"It's the sweat shorts, isn't it?" I said. And then, magically, for the first time in five days, I laughed. "And the bathing suit too."

My father nodded, laughed with me, and said, "It's all bad, really."

Then he put his arms around me and hugged. I was loved; I couldn't deny that.

"Okay," he told me, "I'm arming you with a twenty-dollar bill and a Diet Coke, and I don't care where you go or when you're coming back."

"Oh, you really shouldn't have said that."

"And I know you don't want to hear this"—I cringed into his chest as he started—"but you should forgive Morgan. Clearly this breakup is taking its toll on you. Give him a chance to explain himself at least."

It was a cruel, cruel summer.

"Dad, I hate . . . everyone."

"I know you do, but could you do it somewhere away from the house for a while, please?"

I took the cash, took the wardrobe advice, took the car keys, and bounced.

On Melrose, at Headline, sifting through Bauhaus records and old weird punk stuff, I felt sort of normal again. Sort of. In my rush to get out of the house I'd slipped on my cutoff shorts, the ones I was wearing *that* night, and in the back pocket was his good-bye whatever note. I pretended like I had gunpowder in that pocket, like my shorts were flammable. I pretended like the paper was blank, or just some receipt or movie ticket from ages ago. But it ached again: my heart, my head, my everything.

I would've just ripped it up, but I wouldn't have. Keeping it was better, whether that made sense or not.

My father was right about one thing, though: A toll was being taken. I was paying seriously high rent on an imaginary place in someone's faraway, unbeating heart. It was draining me. I couldn't focus on the racks at Wasteland. Even the soda-fountain soda at Johnny Rockets didn't taste as sweet. And the stupid damn note said he was coming back anyway.

I was walking, dripping sweat, when I saw four kids from my school. They didn't notice me, thankfully, but seeing them reminded me of my real life as a soon-to-be senior and a badass and a lover of fine things like Kate Moss Italian *Vogue*s and River Phoenix movies. It was then, impossibly, hanging out on the cheesiest tourist trap in L.A., that I allowed myself entry to the living world again. On day five—the day God created the weekend—I remembered to try to be human.

It was the kind of L.A. day that'd haunt you forever if

you had to spend an eternity in endless nights: bleached-blue sky, total sunshine, faint Pacific Ocean breeze. I inhaled and exhaled, smelled the burgers, the hot dogs at Pink's, the clove cigarettes, the cheap stupid leather jackets. Every inch of my body was alive to the now, the reality of a warm summer day in Hollywood. It was a very small, not-so-bad feeling.

But "alive" wasn't psyched, and it didn't mean I was ready to interact with people. Morgan, maybe. Baby steps.

I walked back to the Jag and unlocked the door. On the radio was that old band Talking Heads, that "Psycho Killer" song, which is actually kind of dancey and cool and made me turn it up and roll the windows down. After five days of media blackout, hearing the song felt vivid, like a comeback montage, the best part of the movie. I was going to see him again. I *would* see him again.

Then, turning left off Laurel Canyon onto Lookout Mountain, I saw him again.

James whizzed right past me, riding a beat-up old Schwinn ten-speed. I jumped out of the car, forgetting to pull over, park, stop the engine, anything, and sprinted down the street in his direction. I ran like crazy, like the crazy person I'd become. My legs were flying, too fast, faster than the rest of my body, and I shouted and shouted his name. *James. Come back.* I was racing, my head throbbing from the insane heat, then my body tripping over my own feet. I wiped out hard, first landing on my shins and knees, then bombed onto the palms of my hands and finally twisted to a halt on my left shoulder.

I shouted again into the burning black concrete. *James.*

It wasn't a mirage. I had seen his face, that awesome face, and his painfully soft white T-shirt. Something inside of me, a secret sixth sense, felt his presence. James was back.

I was crazy in pain and bleeding, but I didn't care. If James was back, then five days was just an insignificant *pling* in a deep, ancient well when compared to the immeasurable loss I thought I was facing for maybe the rest of my life.

If it had been James. It looked like him, sure, but it was two thirty in the afternoon. In blinding sunlight. A guy on a bike. I felt my insides crashing, crushed. My body was scraped and bloody, but I didn't move. I almost passed out in the middle of the road, Jaguar still running, KROQ still blaring.

Then some cars honked, and I lifted myself against my will.

James was gone. Again. And I was a goner, too, man.

It wasn't so much a bad idea as it was the worst idea ever, but my father had sent me out in one piece, so I couldn't come back in the ten or eleven pieces I was currently shattered into.

Coworker turned life raft, anyone?

Morgan's house was a ranch-style thing, flat and casual and sprawling and rustic. It was decorated like bonkers because Mrs. Crandall was obsessed with collecting weird whimsies and tchotchkes, all that crap Amish families and clueless craft fair moms make for people who love floppy bunnies in overalls, quilts as wall hangings, wheelbarrows, quaint country whatsits. As I walked down the driveway, I lightly kicked an antique, rusted wheelbarrow hand-painted with ivy and tiny burgundy wine grapes that was leaning against the mailbox.

"Hey, don't kick that."

Morgan stood at the bottom of the walk in his swim shorts. His blond hair was wet. His freckled body looked . . . kind of good, stronger than I would've guessed. Or, like, buff. I hadn't ever noticed.

"Why not, is it art or something?" I asked. "Do you wheel stuff around in it?"

"Fine, kick it."

"Sorry."

"I thought you were dead. You look dead." He picked a stray piece of thistle out of my hair. "I thought you were mad at me for telling you you got fired. I thought you were grounded."

"I'm not mad at you."

"You look like you're going to cry."

"Yeah, maybe."

"Well, what's wrong?" Morgan ran his fingers through a few strands of my hair again, but he didn't pull anything out this time.

"It's, like, nothing."

We stood in front of his house for a few minutes, neither of us speaking.

"Can I have a Band-Aid?" I asked, breaking the silence.

He led me in, and I went into the bathroom off the main hallway. I wet a small navy hand towel and dabbed at the blood on my legs and knees, then on my arms and hands. Inside the medicine chest I found a box of Band-Aids and stuck a few peach-colored ones over the deeper scrapes. Then I tied my hair into a loose ponytail, filled the sink with cold water, and dunked my face into it.

Afterward I wandered into Morgan's room and found him lying on his bed, still shirtless, with a game control in his hands. He paused the game as I came into the doorway.

"What are you doing?"

"Nothing. Playing Super Metroid."

"Bo-ring."

"Not even."

"Thanks for the Band-Aids. I'm all better now."

"You still look like you're going to cry."

"Morgan."

"You can totally stay here and hang out. Or you can take a nap if you want."

Sleep sounded like heaven, but I hesitated. Morgan's bed was small, like a kid's bed. Two people might fit on it but not without a lot of contact. In the moment, though, it was hard to resist. I knew for Morgan's sake, for the sake of our friendship and our communal sanity, that I needed to be careful about this kind of stuff. But a stronger part of me just wanted to crawl into a bed and close my eyes. I couldn't calculate all the varying degrees of potential hurt in this situation. I was exhausted and I was lonely. I took out my ponytail, kicked off my high-tops, and spread myself across his ratty old comforter. For just one slight moment he rested his cheek on my hair, then leaned back up. I looked down at the carpet—not an option. I scootched to the extreme right side of the mattress, lying on my side with one leg dangling over the edge. Totally platonic blissful nontouching discomfort. My eyelids fluttered open and shut, revealing flashes of his Green Day poster, then darkness, then *Dookie* poster, then more dark. He left one arm wedged between us and, with the controller in his other hand, unpaused the TV screen.

"I'm going to play Super Nintendo while you nap. Does it bother you?"

I tried to vaguely nod but disappeared into sleep before I could answer.

I didn't dream of anything. Just like the last five days, my eyes opened to a dull gray haze and closed to an infinite black field. I had lost James and would only continue to lose him—the shape of him, the look of him, the feel of him—until he came back. If he came back.

When I drifted awake, Morgan's arm was now cradled around me, some robotic bleeps zinging faintly in the background. I realized from the way his arm was pinned under me, cushioning me, that he was playing his video game with one hand. The gesture felt so sweet, almost noble. I kept my eyes shut.

I tried to imagine what it was like for a human when I showed up unannounced at their house with cuts and scrapes and bloodstains on my clothes. Here I was, wounded and covered in bandages, literally lying in Morgan's lap, and he just went right along playing video games, unfazed and undisturbed. I'd never appreciated this before. I liked humans. They could be so chill.

I pretended to sleep for another few minutes. Morgan's arm smelled good, summery, a mix of chlorine and sweat and a combination of other earthy boy odors. The top part of my exposed shoulder was up against his bare chest, where I could feel his bony ribs. This wasn't the closest we'd ever gotten physically—there'd been numerous hugs, a couple of failed kiss attempts, and a smattering of other short but specific embraces—but it felt like the closest. At least, the least weird.

Then, probably because his arm had fallen asleep, Morgan shifted his body a little and slumped lower, leaning in toward me. The sudden accidental intimacy hit me with a wave: My loneliness was too deep to fight. I wanted everything I shouldn't. I wanted him to drape his body around the shape of mine, wrap me in his arms, bury his face in my hair, show me love. Right then, maybe for the first time, I needed him more than he needed me.

Before Morgan knew what hit him, I hit him. I rolled over and twisted on top of his body. He dropped the controller. I looked down at him, through him, careful not to focus too deeply on his eyes. I didn't want to detect lust or fear or love or disgust, and I tried not to think about what he saw in mine. I held his hands up to my face and winced as his fingers brushed my wounds. Then I moved his hands down my neck, over the outside of my gray tank top, around my hips, the contours of my body. At first they felt like Morgan's hands, then they became someone else's. I closed my eyes and connected with the sensation. Warm human hands. A heartbeat. Teenage nervousness. It was better than being alone. Period.

But suddenly Morgan breathed heavier and flipped me over so that his body was on top. He moved in to kiss me but then froze. "I'm not going to stop this," he said. "Even if I'm not sure you want to, I want to, so I'm going to."

His voice cut through my fantasy and I looked at him, really looked at him. He was Morgan.

"Okay, now I'm going to cry," I mumbled.

"Happy tears, or . . . ?" His voice trailed off.

I covered my face with my hands.

Morgan pulled himself off me, collapsed on his back, and stared at the ceiling. Then he laughed. It sounded distant, kind of scary.

The Nintendo music kept playing along quietly.

"What's funny is I'm not even pissed. It's classic Quinn déjà vu. You're, like, so predictable."

"You're mad at me."

"Get over yourself." Morgan got up abruptly and left the room.

I grabbed my shoes and went down the hallway, through the living room, kitchen, out the back door, to the pool. Morgan was there, by the edge. The sun was just as high in the sky as it had been earlier; it was still scorching.

"Morgan, stop. Wait. I want to say something."

"No," he said forcefully, then turned and dove into

the deep end. He swam back and forth several times, the entire length of the pool, coming up for breath only once or twice a lap.

"It's been bad the past few days," I shouted at the water. "It's been the worst. I won't go into it, but still. This is the best I've felt. I don't know. You were right, we are evolved."

Still swimming, Morgan lifted his arm out of the water and flipped me off.

"Whatever, okay, I deserve that," I continued shouting. "Morgan, damn it, please listen!"

I stepped forward to the edge of the pool and dropped myself down into the water. I sank lower and lower, till I was sitting on the bottom. When I opened my eyes underwater, I saw that my Band-Aids were peeling off and floating away.

I also saw Morgan stop his laps, swim over in my direction, and grab me by the shirt, dragging me toward the shallow end. I didn't resist.

Then my head was above the water and I was gasping for air. Morgan shoved me down onto the pool steps.

"Shake it off, dude, and go home," he said blankly.

Now I was panting for breath, soaked, wearing all my clothes. My scrapes stung from the chlorine.

I opened my mouth to speak, but Morgan interrupted. "Leave it alone, Quinn. For once just drop it."

I climbed out of the pool, my shorts and shirt and high-tops sopping and heavy, and stared up at the sun. I dared myself to think it: I wished I were a vampire. I wished I weren't human. Then I'd be asleep right now and none of this day would've ever even happened. And if it was happening, then the sunlight would hit my skin and I'd burst into flames, become ashes, become nothing at all.

"See you next time we do this," Morgan said finally, then swam back into the pool and resumed his laps.

I kept staring up at the sun until my retinas felt like they were on fire. Then I lowered my eyes and let the red dots and color trails dissolve into Morgan's backstroke.

Under the diving board, barely noticeable to anyone who wasn't looking for it, I saw a soggy white piece of paper floating gently just below the surface of the water. My pocket was empty. My heart was emptier.

12.

BURR

Boiling hot—like a hundred and ten or something—in the valley, on Sherman Way, at Follow Your Heart, waiting for my mother to buy her stupid low-fat whatevers. I looked around at all the granola dorks and hippies and New Agers, and they looked happy. Some of them even seemed to be glowing slightly. They glew.

I myself was a shade past waxen as I followed my mother sluggishly around the store, numbly drinking from a Diet Coke can. Clearly I didn't have the glow. Deal with it.

"Try to enjoy yourself," my mother called back at me from the whole wheat pasta section. "You'll be dead one day, and then what will you think of this moment?"

"Nothing. I'll be dead. I won't be thinking anything."

"This routine may work on your father, but not on

me." She read the label on a soy-cheesy snack thing and threw it into the cart. "So you can just go on acting like a five-year-old. Look around, no one's paying attention. No one cares."

"Yeah, I know no one cares."

People *were* paying attention, though. If I remembered correctly, I was wearing a baggy Butthole Surfers T-shirt over barely visible cutoffs and a metric ton of black eyeliner. Then there were the bandages up and down my arms and legs, my scuffed-up face, and the aforementioned Diet Coke. I wasn't exactly, like, blending in.

"That's right. Just keep that sour puss on for days, doesn't bother me."

"Mom, that's so, like, transparent. And 'sour puss?' Are you serious?" In plain view of her, a shelf-stocking dude, and some other stupid healthy glowing patron, I ditched my empty soda can right between some vitamin bottles of B12 and B complex.

"Make fun of your mother. Very 'cool' of you."

I missed the handwritten notes. Sweet niblets, bring the notes back.

"Bonnie, chill out."

That did it. First names. She banished me to the Lex.

Back in the car, the sun had turned the interior into a volcano. The tan leather upholstery felt white-hot against the exposed skin on my legs. I sprawled across the backseat, letting the backs of my thighs, knees, and calves get bright red and sticky. I could barely breathe, the air was so stuffy and sweltering, the sun burning down through the window directly onto my face. It was like a disgusting sauna. I felt very physical pain. It was awesome.

When the pain finally faded to a distant ache and my body was drenched in a protective layer of sweat, I let my eyes sink closed and just drifted. It was that special almost-sleep of blazing summertime afternoons. I was dimly awake enough to guide my thoughts but too out of it to be fully in control of the outcome. So my thoughts went straight to James. Duh. Obviously.

That night I fell, coming home from Libby's. Out of the shadows, out of some dark canyon ravine, James walks toward me. He moves fast, determined, his eyes more piercing than usual, vague bloodlust in them. I scream out into the blackness for help, but suddenly James is inches from my bleeding face. I sink into him defenselessly, go weak in his arms, an invalid, already dead, waiting for his awesome kiss. He leans in, licks my tongue, the outside of my lips. His tongue runs over some of the blood running down from my nose, and his whole body ripples with pleasure. I stay silent, dipping my head back as James sucks softly on my collarbone, my neck. Then I feel the bite. The slow, deep sucking. And then it's my body rippling, jerking, pulsing. My eyes roll back in my head, and I feel him gently lowering me to the ground. I lie there paralyzed. Ecstatic.

Imagining all this, him, the night, the encounter, I rubbed my hand over the outside of my shorts. I pictured us together on that dark canyon road. In that small, cramped walk-in. Together. I died each death with pleasure, in pleasure. I told James to take it slow, wanting him to indulge in me, but I couldn't savor the moment enough. I couldn't hold on to the bliss.

Then there were voices in the parking lot, people talking, the rattling of a shopping cart's wheels on concrete. I sat up. A car reversed out of its parking space and drove away down the alley. I pulled at the seat belts next to me, curled forward, wet and sticky and red all over, and wept into my lap.

Then just as quickly as I was crying, I was wiping the tears away with the back of my scraped-up, bruised hands. I was losing my mind, or had lost it several times over. I had to get home. To bed, to the pool, to my parents, it didn't matter.

I smoothed the hair around my face and prepared myself to reenter the store and find my mother. I reached for the door handle and instinctively looked up. There, peering down at me through the window with a look that read "concerned on the verge of panic," was James. James the cyclist.

He knocked on the glass and said, "Are you okay?"

I shook my head no.

He put a hand against the window, his big palm facing me. "Do you know who I am?"

I inhaled, exhaled. I pressed my hand against his, through the glass, thinking. Sunlight. Daytime. Freckles and a tan. Eyeglasses. Yes, I nodded. I know who you are.

I rolled down the window and looked at him some more. The sun was shining down from above and behind him, ringing him in a weird halo. He folded his arms against the window frame and leaned in.

"Hey. You were crying."

"Yeah, I know."

"I wasn't following you. I saw you inside and heard your mother say your name. I've heard about you," he said. "I could sort of guess at what you looked like."

"Okay. Sounds like you were following me, though."

He frowned, then smiled; it was a pretty great smile. "Well, I wasn't."

"Okay."

"Want to go get a milkshake?"

"What?" I asked. "No." But a milkshake sounded so, so, so good.

"Come on. Tell your mom you have a friend. She'll be happy."

"Why, because I don't have any friends?"

"Because you're in the parking lot crying."

"So?"

"So come have a milkshake with me instead." When I didn't react, he said, "Milkshakes, mmm."

"I'm not a five-year-old."

"Just come."

What was I fighting? I got out of the Lexus, exhausted, feeling faint.

He reached out and held me by the arm. "Hey, you don't look so hot."

"Well, I am. I'm really, really hot. It's way hot outside."

Then he reached into his pocket, pulled out a pen and piece of paper, scrawled on it very quickly OUT WITH FRIEND HOME SOON I LOVE YOU QUINN, and shoved it under the windshield wipers.

"That's not even close to my handwriting. I'd never write that either."

"You aren't the precious little daffodil I was expecting."

I hung my head down and slouched. Don't I know it.

"Deal with it," I whispered to the ground. I felt only slightly more insane than usual as I followed Whitley Sheets to his car.

I stared at the awkward, greasy waiter in a paper hat taking our order. He scribbled in his book, said, "Two black and whites, okeydoke," then skipped off.

"You took me to Mel's Drive-In?" I glanced around, scowling at the retro kitsch everywhere. "They have a doo-wop jukebox, it's a joke."

"No way, girls love this! Don't you come here with all your friends and listen to tunes and just laugh and laugh until the end of time?" Whit was already making fun of me. "They have good milkshakes. We can get ours to go, okay?"

"Fine. What's a black and white, anyway?"

"It's got vanilla ice cream and chocolate syrup."

"Weird."

"You're going to love it. You're going to shut up and love it."

I watched Whit as he watched me, and there was one thing I couldn't deny: Whit was way cute. Handsome even. He had messy hair, short on the sides and kind of wavy and piled up on the top. His face was freckly in a nice way, kind of tan, and he wore cool tortoiseshell glasses. He also had on a really light plaid men's button-down shirt with the sleeves rolled up and just enough buttons undone so you could see where a small gold chain with a crucifix hung around his neck. Dark denim shorts were cuffed just above the knees with a soft navy L.A. Dodgers hat hanging out the back pocket. And there were those nasty beat-up Converses I knew too well.

"Can we get serious for a sec?" I asked.

"But we're having so much lighthearted fun." The coy, semi-mean-spirited picking-on-me thing was already working.

"You followed me. So you were looking for me?"

"I was somewhat, vaguely, very lazily looking for you, yes." He nodded.

"Why? I didn't tell anyone, I didn't do anything crazy"—I thought about that one for a second—"I'm not like that."

"I had to make sure. And also I wanted to make sure you were okay. I was worried that you might be, like, really scared. Or sad or something."

"You don't even know me."

"So?"

"So worrying about me is, like, pointless. Worry about . . . Naomi."

"She's fine. But clearly you're not."

"Clearly?" Whit came on strong.

"You weren't hotboxing in that car, you were crying. Which means you're sad. And maybe a little goth, which I can get into."

I looked up at him. He reached a hand across the table to me, warmly.

"Hence awesome milkshakes, hence awesome newly forming friendship." He pointed to himself, then me, then back to himself. Us. He wanted *us* to be friends.

"You just want to be sure I won't tell anyone anything, but I won't. I already promised, so you don't have to pretend like you want to be friends with me."

"Fine. I won't pretend."

"Good." Wow, I really wasn't a daffodil. I was one of those pointy, scratchy balls that gets stuck on your socks. I was a burr. Those sucked.

"Can I hang out with you anyway?" Whit looked unembarrassed to ask. "I haven't had friends in L.A. for a couple years, and Naomi isn't in the hanging-out mood. So I'm pathetic, you're cool, I'm begging you, please be my friend. You can even fake it if you want. I have no pride. But I don't have anything to do out here. I've been back less than a week and I'm already bored out of my mind."

"Oh, in that case."

"And, of course, I obviously have to keep an eye on you so you don't ruin the lives of all my family members. Loads of fun to be had."

"Then I should let you know up front that boring's kind of my thing."

"I'm not bored now," Whit said, feigning a yawn.

"Why won't Naomi hang out with you?"

"She's pissed. I wasn't there, but I think . . . you guys did something to piss her off?"

"Ha, ha. Cute."

Calling James and me "you guys" was like the most

random, abnormal thing I could imagine. "You guys" made us sound like buddies, like just a couple of coolies hanging out, like two humans. As the middle child of the Laurel Canyon Addams family, Whit was surprisingly chill on the subject of ampire-vays.

"But even if we did piss her off, you didn't."

"Yeah, I tried that one. Not working."

Our phony fifties geek came back with the black and whites in two Mel's to-go cups. Whit pushed a milkshake directly under my chin and nodded enthusiastically. I rolled my eyes. He paid the bill. He opened the door for me, and we walked across the parking lot to his car.

"Did they have Styrofoam in the fifties?" I asked, holding my cup up for further carbon-dating inspection.

"Has anyone ever told you how adorable you are?"

"No one has ever, ever told me that."

We just sat in his car in the parking lot, not really staying, not really leaving, not even drinking our milkshakes—which were, as Whit had promised, totally rad-tasting. Then he turned to me, suddenly serious, staring at me in a way that made me sink back against my seat.

"Well. You are." He started the car and drove me wherever.

Later, sitting in his parked Camry in front of my house with the windows rolled down and a light breeze tossing through the canyons, I felt kind of okay. We didn't say anything on the drive home from Mel's, but it wasn't tense, just quiet. In one afternoon we already weren't strangers, we weren't really friends yet, just weird knowers of each other's secret stuff. I didn't want to get out of the car. He didn't seem to want to make me. We sat together finishing off our milkshakes in silence.

"So." I cleared my throat and tapped my empty cup against the dash. "You're in college."

"Sort of."

"What's sort of in college? Community college?"

"No," he said, nudging my shoulder. "I dropped out of Brown. Just haven't told my parents yet."

"Does anyone in your family tell the truth? You're like the Olympians of lies."

"Gold medalists in freestyle withholding."

"Silver in men's false pretense." I held back a smile.

"We would have gotten the gold for that, but someone had to open his big fangs."

I stared at Whit, frozen.

"Quinn." He reached out and held one of my wrists. "It's a joke." He sighed and said, "Maybe you are as fragile as a flower." Then he looked down at the scrapes of dried blood where he held on to my arm. "What happened?"

"I was being an idiot."

"Idiot how?"

"I was chasing after you—" I stopped, shaking my head at the memory. "Yesterday, on Lookout Mountain, riding your bike. I thought you were him."

"During the day?"

"I know."

"That should've been your first clue."

"I know." Joking about James didn't work. Even the humor hurt too much. I swallowed hard. "Is he coming back?"

"I don't know." Whit looked at me; we looked at each other. "Probably."

He took our empty cups and threw them into the backseat, then slumped down behind the wheel and turned his face away from me, toward something out the window. The breeze ruffled his hair a little. I would've guessed he was nineteen, but everyone sexy in these hills was a weirder age than they looked.

"Well, do you know what happened? Why James left? Did he tell you?" I stared out my own window.

"No, he didn't tell me anything." Whit thought for a second, then said, "Well, he told me to take care of you."

Even with my head turned I could feel Whit eying my bandages. "I said I fell."

He shrugged.

"Chasing *you*. So if anything, this is your fault." I turned back to meet his eyes.

"You must think he's really great, huh?" Whit asked.

I shifted in my seat. "So?"

"So nothing." Whit put his hands on the steering wheel and looked ahead at the empty street.

"What, he's not?"

"No, he's awesome." When Whit said it, I could tell he meant it.

More silence, more weirdness.

"Told you I'm boring."

"Yeah," he said, and laughed. "This sucks, dude."

"Let's talk about the ways in which you're a screwup now that we've exhausted the topic of my sorry-ass life." I stretched my legs out on the dashboard and picked at a tiny scab on my thigh. "You dropped out of college? So you're an academic failure?"

"Maybe this would be good for our next hang-out."

I dropped my legs. "Fine."

"It's late."

It was like four thirty or something and James, wherever he was—assuming he was still in the Pacific Standard time zone—wasn't even awake yet.

"Yeah."

Whit jiggled his key chain hanging in the ignition. The members of this family could not get rid of me fast enough.

I reached for the door handle, then paused. "You want

my phone number or what?" It was lame but whatever. Had to ask.

"Yeah, you want mine?"

"Have it." I finally opened the door, grabbed a pen off the dash, and scribbled my digits on his hand. "Call if you feel like it."

"I'll call tonight."

"Really?"

"Yeah, we have to make plans for tomorrow. Know what you want to do? And don't say Mel's Drive-In, we already did that."

I knew what I wanted to do.

"Nothing too boring," he warned.

I nodded, shut the Camry door, waved, and watched Whit take off.

Okay, Libby, I thought, *make it through tonight. Libbits Casey Block, just make it through tonight and we'll be solid.*

At dinner my mother stared across the table at me with a smile that said, *I know what you're up to, missy,* but in a totally, like, okay-with-it way.

"So," my mother said, blowing on a piece of steamed broccoli speared through her fork, "tell your father what you did today."

"Um, you know. Hung out with a friend." I shoved the hot vegetable into my mouth, hoping it'd scar my tongue and render me unable to elaborate on the matter.

My father nearly choked at my casual use of the word "friend." This was *news*. It was, like, the headlining topic of tonight's local news. Then I had to endure this:

"You did? That's so great, Quinny." Dad.

"She did. Isn't it wonderful?" Mom.

"Is this person special?" Dad.

"Do we know this person?" Mom.

"I just think it's really positive." Dad.

"Would this person like to come over for dinner?" Mom.

"We thought, well, we were worried, for sure." Dad.

Whoa.

"Are you guys retarded?" I asked, actually expecting an answer.

"Quinn." My mother held her fork in the air, using it as a wand to conduct the words: "We are not 'you guys,' we're *Mom* and *Dad*."

"Yeah."

The thing was, and even I couldn't really express this in any way that would make sense to anyone, it *had* been a pretty good day. Skip the health-food-store part and the crying-in-the-car part, but past that—all through and even up to the part where Whit sort of kicked me out of his Camry—was actually nice. So I didn't really want to talk about it too much, because if I couldn't understand it myself, then I didn't want to ruin the not-so-bad vibes

I was feeling by analyzing them to death. I just wanted to go upstairs, drink a Diet Coke, jump on my bed, listen to some songs that reminded me of this exact situation, and in a mainly relaxed way wait for Whit to call. That's how I would have done it . . . before. And not just before James left, but before he came along too.

Normally this would also be the juncture when I peaced out of the dining room. My plate was basically one-fourth finished, I felt like I had nothing left to say but dull, passive-aggressive things, and my parents had switched their attention from my hang-out to such amazing topics as what was in the mail and who called and who left a message and how good *is* this bok choy! But in the past week I'd set this new precedent where I acted like an actual member of the family, so I decided to just sit it out till the end. Yesterday my parents were so bummed for me, and today they were so pumped for me. Ugh, the guilt was so boring.

I clanked my fork against the plate. "His name is Whit. He's pretty cool, he's a nice guy, he's my friend. We're hanging out tomorrow."

My mom reached across the table and lightly yanked on one of my braids. "See, was that so hard? It didn't kill you."

"I think it's great," my dad said, and winked.

Then, as if I'd shown them an X-ray of my mended

heart with a doctor's note saying everything was fine, my parents moved on. Something besides the bills *had* come in the mail. Invite to a Fourth of July party at the club near Griffith Park, and suddenly I was old news.

I didn't have to wait long for Whit to call. Even his ring sounded confident. I was lying on my bed reading an article in an old issue of *Sassy* magazine about the perks of dating older guys. One, confidence. Two, loyalty. Three, experience. Gross.

"Hi," I said.

"Hi, you," Whit said.

"Are you in your bedroom?"

"Yeah."

"I've been in that room."

"Did you get yelled at for trespassing?"

"Only after I tried on your shoes."

"You tried on my shoes? That's nasty, dude."

"I liked all your stuff. I liked your life."

"Well, my stuff isn't my life."

I looked around my room. My stuff was, like, pretty much my entire life. Once I'd added James's blue T-shirt to the archives, my stuff meant everything to me. Total definition.

"Care to elaborate?" I asked.

"Obviously. Who doesn't want an excuse to go on and

on about themselves?"

"That's what I'm saying!"

That made him laugh, and we laughed together.

"Hey, Whit?" I said after we were quiet again.

"Oh, you want to get serious, don't you?"

"I need your help."

"Done."

"I'm serious."

"I'm serious too."

"This isn't a normal favor to ask. It's awkward as hell, and totally out of line, but I'm desperate. And it can't wait."

"That's cryptic. Translation, please?"

"Help me, Obi-Wan Kenobi, you're my only hope."

"Becoming clearer . . ."

"And James won't want you to do it."

"Explain, lady."

I tried to hold back, but it came out in a gush. I told him everything—it already felt so natural to—*except* . . . for that end part, that last bit, when Stiles told James he'd come after his family if anyone messed with Libby again. That we had to leave them completely alone or something terrible would happen to the Sheetses.

I couldn't tell Whit about that stuff or else he wouldn't help me. But I also wouldn't have asked for his help if I didn't believe that Sanders and Stiles would only come after *me* if something went down, not him or Naomi. Not

James, because James wasn't around.

But otherwise I told him everything, the past, the present, and my plan for the future, where we raided their lair during the daytime and rescued my best friend. And the cherry on top: Libby's aunt Lynn in the desert. Crucial witness protection pad. I rambled and rambled until I hit a crescendo and couldn't think of anything else to add.

"Yeah, I'll do that," Whit said nonchalantly.

"Wait, really?"

"Yeah, they'll be asleep. It'll be fine."

"And we just go . . . get her?"

"Yeah. I know how this works."

"Then that's it?"

"Then we can listen to *The Chronic* in my car."

"I think Libby actually likes that album."

"And then eat some pizza."

"Wait. Pizza? Milkshakes? Are you trying to make me fat?"

"Yes."

"That's unique."

"I'll pick you up at two. Wear something big so you can eat a lot of pizza." Then he hung up.

I liked Whit. I loved James. I guess older guys *were* my thing. Confidence, loyalty, and experience. Not so bad.

13.

CONFETTI

Maybe I woke up before noon, but maybe I never fell asleep. I was exhausted or I was wired. I was both. There is no getting ready to do the stupidest thing a person could ever do. So I did the only things I could do. I fastened twenty necklaces around my neck for armor; I drew on so much eyeliner I looked like a sobbing drunk raccoon on a tequila bender; I plowed through a third can of soda.

I felt alive, wildly so, because I was scared out of my mind. My heartbeat thumped out louder and louder and crazier and louder to all the hibernating vampires in the Los Angeles hills. My insides were insane, ribs rattling, lungs hyperventilating, my whole human teenage form dissolving into a permanent panic attack. At two, when Whit was supposed to pick me up, I thought I might die or shatter or explode or melt—whatever happens to a person when they're never going to be the same again.

Then I heard a car horn honking twice from the street. I peeked out the blinds. Whit was thirty minutes late, sipping from a Starbucks cup, his head in his hands, looking sleepy.

I hurried down the walkway and into the Camry.

And we were off. Whit sipped his coffee and shot me a bleary smile now and then as we wound through the hills. I stared out at the houses passing by. It felt like we were going eight miles an hour. If a car could crawl, Whit's was on its hands and knees.

I couldn't unclench my insides. I needed origami to unfold. I wanted to rip paper into confetti.

"What's going on with this?" Whit tugged on the giant Mickey Mouse tank top I was wearing as a dress.

"Distraction tactics."

He looked from the road to my naked thighs, then back to the road. I looked down at my lap too. The color of flesh; I was still human.

"Distraction achieved."

"What are you wearing, a Celtics jersey?" He was. He had on a green-and-white jersey with those stupid cute jean shorts from yesterday and his nasty Converses. Kobe might have actually been comforting. Even Shaq would've been cool. "Traitor."

"Imagine how crazy they'll go when they see this."

I nearly choked. "You said they'd be asleep."

Whit sipped from his cup, shrugged.

"No." I grabbed his arm and squeezed hard. "You said you 'know how this works' or something. That's what you said."

He pulled his arm away and adjusted his glasses. "They'll be asleep, it's daytime. Chill. Let's listen to something."

I dug through his CDs, not really paying attention to the writing on the spines.

"Not *The Chronic*, though," he said. "That's for our victory slice."

Ugh, pizza.

I picked up the first CD in the pile, but when I moved to slip it into the player, Whit grabbed my wrist. I followed his eyes to the object in my hand.

"Not that one either, okay?" It had hearts all over it and stupid shiny stickers.

"Okay, fine." I put it back.

We were both on edge and a long way from some pizza-Dr.-Dre-confetti-Libby rescue celebration.

Who knows what album we settled on? Sounded like the last thing I'd ever hear.

Finally we cruised to a stop in front of the twins' guesthouse. It was three. Outside it was hot and sunny and normal. Inside the car it was a panic room.

I tried to relax my muscles and visualize my plan working, but now that we were here I couldn't. So my only choice was to pretend the plan still made sense.

"Don't turn off the car," I said, putting my hand over Whit's on the gearshift. "Keep it running. I'll be ten minutes, tops."

He shook his head, shut off the engine, got out of the car, and started walking down the long, narrow drive. I almost tripped over myself sprinting to catch up.

"What the hell?" I grabbed his jersey and yanked backward. "Stay in the car."

He spun around and glared at me, his face stern but scared. "No way."

"Seriously," I whispered, shaking. "Just stay in the car."

"You're not going in alone."

"Someone has to keep the car running."

"They're going to be asleep. They have to be."

I started to argue more, but Whit silenced me in a crushing bear hug. James had never held me like this. Maybe no one had. He shoved his face in my hair. I could smell his hot coffee breath on my cheek. For one moment it was the only thing in the world.

"Listen," he said. "If you see Libby, you're going to lose it. I have to be there."

I didn't have a choice. I could only trust him.

I nodded. He let me go.

"We're going to grab her and bail, that's it. That's all." He stared at me, inches from my face.

I nodded more. Whit's lips began to slowly open, like they would for a kiss, but he spoke instead. "Okay, Quinn?"

"Okay."

"Okay."

Then he turned, and we silently walked the rest of the way to the guesthouse's front door. Then Whit's hand was on the doorknob.

I closed my eyes.

James.

I love you.

Then Whit turned the knob. There was a tiny click sound and it opened. Stupid, trusting, supernatural Spaders.

He gently pushed the door inward, and we peeked inside. There was dead silence except for the dull drone of the refrigerator. Everything was the same: the same couch, the same kitchen countertop, the same heavy curtains pulled tightly shut. And with the curtains shut, it was cool and way dark. Whit left the door open and we stepped inside, trying not to make a sound.

I stood by the door and looked around. Whit tiptoed

toward the main set of curtains and slowly pushed the thick drapes to the outermost edges of the windows. Blinding sunshine poured in. I reached over and fingered the heavy, multilayered fabric of the curtain. It felt like the stuff they used in Vegas hotel rooms so you can't ever tell what time it is. But you could tell now. It was bright as hell.

This was going to work.

Suddenly Whit froze. "Where is she?" he whispered.

I shrugged. My eyes drifted to the lone long, dark hallway.

Whit followed my eyes, counted two closed doors and one open bathroom door, then collapsed into a chair, his hands rubbing his face.

I looked down the hallway again. She was in bed with Stiles. Duh, my God, I hadn't even considered that. I felt my whole soul fall away. I sank to the carpet.

Whit snuck over to me and grabbed my shoulders, scream-whispering, "Why didn't you tell me that she'd probably be in bed with him?"

I went limp. I went empty.

"Damn it, Quinn. Damn it." There was dread in his voice.

He got up and went into the kitchen. I heard him opening some drawers. Seconds later he was back in front of me, holding a butcher's knife. This was getting too slasher.

"What are you doing?" I said, trying not to understand

why Stiles and Sanders had kitchen utensils when they didn't eat.

"I'm going into their room."

"Whit, you can't."

"Shut up and get under the window."

"What?"

"Get. Under. The window." He pointed to where the sunshine was flooding in. "Now. In the light." He started to wrench me to my feet.

"Okay. Okay, okay, okay." I crawled in front of the window and let the light wash over my body. Lying on my side, I pushed my knees into my eyes hard, until I could see spots and stars rushing through blackness.

With my head buried in the carpet, I could hear Whit's footsteps carefully padding down the hall. I counted seventeen steps, then nothing.

Then I heard his feet stalking back my way and felt his hands on my shoulders.

"It's locked, we're leaving."

I couldn't move.

"Quinn, get up! The door is locked. We have to go."

"I'm sorry," I whispered.

He said nothing.

I said, "I'm sorry" twice more. I stared down at the floor, at perfect peach carpet, at nothing. At failure. I moved to stand.

And there was a sudden, small creak. But it wasn't from me. It was from away. From down the hall.

Whit went rigid, his hand tensing on the knife. The creak creaked longer, the sound of a door. Opening.

"What," Whit started to whisper. He leaned to peek down the hallway. I snuck in behind him, hugging up against his back. We craned our necks into the path of the hall.

Libby, in faded green cotton underwear and a holey Nine Inch Nails shirt I'd lent her weeks ago, was shuffling into the hallway, out of the cool darkness. She looked wan, anemic, barely there, a photocopy of a ghost.

I saw her like that for a single frozen moment: It was my best T-shirt, on my best friend.

Whit dropped the knife and whisked down the hall and scooped her up into his arms and mouthed, *Go, go, go, go, go, go* at me as he speed-walked back across the living room and out the front door. He and Libby were in the front yard before I could even get my legs to move, but once they did, they ran. I slammed the door, leapt down the four steps onto the grass, and raced for the car.

We had Libby, *we had her.*

Outside it was hot and sunny and normal, and I kissed the dashboard of the Camry as Whit sped out of the canyons and down toward the highway.

*　　*　　*

Every few minutes I turned around and checked for vital signs in the backseat. Libby's pulse was a crawl. I could only feel it beat about three times a minute. If I hadn't already seen her physically moving in the hallway, I might've thought there was a chance she was actually dead. Our triumph wasn't pure. Things were too twisted, too dark. No call for confetti.

Whit tried to act confident. "She'll be okay," he said several times.

I nodded. I wanted to believe him.

"Where is it again?" he asked once we were on the 10 heading east.

"Joshua Tree. Lynn knows we're coming."

Earlier this morning, sometime between my second panic attack and third Diet Coke, I'd dug up the number for Stella Block's sister. Libby and I had visited her a couple of times together in junior high. She'd retreated to the desert about seven years ago to read chakras, live on sprouted food, and believe in the oneness of whatever. When I called, she acted like she remembered me, sort of. I told her Libby was in a bad way. That was all Aunt Lynn needed to hear.

I looked back at Libby again, dead asleep or just dead, her long legs folded up under her in an uncomfortable position. Whit caught a glimpse of her splayed out in his rearview mirror and patted me on the lap. He was, at that moment, the closest friend I had in the world.

"I brought one of Naomi's dresses," Whit said, pointing to the back. "It's under the seat in a bag."

I rested my head on his shoulder. "Thanks, Whit." I meant it so much.

"Sure."

"How did you know she'd be, like, half-naked?"

"I didn't. I thought she'd be covered in blood." He forced a small laugh, but it didn't fly. "Sorry."

I turned around and looked at Libby some more. The *Downward Spiral* shirt she had on was bunched up around her waist, exposing her underwear. Her skin looked waxy and sort of translucent. I could see the thin veins running up her thighs. Her bracelets were gone. I tried to remember the color of Libby's eyes. Brown or something.

"I'm not an expert on this stuff, you know," Whit said. "He and I don't really talk about this kind of thing."

"What do you guys talk about?"

"I don't know. How to deal with my parents." He half laughed. "School. Girls. Whatever."

"What does he know about girls?"

"Not much." Whit looked over at me and smiled. "Don't worry, I do most of the talking."

Obviously. I reached back into the CD case and grabbed the one with hearts and stickers and junk all over it. The cover read LOVE SONGS FOR WHITLEY, in handwriting sweeter than soda. I held up the plastic case as evidence and arched my eyebrows. "What do *you* know about girls?"

"A little."

I frowned.

"Too little."

"Yeah, right. You've got two high school chicks in your Camry right now, you must know something."

"Normally I'd say that doesn't count for much, but since you're both wearing only T-shirts and underwear, I'll take the points."

"Good call." I high-fived him.

Cool beans, Libby would've said.

I stuck my head out the window and let the highway wind blow my hair in a billion directions. Ugh, smog. I pulled my head back in and rolled up the window.

"So . . . how's Naomi?" I'd been wondering, why not ask?

Whit shrugged. "Naomi's . . . Naomi."

"Right . . ."

"I just mean she's the same as before."

"Before what? Before she met me?"

"I suppose there *are* only two ways to divide history: that which came before Quinn, and that which came after."

"Works for me," I said, mussing up Whit's hair till he

pushed my hand away. "But, like, what was her deal?" I bit at my thumbnail. "Before everything."

"Like another brother, kind of. Tough and smart. And she was sweet, too, in her own way."

I muttered, "That's news," but Whit ignored it, staring ahead into the highway.

"Losing James was worse on her than it was on me."

"You two are still close, though."

"I don't know. I don't really think she likes me that much anymore. And I know she doesn't like James." He gave a weak smile, pushed his glasses up the bridge of his nose. "Naomi used to always want things to be so perfect. Even when stuff was normal, I never thought of us as a perfect family or anything, but I think she did."

"Naomi's still perfect."

"She'd be stoked to hear you think so." He laughed a short *ha* sound, and after that there was nothing but the steady muted hum of transportation.

A few miles later I reinspected the mix CD. "Should I pop this dude in?" I shook the jewel case, made it do a little dance on the dash.

"What's playing now?" He pretended to strain his ears to hear through the silence in the car. "I love this song."

"Sorry"—I read the name on the spine with only the faintest, tiniest, barely noticeable hint of jealousy—"Courtney, but the Joni Mitchell concert is over. Time to go home." I shoved the CD in between my seat and the door. "Whoops."

"Don't be jealous," he said. "You can make me a mix too if you want." When he said it, he sounded like Milkshake Whit.

"Yay." I missed Milkshake Whit. It already seemed like forever ago.

We passed on through San Bernardino, heading deeper into the desert. It was already six thirty. The 10 East stretched out into the horizon. Traffic was brutal but it didn't matter; we had all the time in the universe. And more crucial: We had Libby.

"So what happened at Brown?"

"Do you like long stories as much as Courtney does?"

"I like them better."

Whit relaxed in his seat. "It's not that dramatic. I was a creative writing major. Mainly plays."

"Were you a good writer?"

"Doesn't matter."

"To the story, or in general?"

"Doesn't matter in general. If I'm a good writer, I'll just write. School's useless. I'm more interested in life."

"Ah, don't tell me." I held up my hand like a stop sign. "You've been to Europe."

"That was funny. You're pretty funny."

"I try."

"Well . . . I studied abroad one semester, but that's not what I'm saying."

"What are you saying?"

"The thing that no one ever tells you, the thing my parents never told me, is that you don't need to go to college. If I want to write, I need life experiences, not chemistry, not Rocks for Jocks. Not math I'm never going to use." He shook his head, convinced. "It's pointless. I realized that. Brown wasn't for me. So I bailed."

It sounded like a speech he'd given many times. Or like a speech he was preparing himself to give. I was buying it, but I was no Brown candidate.

"What are your plays about then?"

"I don't know." He laughed. "Divorce, class struggle, death and dying, the truth."

"The truth is depressing."

"Dude, Quinn, you have no idea."

The sun was starting to slant in the sky, the temperature dropping, the rocks and desert shrubs were turning that shadowy lavender mystical color. I loved L.A. highways. I loved Southern California. My lingering fear faded, giving way to a gentle sense of accomplishment. Maybe not a job well done, but at least a job done. We saved Libby; it really had happened. We'd be at Lynn's soon.

"Well, what about you?" Whit asked. "What do you want to do?"

"When, now? Or in . . . life?"

"Yeah."

I hadn't actually thought about it much since I was eight, so I gave him the old stock response: "Either be a bride or a mermaid."

"Shoot for the stars. How about a mer-bride?"

"Libby's going to be a hologram." I sighed, remembering her own eight-year-old life quest.

"Whoa, sick."

"I know."

"Oh, damn, I forgot the pizza! Our victory slice!"

I put my hand over my stomach. The idea of pizza, even the smell of it, was not cool beans.

"I'm not hungry." I leaned back and let dusk begin to settle down over our universe. "Like, at all."

"Whit, I'm starving." Twenty minutes later, waking up groggily from a car nap, deep in the empty desert, hunger pangs came on like a beast. A giant honey-mustard pretzel beast. "And I need a Big Gulp."

"Tall order."

"Rest stop," I said in a monotone. "Seven-Eleven," I said like a zombie.

"You were a lot less demanding when you were drooling."

"You wish. How's Libby?" I turned back to look at her. No significant change.

"She's a party animal. Apparently she danced her pants off."

Whit's charms were working. I felt okay. Libby was with us and we were miles away from evil guesthouses. The early evening air was cool. Big Gulps and things flavored cool ranch were in my immediate future.

Whit steered the Camry off the freeway and into a gas station. After he'd parked the car, we both turned around and stared at the body in the backseat. To a Video Journeys customer I'd describe this part of the movie as *Weekend at Bernie's* meets that passed-out chick in *License to Drive* meets, um, vampires.

"I guess I should put that dress on her."

"Yeah, probably."

Whit got out of the car, leaving Libby and me alone together for the first time since we'd kidnapped her. She hadn't said a word or made a single sound or even opened her eyes for hours. It was hard to remember she was alive.

I scooted back to the seat next to Libby, propping her into an upright position. She slumped forward limply. Predictable.

I grabbed the soft flower-print dress from under the seat, placed it at Libby's feet, pulled it up her long legs to her lap, and then worked my best gym-class locker-room magic. I got her arms through the T-shirt sleeves and into the dress straps without a topless moment. Then I slipped the NIN shirt off her head and, voilà, she was presentable. If you were nearsighted.

At least she was fully clothed. Minus shoes.

I was out of breath. I opened my door and walked around to her side.

"Come on, Libby. Time to get up." She stayed like a rock. "They have Cherry Coke Slurpees." I leaned there against the open car door, staring down at the sad mess in Naomi's sweet cotton dress.

"I bought one of every gross thing," Whit said from behind me. I felt his hand on my shoulder. It was warm and sticky on my skin. His other hand held three plastic bags full of crap and a drink caddy crowded with two massive sodas.

"Look at her, Whit."

"She'll be fine."

"No, I mean look at her. She's still so beautiful." She was. Stupid girl was gorgeous.

I tried to smooth down Libby's bed-head hair. I put some of my ChapStick on her lips and one of my chains around her neck. What else could I give her? My high-tops? My Big Gulp? Everything I had, which was seriously, literally, nothing?

"I'm going to cry, okay?" But tears were already

starting to drip-drop down my cheeks. Then I drip-dropped to the ground. Everything went blurry. I could dimly make out cars pulling in for gas, a family waiting in line for the bathroom, bugs swarming around a parking lot lamppost.

For the second time today Whit hugged me deeply, trying to crush the grief out of my bones with his tender strength.

"I know Libby's your best friend," he said.

I shook my head. "She's not really that good a friend actually, but whatever."

"Is that how you really feel?"

I shrugged.

"Well, I'm sorry, but I don't get that at all."

"Libby can be her worst around me. We love each other."

"That doesn't make any sense."

"Who says love has to be even? Who says Libby doesn't give me certain things I can't give her?"

"I don't know her."

"Yeah." I rolled my eyes. This conversation sucked.

"How can that kind of friendship make you happy?"

I told him, "It used to make me happy," but even while saying it, I didn't know if it ever did. I'd never thought about it in those terms. I loved Libby; therefore she made me happy. Right?

"Well, you saved her life. Doesn't matter what happens now. She owes you one permanently."

"*You* saved her life. I was over by the window sunbathing."

"Hey, you're right. This girl owes *me* everything. Guess she'll have to be my slave now." Whit brushed the hair out of my face and used his Celtics jersey to blot the leftover tears.

"She's pretty used to enslavement."

"Harsh, man," Whit said, grinning. "But nonfiction nonetheless."

He hugged me again, then released me again. He lifted me up and handed me one of the plastic bags of snacks. My empty stomach rumbled. A bag of jalapeño Corn Nuts had never seemed such a sweet and heroic gesture.

"So if Libby's my slave," Whit started as he straightened my tank top, "and she has to do whatever I say, then after I squash her dreams of becoming a hologram, what do you want from her? I'll make her give you anything."

What I wanted was for Libby to wake up tonight with complete amnesia of all things Stiles-related. But that didn't seem likely. So I compromised: "Uh, that's my Nine Inch Nails shirt, for the record."

"Done." Whit reached over Libby's body, grabbed the

T-shirt, and shoved it into my hand. "I knew this shirt belonged to more of a badass. Here. Consider this the first of many thank-you gifts from your best friend Libby."

I looked at the shirt, then at the sleeping beauty. Snacks, sodas, and so few miles to our destination: I had seriously so many gifts.

I tossed the shirt back in the car. "Whatever, looks better on her anyway."

Two minutes later we were back on the road, stuffing toxic waste in our mouths, finally, *finally* listening to *The Chronic*, talking trash, watching dust and dirt and nothing, shaking it all off. Then we started spotting the faint silhouettes of Joshua trees out in the desert. That meant Aunt Lynn's cosmic vibes weren't far away.

I knew some things never changed, but some things I wanted to. This would change Libby and me. Good.

Aunt Lynn was perched on a wooden porch swing when Whit pulled the Camry up into the dirt driveway. She got up and came out toward us, smiling, her arms outstretched, her blondish-gray hair piled into a loose bun on top of her head.

Although she was immediate family, Aunt Lynn was nothing at all like Stella or Libby, the Block glamour girls with their legs for days and their effortless city cool. Lynn had spent some time in that world, but then something else had called to her, something weirder and more spiritual. So she'd said her good-byes and come out to the desert to wear giant white linen dresses, no makeup, and long crystal necklaces. And here she was, beaming, barefoot, happy in her outsider life, hugging Whit and me like we were her own niece and nephew. A set of wind chimes clanged peacefully from the porch like a good omen. I exhaled.

We exchanged the shortest pleasantries:

Haven't seen you in so long. Look at you, you're a woman now. Whit, Lynn. Lynn, Whit. He rescued Libby from bloodsucking male models. His older brother is one too. That's the one I'm in love with.

All caught up.

I cringed when Lynn finally opened the Camry's back door and found Libby crumpled up and unconscious in what she probably could only assume was a postdrug stupor. But she didn't freak out. She just scooped Libby up, propped her against her shoulder, and began hobbling her niece toward the house. They were both barefoot, their bodies one mass under the porch light, angel and ghost.

We followed them into the house, and Lynn led Libby away down a hall while Whit and I seated ourselves on huge Japanese pillow cushions on the floor in the sparsely furnished living room. There wasn't a couch, just the cushions and a low, long cherrywood table.

Then Lynn came back and brought us a small ceramic pot of tea with two cups. She told us she was so happy that we'd all be here when Libby woke up.

But I did *not* want to be here for that. I pinched Whit on the arm. He caught my drift.

"You're staying for dinner, of course," Lynn said suddenly, as if psychically picking up my escape signal.

All we could do was consent and relax back on the cushions and sip our tea. Lynn smiled, said, "Wonderful," and disappeared down the hallway.

As soon as we heard the door close, Whit turned to me. "She's taking this well. We dropped off a very, very damaged package."

"Maybe she has faith. Third-eye stuff." I felt it: Libby was safe here.

But were *we*? Was *I*? Dusk was close, the undead—wherever they were—were stirring, and dinner was only a meal. We couldn't stay here forever.

"What do you think's going to happen when they find out she's gone?"

Whit looked at me and rubbed his eyes. "Nothing. She'll be gone; they won't know where. Or how."

"What if they guess?"

"They won't."

I felt my nerves crawl. "I don't know." I looked out the window into the dark.

"Quinn, they won't."

Then there was a light creak down the hall, then footsteps, then Lynn came into the room, and in her hand was the bony hand of an old best friend of mine. Libby's eyes were open—they *were* brown or something—and she was walking, one foot in front of the other, very slowly. Her free hand dragged itself absently along the wall.

"How is she scarier now than she was before?" Whit asked under his breath.

Somehow, with her eyes open, Libby's head looked more like a skull. And with her spine upright and limbs moving, her body looked more like a skeleton. Seriously freaky.

Lynn whispered something in Libby's ear and they separated, aunt to the kitchen, niece to the living room. She came in and collapsed in a heap on a cushion, her eyes huge and glassy. She showed no sign that she even realized there were other people in the room.

I leaned in to Whit. "We would know if she's one of them, right?"

Whit squinted behind his tortoiseshell glasses. "Not until she kills someone."

I glared at him. "Cool, Whit."

"Or until she eats some food maybe?"

Lynn started bringing out huge bowls of salad. Me and Whit picked at ours, said thanks, took some bites.

Libby just sat there, staring ahead in an unfocused way.

When Lynn got up to get dulse flakes and cayenne pepper from the kitchen, I turned and grabbed Libby's hand. She moved her head sluggishly in my direction. Weak, but a sign of life.

"Hi," I said.

She just stared at me, vacant. I noticed the whites of her eyes were very white. I didn't know why, but I'd thought they'd be bloodshot.

"Hi," I said again, softer.

Her mouth hung open for a second, and then she managed a hollow, distant "Hi." Her first word.

"How are you?"

Her mouth hung open again, but nothing came out. Her face twitched slightly. I scooted over toward Whit. No one was home at Libby's. Not right now.

Lynn returned and sat back down. "Eat, eat," she encouraged.

So we did—three-fourths of us at least—and tried to enjoy being together on a summer night, on soft cushions, with giant salads. I said a small, human prayer for such small, human things as these.

Aunt Lynn tried to persuade us to drive back in the morning, but we politely declined. I told her Bonnie and Elliott were expecting me. Whit said Naomi would be alone in the Sheets house. We made no return plans to pick up Libby. For now this was a one-way trip for her.

As we moved toward the door to leave, I stopped and stepped back close to Libby, hugging her till I'd lifted her up off the ground for a second. *One baby to another says I'm lucky to have met you*, I hummed.

But it probably wasn't true. That baby probably wasn't lucky to have met that other baby at all. I bet even Kurt had known that.

"See you senior year," I thought I said to her, but when I was back in the Camry, I couldn't remember. I may not have said anything to Libby when I hugged her good-bye.

The drive was fast. Short. Whatever. There was nobody on the highways, it was too late. Whit and I didn't say much, but it was okay. We rolled down the windows and let the warm night air do the talking.

When Whit finally parked in front of my mother's tea lights, it was almost midnight. My parents were totally asleep. I got out of the car and Whit followed up the stone steps, to the front door, inside, up to my bedroom. I was too sleepy to convince him I'd make it to bed on my own. And maybe I wouldn't have. Maybe I would've passed out right in the foyer, my cheek pressed against the cold tile floor until morning, when my parents found me. As if my sanity wasn't already in question. I waited to see if Whit was actually going to try and tuck me in or something.

"I thought it'd be messier in here," he said, and yawned.

"It was." I slunk down to the carpet.

"Going home." Whit kicked me lightly on the leg. "See you tomorrow."

"Tomorrow? Are you crazy? You want to hang out again?"

"I miss the boring times. Those were classic." He said it wistfully, as if we'd even shared more than twenty total hours between us. "Tower Records and In-N-Out?" he asked, already halfway out the door.

"Whit, soon I won't fit into any of my pants," I whined.

"Like you wear pants." He knocked once on the door frame, yawned out "Tomorrow," and was gone.

I felt like falling asleep in my Mickey shirt and dirty sneakers and leaving all the lights on too, but for some reason glanced at my answering machine first. The red message light was blinking. I didn't feel like dealing with it, but I pressed the play button anyway. It was Morgan's voice, so I started to zone it out, but then I realized what he was saying and my blood drained down to my toes.

"Dude, I don't know what you did, but the twins came into the video store tonight. Does the word 'warpath' mean anything to you? I told them you don't work here anymore. I told them you were on vacation. You better hide out, man. It was some evil stuff."

I was already flat on the floor, so I couldn't fall down farther. I was already on my knees, so I prayed to Santa Ana: Blow it all away.

14.

QUAKE

I couldn't sleep until I eventually fell asleep and, once asleep, my body knew to stay asleep. I woke up briefly every other hour, just for a few minutes, to the sound of the garbage truck's mechanical crunch or our housekeeper Carmen's *ranchera* radio/vacuum combo or, finally, my parents sighing loudly as they stood beside my bed, staring down at me.

"I thought we were done with this."

"Look at us, Quinn."

I slowly pulled the blanket down to my chin and looked at them. They were dressed up for some party. My mother was carrying the tiniest clutch bag, my father held his reading glasses. Upon seeing me, their faces fell. I wondered what I looked like. How bad I'd really gotten.

"What are you doing?"

That was me.

"What are we *all* doing?"

That was my dad.

They waited. I rubbed my eyes, blinked out the moisture of old tears.

"Going to the . . ." My mother started out the words slowly and moved her hand as if to say, *Join me in finishing this sentence, Quinn.*

"Going to the . . . Going to the . . ."

"Hollywood Bowl!" my father jumped in.

No, that didn't sound right.

I said, "I'm not going to the Hollywood Bowl," but not in a defiant way. I said it like clearly, obviously, I'm in no condition to be going to the Hollywood Bowl right now, because I'm terrified and because I can't be out at night.

"Don't pull this," my mother said.

"Quinn, we've had these tickets for two months. Can't you put your problems on hold for one night?" My dad reached under my arms and lifted me up out of bed like a sack of flour. "How about for Harry Connick Junior?"

"Harry Connick Junior," I repeated. No way I'd agreed to that.

"How about for your old mother and father who want to spend some time with you?"

I dropped my forehead into my palm. I let out the

smallest whimper. "We can rent a movie. We can play Trivial Pursuit." I grabbed my father by the elbow.

But they didn't see the pleading in my eyes. Or if they did see it, they didn't know what it meant.

"We're going," my mother said.

"Get dressed, kid," my father said.

I dropped to my knees. I wrapped one arm around each of their legs and held tightly. I pressed my head between them. I couldn't go. And they couldn't go and leave me here alone. I didn't know where the safe zone was. Was my house safe? Were my parents safe outside, after dark, as long as they weren't with me?

No one said anything.

Maybe my parents were having a silent conversation above me. Maybe through their eyes and facial expressions they were discussing what to do with their crazy daughter. Maybe something like that was happening, but it was quiet in the room.

Then I heard, "Fine," and realized that I'd ruined my mother's night. Week. Summer?

"They're season passes," my dad said, then patted my head. "The Bowl's always going to be there."

I let out a small gasp and squeezed their legs together. "I'll get dressed, I'll get dressed and come down for dinner," I said, so happy to be staying in that the words gushed out of my mouth like a shook-up can of Coke.

As my parents wriggled free from my grip, I noticed the sun out my window dipping just below the roof. I reached out for them again, but they'd left the room. In the hallway someone mentioned something about Thai takeout and Blockbuster.

Hiding from vampires was a monotonous scene. At night. During the day my life was packed, thanks to Whit: at the MOCA downtown, the Armand Hammer, chili-cheese dogs at Oki Dog, free samples at the Fairfax Farmers Market, pretending to shoplift at the Virgin Megastore followed by a bad indie at the Sunset 5 and crappy Chinese chicken salads at Wolfgang Puck's, trendy-band-of-the-month at the Palladium, people-watching and trash-talking at the Galleria, friendship bracelets and potato tacos on Olvera Street, car wash-ing, lip-synching, pool dunking, anything, everything random.

Even though I'd never told him about Morgan's answering machine message—the less he knew, the safer he was—Whit sensed my generally freaked-out vibe and seemed anxious to chill it out. He called all the time just to talk or listen to me talk, and his list for possible hang-out plans was endless. Maybe he thought that if I was too physically and emotionally wiped out from nonstop daytime activities, I'd be too exhausted to panic about potential Libby revenge attempts and weird sounds outside my window at night.

I tried to play down my paranoia by keeping up my usual act: sarcasm, post-irony, feigned disinterest, parade-raining-on humor. But Whit knew me too well now to fall for all that. He had this rad ability to deflect everything tense and heavy and ominous about our situation and turn it into something lighter, more manageable. He did believe in supernatural stuff—both good and bad—because it was a reality in his life, but he also knew when to be human and let things be quiet. And when it got too quiet, he let me pretend like that was fine. Sometimes when we were together he'd touch me in some way, on the soft part of my forearm, or a pat on the head, or a side hug, or a high five where he held my hand and didn't let go. But mostly he just tried to make me laugh and stay okay and helped keep my blood inside my body where it belonged.

Everything was super present tense with Whit, too. He didn't get into prologues or origins or deep history. I assumed when he felt like opening up about what life was like as a Sheets boy in the midst of two brilliant explorers, one sexy dead dude, and an award-winning priss, he'd bring it up himself. I also assumed if he wanted to know about my far less exciting, far more normal—but getting less normal by the day—seventeen years of existence, then he'd ask. Not so much.

This would've bothered me before. But before, everything bothered me, so whatever.

We avoided upsetting conversation topics like Libby's health, the whereabouts of the twins, and what would happen when the Sheetses came home or the fall semester began or the Laurel Canyon branch of Hellmouth reopened. We definitely never brought up James. We never ever mentioned Naomi. But I saw her once.

It was three days after Joshua Tree. We were on our way to Think Ink in the Valley, where Whit was going to re-ponder the possibility of finally getting his first tattoo. We had just left the Sheetses' when he realized he'd left his driver's license on his desk, so I waited in the Camry while he ran inside to grab it.

Whit had been inside for only a couple of seconds when I saw her. She was just finishing a jog. Her whole body moved like in slow-mo, each limb pumping in hyper-focus, covered in sweat. Then her eyes locked on mine, pure poison, never blinking. I couldn't slip any lower in my seat without literally crouching down into the foot space, and I felt like that's exactly what she was hoping I'd do—cower, flee, go underground. I would've if I could've.

Instead I leaned an arm on the window, forced a pathetic smile, and threw up a peace sign. Mine probably looked guiltier than Nixon's.

When Whit passed her coming back to the car, they exchanged a few words. *Don't murder her*, I imagined Whit saying. Then her saying, *But I want to.*

Minutes later we were out of the canyons and onto the 101, cruising north.

"God she hates me," I said.

"No. She's just happy you haven't met Henry yet."

"Who's Henry?"

"Our other brother."

"Oh, you've got to be kidding me!"

He took his eyes off the road and put them on me. "Yes, Quinn. I am kidding you."

I was a sucker.

And those were our days. Not un-fun, kind of cool, and filled with a decent amount of wacky field trips and comic banter. I stuck to a semi-tight schedule, though. I wasn't exactly Cinderella, but when the clock read six, sometimes seven—but almost never later—the curtain closed, Whit dropped me off, and my nights began. And those were much less awesome.

I didn't totally sink into my old black hole—and for that the entire Lacey family was grateful—but there was a lot of numb TV-watching and nervous hair braiding going on. Saltine-and-soda dinners were definitely back on the menu. My parents didn't really seem to notice. Maybe because it seemed so realistic.

But most nights when dusk settled and I sat in my room, nothing could block out the thoughts that haunted me: Libby lost in the desert, bloodless and brainwashed; the twins prowling the hills for payback; James, far away and getting farther every day. My parents bustled around downstairs, listening to records with the windows open while making dinner, enjoying the summer nights. Whit called and told me what good shows were on TV, and we'd talk and kill time.

And every night I'd lie there in bed and look out at the hills behind our house, listening. I knew there'd be consequences, there had to be. Actions meant reactions. Sunrises meant sunsets. Every new day was just another new chance for Stiles to catch me at my weakest moment. My fear was too permanent, lasting longer than eyeliner, something I wore every day and didn't wash off.

Still no sign of him. Or *him*, either.

I'm afraid I'll forget you, James. I'm afraid I'll forget who I was with you.

It had been a week and a half since Whit found me in the Lexus and a week and a half minus one day since we'd rescued Libby. How we'd jammed a summer's worth of trivial activities and casual bonding into such a short span of time was a mystery and a miracle. One that Whit and I decided to finally celebrate with a victory slice of pizza.

So we went to a Round Table Pizza in the Valley on a sunny afternoon and claimed a booth in the back. We ate too much and told dumb stories and asked for refills on our unlimited fountain drinks. We got grossly stuffed and didn't care.

"Ugh, pizza," I moaned after my fourth slice. "No more."

"They'll have to roll us out of here," Whit groaned, holding his stomach.

"James is going to dump me when he sees how fat I've gotten."

"Weren't you always fat?"

I stuck out my tongue at him. "Weren't you saying James might be coming home soon?"

"No, I never said that." He nibbled at a piece of half-eaten crust.

"Yeah, you did. You said he was probably coming back."

Whit stopped chewing and got sort of serious. "Look, you know when Robert Plant says, 'Baby, baby, I don't want to leave you, I ain't jokin', woman, I got to ramble'?"

"What?" I blinked over and over.

"'Babe I'm Gonna Leave You.'"

"What?" Blinking. Blinking.

"Led Zeppelin."

"Are you, like, a hundred?"

"Yes," he said sarcastically. Then he folded his arms. "No, I'm not a hundred, I'm nineteen, and in six months I'll be twenty. Then I'll be twenty-one, then twenty-two, and on and on until I'm old and gray and cussing at buildings and small children. Then I'll die, hopefully in my sleep, and stay dead forever."

Damn.

"Never mind." He stared off at the arcade games.

"Whatever, Whit."

"Yeah."

Major tension. But the tension didn't last long, because suddenly some stoner dude in a ragged Depeche Mode shirt was standing next to our booth, reeking, giddy, hovering over us.

"Sh-sh-sh-Sheets, Sheets," he said like he was scratching a turntable.

Whit reacted slowly. "Hey, Jody. It's been a long time, man."

"It's been *forever*, man!" Change that: super stoner. "How've you been? Who's your lady?"

"Quinn, this is Jody Bennett. He's—" Whit paused, thinking of a word, but gave up.

"Hey." I waved.

"Hey to you." He turned to Whit and said, pointing to me, "Nice, man."

"So what's up?" Whit looked tired of this already.

"Here's the deal: You guys *have* to come to this thing I'm having."

"A thing? Like a party?" I asked with a bit more disgust than was polite.

"Yeah! You like to party?"

I sank lower into the booth.

"She loves it," Whit interrupted. He raised his eyebrows, daring me.

"Really?" Jody moved his red, weeded eyes from Whit to me to Whit and back to me. "*Killer.* It's tonight at my house. You're gonna come, right?"

"Totally, Jody." Whit gave him a thumbs-up.

"Awesome. Don't bogart the babe, man," he said, looking at Whit but pointing to me again. "Do not be a Bogart."

"No way, man."

Jody held up both of his hands for Whit and me to high-five. When we both sort of lazily complied, Jody clasped our hands in his and then brought them together to form one giant hand-holding clump. Then he dropped the clump, put a hand on each of our shoulders, shook us lightly, bowed his head, lifted his head, said the word "tonight" like it had any other meaning than just a portion of the day, and walked away.

"Best friend from middle school?" I asked, watching him leave.

"Something like that."

"Jody sucks."

"Maybe," Whit said, pretending to consider the matter. "But he's such a lover of fine things. Like Humphrey Bogart. And parties."

"Yeah."

"So you'll come?"

"You're kidding."

I hadn't been to a nighttime social gathering since . . . since Joshua Tree. That just wasn't something I did anymore.

"Aren't you getting cabin fever?"

"Cabin fever, cabin flu, cabin measles, cabin mania . . ."

"So come." Whit reached over and touched my hand. "Please? Jody thinks you're"—he made quotation marks—"*nice*."

"Jody sucks."

But it wasn't a no.

Whit dropped me off at six-twenty, per usual, but promised to be back by ten to drive us to the party. That gave me more than ample time to scheme a story for my parents, float in the pool, put on more eyeliner, drink a Diet Coke or two, listen to a Fugazi tape, break into a good cry, fear for my life, then pull the whole mess together with a pair of party pants. Seriously. I decided I was going to rock these super-fitted black matador pants with little red pom-pom balls going up the sides that Stella scored from some nineties Madonna video shoot she had styled. She ended up giving them to me because they were too small for her and too short for Libby's legs, but I fit into them fine. Just like Madonna. Madonna danced in my pants.

It was a rare feeling, but tonight I had to admit it: I looked kind of pretty. Despite my annoyance at having to attend a real party, my anxiety at having to seem charming to some of Whit's older friends, and my faint terror at being out past midnight at some stoner's house in Bell Canyon where anyone could stalk up the hills and nab me and suck my blood—despite all that—I thought I looked okay. My eyes were bright and awake, my lips felt full and shiny under a layer of cherry ChapStick, my skin was slightly tan, my bruises and scrapes were gone, and my long brown hair had that cool, chlorinated, wavy thing going on. I didn't know when—if ever—I'd get back that way James made me feel, but I'd take just feeling pretty, at least for tonight.

I scavenged my room for some accessories to complete tonight's look. Under some magazines I dug up my single pair of eighties thrift-store pumps, which I'd totally forgotten even existed. Then I tucked a silky white camisole into my party pants—because Courtney Love would have done that—and put on literally every piece of jewelry I owned.

I was just about ready when I heard the doorbell ring

downstairs, then the door open, then my father's voice. Oh God, Elliott and Whit. I snatched the ChapStick off my dresser and downed the rest of my soda.

"Quinny," my dad shouted, "Morgan's here to pick you up."

I dashed down the stairs without remembering I had high heels on and so stumbled the last few steps before wiping out into Whit's arms.

"Careful," he said, propping me up.

He was wearing a white V-neck and a pair of tight ripped-up Levi's with his usual high-tops and that stupid necklace with the crucifix pendant. Whit was dressed just like him and it sucked.

"Thanks, Dad, leaving now." I waved good-bye and pushed Whit out the door, shutting it behind us.

"Your dad thinks I'm Morgan," he said.

"It's possible my dad thinks *I'm* Morgan."

"Hey." Whit stopped me as I was opening the car door. "You look good."

I didn't know what to say, so I said, "Oh, cool."

Up Bell Canyon, still inside the car, parked a couple of houses down, waiting a full ten minutes before we made our entrance, Whit rested his chin on the top of the steering wheel and stared out at the night.

"I want to talk about earlier."

"No, you don't," I said. I didn't.

"What I meant about Led Zeppelin," he started, as I rolled my eyes dramatically, "is that Plant really loves this chick, like there's no question about that, but he's still got to leave her, you know?"

"Is he bummed about it?"

"Dude, he's, like . . . so, so, so bummed." Whit turned to look at me. "He's in major pain."

"I'm in pain." It was the first time I'd said it out loud.

"You haven't seemed so bad."

"I've gotten better, I guess."

"That's good." He touched my shoulder.

I shook his hand off and said, "Why are you wearing that?" I looked at the shirt, the necklace, the messy hair. I was getting déjà vu bad.

"Why am I wearing what?" He looked confused.

"I don't know."

"What are you talking about?"

"Forget it." I opened the door.

Whit got out too and locked the car, and then we headed toward Jody's house.

"Hey, don't ditch me in there," I said.

He threw an arm around my shoulder and kissed me on the top of the head. "Where'm I gonna go?"

No one answered the door when we knocked, but it was unlocked and we could hear music so we just went in, through a foyer into a wide living room area that sprawled onto a sweeping back balcony with a stupidly stunning cityscape view. We helped ourselves to glasses of what I guessed from the label was fairly expensive red wine and then wandered out to the deck, which was draped with several canopies of tiny multicolored lights and paper lanterns. There was a nice desert breeze drifting up the canyons, and it struck me then with weird force: Night was beautiful. I'd missed it during my past two weeks of self-enforced house arrest.

I leaned against the wooden railing and closed my eyes, letting the night air float across my face. Then I heard several voices behind me greeting Whit. Everyone said hi, hello, and soon he was deep into a story about a recent run-in with an old mutual friend.

Five people stood in a semicircle around him, rapt, eyes sparkling, mouths on the verge of laughter, waiting for the next punch line, eating up his impression of Howie or Huey or whatever this random guy's name was. I slipped in beside him while he talked, sipping my wine. I felt somehow in awe. Whit was my best friend now, so I obviously knew he was clever and cool and cute and charming but tonight, under the glow of the lanterns, on my first night back in the real world, his presence was like a revelation. He was the center and, when he reached his hand up and rubbed the soft part of my back, so, so centering.

A few dudes came up and offered me a drink and tried to flirt, but not a ton. And that was fine. I was happy just to stand near the glow of Whit's magic, silently sip wine, stare away into the shadowy canyons, and sway slowly back and forth to some Nina Simone record Jody had thrown on. My dad loved Nina Simone, so I felt doubly protected as her heavy, honeyed voice washed over me. Or maybe it was the dry L.A. wind drifting through my hair. Or maybe it was my third glass of Shiraz.

I thought I was doing a good job of hiding my wooziness until one of the dudes who'd been smoking with Jody all night tapped me on the shoulder and asked if I was feeling all right. His shirt said LOSER across the chest in giant black letters, making it hard to concentrate.

I tried to nod like a sober person. "I'm . . . awesome."

He introduced himself as something that I knew wasn't Owen but sounded like Owen, so I said, "Cool to meet you, Owen," and held out my hand for a shake. But because he was holding a joint in his right hand I awkwardly grabbed for his left one. And then, because I was so out of it, I didn't let go.

"Oh, feels nice. Your hand is so cold," I said, still shaking.

"Are you cool?"

"I don't think I understand the question."

"How old are you?" He finally pulled his hand free from mine.

"I just need some fresh air, you know?" I stared at his chest. LOSER, LOSER, LOSER.

"We're outside, man." Owen took a deep hit and blew the smoke behind him, gesturing with his face, the joint, the smoke, his whole body, that we *were* in fact outside. "I should get Whit before you go bananas or something." He nodded above my head and immediately Whit was there, pressurizing the cabin, checking for vitals.

"I'm okay, I'm okay," I stuttered.

"I see you've met Joey," Whit said, indicating Owen.

"Joey, yeah." I tried to shake his hand again, but both of them were full this time so I sloppily shook his elbow. "Don't drive home," I said as steadily as possible.

"*You* don't drive home." He laughed, already walking away.

Then it was just me and Whit. Like always.

"You don't have to get drunk." He leaned in, serious. "No one's going to hurt you here."

Before I realized I was saying it—before I even knew I was really feeling it—I said, "I'm scared." Then I couldn't hold it in. "They're looking for me. They want to kill me."

"They're not looking for you, Quinn. They have no idea about anything."

"*You* have no idea." I tried not to cry. The music was louder now. There was a small blurry dance floor in the living room. The lanterns gave everyone's skin an eerie glow.

"Calm down, okay?" He held me at the elbows. "They don't know it was you."

I shook my head. "Yes, they do."

"How do they know that?"

"I can't tell you."

Whit tensed up. "What are you talking about, Quinn?" His fingers squeezed harder.

"They know where I live. . . ." My words drowned in drunken slurs.

"They're not going to—" he started to say, but a voice somewhere called out Whit's name. He held his hand up, yelled, "One second, man," and leaned in even closer.

"Do you want me to take you home?"

"No." I wanted to go to his place. His room.

"Quinn. You're safe here. I promise."

I rubbed my eyes.

"Nothing's going to happen. Please try to have a little fun."

"I am having a little fun."

"Well, you don't exactly look like it."

"Sorry."

"It's okay. Come on, I'll introduce you to some people."

"I have to go to the bathroom first."

He shot me a distrusting look.

"I do."

"Fine. But come right back, okay?"

"Okay."

He gave my elbows a final squeeze and headed over to a group of people down at the end of the deck. I wiped my eyes again and then slid open the sliding doors, went through the living room, past the five people on the couch watching a movie, past the trio snacking from a bowl of popcorn on the kitchen island, past the couple Frenching up against a collection of Jody's baby pictures hanging in the hallway, and into an enormous Italian marble bathroom. I stood staring at the two-person Jacuzzi for about five minutes before I climbed in. I collapsed in the empty tub and tried to keep my eyes closed, but too many bad things were swirling beneath my lids, so I stood up and looked at myself in the mirror. My eyeliner was smudged, but that was nothing new.

On the wall next to me, right above a shelf loaded with shampoos and conditioners, was a small cream-colored telephone. I hit my head with the palm of my hand. There wasn't a doubt in my fuzzy, sloshed mind that I was going to use that phone—and for evil, not good. This was really happening. I was really dialing his number.

It rang twice.

"Hello?"

"Hey."

"I thought you were dead or something."

"I am. Sort of."

"So you got my message. Thanks for calling me back."

"I am calling you back."

"Are you drunk?"

Then someone knocked on the bathroom door.

I cupped my hand over the receiver. "Hold on!"

"Who? Me, or . . . ?"

"Not you."

"Where are you?"

"Uhh . . ." I looked around, unsure of the right answer. Bell Canyon. Jody Bennett's. A Jacuzzi. None of it really made sense.

"Never mind."

"Yeah, it's weird."

The person at the door banged some more.

"So you're okay then."

"Yeah."

"Then I'm gonna go."

"Right."

"Say good-bye, Quinn."

"Thanks for lying to the Spaders for me, Morgan."

"Good-bye, Quinn."

He hung up. I listened to the dial tone and the banging on the door for a few seconds before climbing out of the tub.

"Okay, okay," I said while unlatching the lock and opening the door. Then my heart lurched: A pale guy in a polo shirt with black hair was standing there glaring at me, arms crossed.

"What the hell?" he asked, annoyed.

I shook the flashback out of my head and pushed past him.

Either I'd somehow gotten way drunker sitting in the tub or there were three times as many bodies as before. I scanned around trying to spy Whit or Jody or even Owen, but the lighting was too dim, everyone's faces looked the same, everyone's clothes were the same dark blur. Anyone could've been Cooper. I thought I saw Dewey for a second over by the kitchen, but when he turned it was someone much older. My heart beat erratically. I bit my lip. Every exhalation was a tiny moan.

I weaved through the crowd to the deck's edge and leaned against the railing. The hills were blacker than before, no stars and no moon.

Then the ground began to shake. I felt the deck rocking beneath me. Abandoned wineglasses and beer bottles on the railing started to shift, clinking against one another. The overhead lights swayed. The needle on the record player skipped and scratched and then went silent. Everything was vibrating to a low rumble. Everybody grabbed something for support: furniture, a wall, each other. My insides rattled, the wine sloshing against a stomach full of anchovies and mozzarella. I gasped for breath. The planet was tossing us around, trying to swallow us whole. I crouched down into a ball, waiting for glass to shatter, the roof to cave in, the balcony to crash down into the canyon.

And then it was over. Everyone froze for a second, braced for a second quake or a follow-up tremor. But nothing came.

Then the entire party erupted in cheers and shouts and cuss words and drunken *whooo*'s. I felt hands on my back; Whit had found me.

"There you are!" he said. "Can you believe that?"

Weakly I said, "Yeah, I can believe it."

"Are you okay?"

"I don't know."

People everywhere were still screaming, celebrating.

"Hey, why don't we go, okay? Meet me out by the car. I'll be there in one minute." Then he was gone again.

"Did you feel that, man?" Joey/Owen yelled above the noise.

"Totally." I staggered, still buzzed, fried.

"How L.A., right?"

I nodded. Then someone put on a new record, "Bela Lugosi's Dead." Definitely my exit song. I cut through the chaos all the way to the Camry.

Whit was sitting on the hood of his car when I got there. He looked tan, happy, untroubled. He said, "Hey, you."

"Hey."

"How insane was that?"

"Crazy."

He looked up at the stars. "Kind of a special night." He paused. "It was good I dragged you along."

"You always drag me along." I smiled at him.

I thought about the past ten days, the time it'd taken me to go from meeting Whit to knowing him to trusting him to even loving him. Already he'd been in my life longer than James had. And every extra day that James was gone was another day that Whit was around, driving me all over the city, stuffing my face with goofy foods, drying my tears, making me live, helping me forget. Things were still far from okay, but maybe we were getting closer. I drank in Whit's face, dark and quiet in the nighttime, already so precious to me. Already transformed from the strange imitation I used to see into an original.

He slid off the hood and stood next to me. "I feel like the earthquake was a sign or something, don't you?" He was excited.

"Maybe. I hope so." I looked up at the sky, at the no moon and no stars. I felt like I was back on earth, like I'd been away for a while. And Whit was the one who'd brought me back.

But now Whit was distracted, his eyes on Jody's front door, waiting for something. Then the door opened and a prim redhead in a tiny turquoise dress skipped out toward us, a small leather bag in one hand and some heels in the other. She was swinging a perfect French braid from shoulder to shoulder. When she got close, Whit hugged her around the waist. What. Was. Happening.

"Quinn, this is Tori," he said.

"Tori?"

"Sorry to make you wait, had to find my purse," she sang to Whit, then turned to me. "Whoa, crazy pants."

"Madonna wore them in a video," Whit said.

"Crazy." She made a crazy face.

"No." I glared at Whit, then stared at Tori. "She never actually wore them. She only tried them on."

They both looked confused.

"Different pants are in the video," I explained.

Whit shrugged. "Okay, whatever."

"Yeah."

"My ladies ready?" Whit asked. It was, like, the grossest thing ever.

"I can ride in the backseat," Tori said, opening the door behind Whit's.

"Well, we're actually dropping Quinn off first, so . . ."

My head was trembling. Another earthquake? Another seismic convulsion?

I got in the back. I tried to stare away out the window during the ride home, but I kept catching glimpses of Tori rubbing Whit's thigh across the armrest. In my head I told myself it didn't matter, me and Whit were closer than this, I obviously meant more to him than some airhead in a miniskirt. We had something special, we were more . . . evolved. It didn't help.

Whit pulled into my driveway and left the car running while he opened my door to help me out.

As I was getting out of the car, Tori turned her cute little head around. "Bye-eee. That's so cool about Madonna."

"Yeah, bye."

I walked up the stairs, realizing I was still drunk, past the tea lights, to my front door. Whit followed. At the door he reached out to fix my hair, moving some strands behind my ears.

I threw his hand off me. "I got it."

"I just want to leave you as pretty as I took you."

"Can you not say that, please?" My hands were balled into fists at my sides.

"What's wrong?"

"Have fun with Tori." I said her name in the bitchiest way possible.

"Cool, you're being adorable right now."

"So you're going back to your house or what?" I

didn't even try to hide my pissiness.

"What do you care?"

"I don't."

"You're being lame."

"Not really."

Then Whit said, "I'm not him." He was staring me down. "You love him so much, just wait for him then. Jesus Christ, Quinn."

I touched his cheek, palmed the side of his face. *No, you aren't him. You're someone totally different. You're alive.*

"Sleep it off, okay? Call you tomorrow." Then Whit was gone, driving somewhere with Tori to do something I had no right to know about.

I stalked through the house stripping, throwing clothes wherever—my high heels and pants on the foyer floor, my purse and keys on a stool in the kitchen, my blouse slung over the back of the couch. The house was silent and dark. Through the sliding glass door, the backyard looked silent and dark too. The pool was glowing and blue.

I climbed down the ladder into the deep end and let my body sink to the bottom, let the night sink away too. I slouched on the floor of the pool, my back against the wall under the diving board, and stared up through the water at the sky. Earlier tonight at the party I hadn't been able to see any stars, but now there they were, a few scattered points of light, shining faintly. Then less faintly, as one of the sparkling shapes grew brighter and closer until suddenly it landed softly on my thigh. Not a falling star; a single silver bracelet.

I knew that bracelet.

I gasped and accidentally breathed in and started to choke, racing for the surface, swimming through a half dozen other silver bracelets already drifting down through the water. My head broke the surface and I spun around, scanning the backyard. Then I saw them: along one edge of the pool, fanned out like a display, twenty or more of Libby's bracelets.

The trees swayed in the breeze, but otherwise there wasn't a sound. The diving board bounced gently, but nothing else moved. He was playing with me. I hurried up the pool steps and ran into the house, double-locking the door behind me. I stood there dripping wet, shivering in the air conditioning, for a few minutes before I finally forced myself to dry off and go upstairs.

It was two thirty in the morning when I stumbled into my bedroom. I ditched my wet underwear and reached for a T-shirt and slipped it on, not realizing at first that it was soft and blue and smelled like a room with no windows. In the darkness I watched the shadows play across my ceiling, feeling the aftershocks, trying to calm down.

Then the shadows subtly changed shape. Something blocked them, eclipsing the straight slits of the blinds with the outline of a human figure. I jumped up. My nerves burned and my heart pounded.

Stiles. He hadn't left.

I leapt out of bed and backed up against the wall, away from my window. The shape was closer to the glass now, more familiar, but still in shadow.

It was Whit, on my roof, outside my bedroom, looking in at me. His hand was pressed against the glass.

Something made me step forward. Something made me hold my breath, or maybe not hold my breath, but forget to breathe altogether. I moved closer to the window. Looked at the eyes.

No. Not Whit.

I cried out, felt my heart lose control. Was it? It was.

James. My James.

15.

AFTERSHOCK

I couldn't get the window open. Then I panicked that if I couldn't get it open, he might just leave; if I couldn't get the window open, maybe he wasn't there at all.

But he was. James tapped on the glass and pointed to the middle of my room, motioning for me to step back. I thought he might break the window, but he just lifted the glass off its frame and stepped inside and leaned the pane of glass against the wall. He studied me in his old blue T-shirt.

I flipped out.

I wanted to throw myself at him but threw myself into the carpet at his feet instead. I lifted my face but didn't look at his face, didn't make it past the knees of his jeans, his holy holey Levi's. They were the same, no dirtier, no more frayed, and it was crushing to think that time hadn't passed for him the same way it'd passed for me. I moved enough to reach the hem of his shirt and fingered the fabric. Impossibly, this had gotten softer. And then my body loosened, I got softer too, and my legs wouldn't stand.

"Hey." His voice.

"I can't get up."

"It's cool," James said, and kneeled down next to me. He hugged me and I leaned in, burying my head into the fold of his neck, my lips against the side of his throat. There was that inner stillness, that no pulse, and it scared me more than it used to, but it also comforted me more than I was expecting. This was the sound I'd been waiting to hear: the sound of no sound, of no heart.

Then James looked at me, and even though I wanted to be held, I wanted to be looked at too. I went from drunk to drunker as we drank each other in. The room swam, the walls around him were woozy, but James was just like he was that first night. It was as if he'd stepped out of my memory and into my bedroom. Out of a memory I'd thought I'd lost.

But I knew I wasn't like his memory of me. I was older, weirder, darker, crazier. I felt like I'd come apart and someone had only just begun to stitch me back together. I was half-alive, half in pieces. I'd become a strange creature myself.

"I thought you were Whit," I said, already disappointed

at my first words. "I thought he was you."

"Why would Whit be here?"

"I don't know." It wasn't what I wanted to be saying. "He just dropped me off."

"So you were out with Whit tonight."

"James," I said.

He leaned back against the dresser and eyed my naked legs. Then he looked at his soft blue T-shirt on me. I knew that look, but I'd only seen it once.

"You have to take your shirt off," James said.

"What?"

"Take off your shirt."

Then he wasn't leaning against my dresser, he was crawling toward me. And I wasn't taking off the shirt, he was taking it off for me.

"James." It felt amazing just to say his name, but I wanted to say something unforgettable. Something about love and the oneness of us, something he'd be happy he returned for. But all I could say was, "I missed you."

Now he was over me, touching the outside of my underwear where the elastic met my hip. I arched my back against the carpet, closed my eyes. His knees knocked mine and I cringed and made a small, pained sound.

"Are you okay?" he said, moving his fingers from the elastic band to the bruises on my knees.

"I'm okay."

"Does it hurt?"

"Relatively."

Then he forgot about my wounds and pinned me to the carpet, roughly.

"I need you," James said, smelling my hair, my breath.

"Me too."

"Right now." He made his way down my body, his tongue on my hipbone, his hands pulling at the only piece left of my clothing.

"Yes."

"I'm back." He smelled my thighs, kissed them, licked the inside of them.

"You're back."

It hurt less and more this time, but James was better because he didn't have to look away, he didn't have to hide his teeth from me. We each bit down on our lips. As always, our union, pleasure and pain.

Exhausted, sobering up from the wine, still trembling from his touch, naked, lightheaded, about to laugh, about to fall asleep, touching the tips of my fingers with the tips of my other fingers, I noticed James smelling me again. But not in the sexy way from before.

"Yeah, I need a shower." I didn't remember having taken one since he left. I usually considered a dip in the pool a sufficient washing.

"You smell like me," James said, his head in my hair.

"Then I don't ever want to shower again." I looked up at the Hole poster on my ceiling. "Unless . . . do you shower?"

"Sometimes." He laughed and touched his greasy hair. "Come with me," he said, getting up off the floor.

He helped me stand and led me to the bathroom. In the darkness James turned the faucet on. I stepped over the edge of the bathtub and lay down as he filled warm water up around me. When it came to just below my shoulders, he turned it off.

I dunked my head down, slid up, knotted my hair into a wet bun. James sat on the bathroom floor, arms folded on the side of the tub, his head resting on his arms, his eyes watching me.

"So." I blew bubbles on the top of the bathwater.

"So, I'll tell you."

"Okay, tell me."

"Let me ask you first . . . you've been hanging out with Whit this whole time?"

I blew more bubbles. "Kind of."

"So he's been taking care of you."

"It's been bad. The worst."

He picked up a bar of soap and rubbed it across my neck, my shoulders, down my arms, across my chest. "I told you I was coming back."

"I didn't know."

"It's been, like, two weeks."

"It's been, like, forever," I said quietly, and took the soap out of his hands.

"I know forever."

I nodded apologetically but whatever, two weeks for me *was* an eternity. A lot changes, and a lot had changed, and I wanted to tell him that.

But he said, "What kind of stuff have you and Whit been doing?"

"What do you mean? Who cares?"

What hadn't we been doing? Kissing. Talking about you.

"Maybe I care, dude."

"Lots of random daytime stuff."

"Daytime stuff. Doesn't ring a bell."

"Aw, you're making a joke."

"Am I such a bummer?" He lathered shampoo into my hair.

"Not even, like, a little bit."

"Whit's funny."

I dunked my head. Whit was totally funny. He could make a lonely, pissy, bratty burr laugh. He could make a dead girl crack up.

"Yeah."

Even though James was back, Whit wasn't gone.

I said, "We're close. I think."

"Close is cool," James said.

In a rush I said, "We're not that close," but it sounded forced. "I mean, I'm not in love with him." I didn't know why I said it. But there was the truth—I felt love for Whit—and there was the deeper truth. Whatever that meant.

"Well maybe *I'm* in love with *you*," he said.

"You just love my bloody nose." I splashed the water across from me. "Get in here."

James, still in his boxers, climbed in the tub.

I flicked some water at him. "Talk, you."

"You haven't told me anything you've been doing."

Blah.

"You haven't even mentioned Libby."

Double blah.

"She's whatever." I looked down in the water at my pruned fingertips.

"Fine. I went to Cambridge. I tried to convince some friends to come back with me."

"And?"

"And they weren't in the mood for a fight."

"I thought they loved to fight."

"These are good dudes."

"But good dudes fight bad dudes," I said, certain of it.

He shook his head. "Why would they kill the twins for doing exactly what they exist to do?"

"I guess."

"I went for you."

"Don't say that, I didn't want you to go."

"I know. But I had to try."

I squinted at him. "Did you try hard enough? I mean did you tell them how Stiles and Sanders are evil and that they deserve to die or whatever you call it?" I tried to keep my voice even, but I could feel myself getting frantic.

"So they deserve to die but I deserve . . . you? How does that work?"

"Now you're on their side?"

"Quinn. I'm kind of permanently on their side. If there are sides."

"No, you're on my side."

He rubbed his temples, looked frustrated with me.

"Because you hate them, James."

I pulled his hands away from his face.

"Because you love me."

I touched his forehead to mine.

"And you'd never hurt Libby."

He closed his eyes and said, "I've hurt tons of Libbys," like I didn't get it.

But I didn't want to get it. His fate was mine now. "Don't say that."

"Everyone's someone's Libby," he said.

"I know that," I shouted, climbing out of the bathtub, splashing water everywhere. Then I slipped on a puddle and banged my knee right on the most banged-up part of my knee and shouted again. James started to move toward me, but I held up my hand. "So I'm supposed to wish you didn't exist. So I'm not supposed to love you. Great, cool, I'll do that."

He said, "Quinn," but before he could say anything else I grabbed a towel and walked out of the bathroom.

In the bedroom he found me already under the covers, facing away from the door, my nose an inch from the wall. I felt him come beside the bed and sit on the edge of the mattress.

"Go home," I said. I couldn't tell if he was looking at me or looking away. "Go home and tell Naomi and Whit that we've agreed not to love each other. They'll be thrilled."

He didn't move.

"Go," I said.

"What's happening?"

"I'm telling you to go."

"I just got back."

"I know." It shouldn't have taken all my strength to not screw everything up, but it did. I couldn't unclench my muscles. And I still held on to a sliver of that anger until he slipped in bed and lay next to me. We stared up at the shadow patterns on the ceiling, not talking. But I didn't resist when James made a move and held my hand.

"What did Whit and Naomi say when they saw you?" I whispered.

"I haven't seen them yet. I came straight here."

"Oh. Whatever, they'll be happy to see you."

"It's pretty dangerous for them when I'm around."

I couldn't say we'd be safer without him. But what was "safer" anyway? I'd still be hiding out. I'd still be hyperventilating every night when the sun went down. James may have pissed the twins off, but I'd done my own damage.

"Tonight was the first night I've been out since you left," I said.

"Because you're afraid."

I nodded.

"Don't be. Nothing's happened. They have what they want, that's all they care about."

"Didn't you come back to fight for Libby?"

"No. I came back to be with you."

I didn't say anything to that.

"I can't start that kind of mess. It wouldn't end."

I didn't say anything to that either. I was already wishing I hadn't mentioned Libby's name.

"I called Whit, didn't he tell you?"

"No." It stung. "He told me you had to ramble, or something."

"What?" James paused, then said, "Doesn't matter, I guess."

"Well, if you won't fight you should've stayed in Massachusetts." I folded my arms.

"I was worried. I thought you'd . . . I don't know." He thought I'd be stupid and try to rescue Libby.

"Never mind," I said. "I'm happy."

"Me too."

"One more time, James, before you go tonight."

It was complicated, but so was everything.

I tried to be sexy, but there was nothing to strip off. I tried to move closer, but we were already on top of each other. I felt like a decadent body, like I deserved to feel this good forever.

And now I could sleep. The kind of sleep I'd been without for days, the kind that I couldn't have when James was gone. Between slow, heavy nods I watched him slip into his T-shirt and jeans. I held loosely on to one of his belt loops while he sat on the edge of my bed to tie his shoes.

The earth had opened up tonight. But it hadn't swallowed me.

"I want to wear your blue shirt," I whispered. He grabbed it off the floor and put it on me.

"The sun's coming up. I've got to take off."

"Can't you sleep over?"

He didn't answer, just pointed to the shadows above our heads. Across the ceiling the thin slits cast from my blinds looked more menacing than I'd remembered. At dawn those thin lines would light up the room with morning.

"Toaster caked, huh?"

He nodded. "Listen, I know you're freaked out, but you don't want this Libby back. Time to move on."

I held my breath. I closed my eyes as tight as I could. Then I told him, "We got Libby back."

There was a bad pause.

"How'd you do that?" he asked, too calmly.

"Wait, look." I peeked at him. "I'm safe, Whit's safe, Libby's safe. It's cool."

"Is it?" He raised his eyebrows. "Is it cool?"

"I had to."

"Whit helped you." Not a question. Didn't need a response.

"You told him to take care of me."

"I told you to let Libby go, I told you to take care of yourself. I told you I was coming back. Didn't you believe me?"

"Not really," I whispered.

"Why?" His voice weakened, emptied, hollowed out with one word.

I didn't know. I had an answer but it was pitiful, weird, boring: because I figured I loved him way more than he did me. I imagined he'd be relieved to not have to worry about loving me or hurting me or saving me. Or killing me.

"I was being stupid," I said.

"So . . . what are you saying? Now the twins are after you?"

"I don't know. Maybe."

"What about Whit?"

"They don't know about him. It's just me they want."

"And me." He shook his head. "You've made this worse. They'll be vicious now."

"They were vicious before."

"You've made it worse."

"I know."

"They'll try to kill my family."

"No."

"Damn it, Quinn. Damn it."

I remembered the last time I'd heard someone say that: in Stiles and Sanders's living room, under the window, burning from the heat, sticky with sweat and tears, ready to make the decision that would take me here to this moment, to the moment James would yell the same words as Whit. This just kept being my fault, over and over.

"I love you, but I don't know what to say. They're after us," he said.

"It's been over a week."

"They're waiting for something."

"How do you know? How do you know?" I looked into his eyes.

He didn't have to reply. He knew because he knew.

"Okay, okay, okay." I only had repetition and his soft blue shirt. I clung to both. "Okay."

"We're going to Libby's tomorrow." James stood up. I could see the pain in his face, but the sun was coming. He had to go.

"She's not there. She's in the desert." I reached out for him, but he wasn't interested in my hand. He was by the door.

"We're going wherever she is."

"Please, we can't bring her back."

"We're not bringing her back, we're using her. We have to find out whatever she knows."

"She's fried, she won't remember anything."

"We have to try."

I knew we weren't running away from them now; we were running toward them.

"Okay." I kept my arm reaching.

James was across the room from me. He wasn't getting back in bed.

"I've got to go."

"I know." I wouldn't ever be able to say the word good-bye.

"I'll be back." Was he down the stairs?

"I know." He would be back. Tonight. The second the sun went down.

He said, "I love you," in a weird way. From outside?

I love you too, James, so much it hurts. I love all of us. It hurts times all of us.

16.

SUCCESS

The morning was the rudest awakening. It sounded like my bedroom was the Enchanted Tiki Room. It sounded like there were birds in my bed. I threw a pillow at the chirping noise but hit my mirror instead. I tried to shut it all out, keep it together. No luck. Because glancing up I noticed, over in the corner of the room, leaned up against the wall like a silent spectator to my deranged and erotic nightlife, the large rectangular pane of glass that used to be my window.

There it was as if to say, *James didn't come to you in a dream. You didn't make it all up.* I stumbled back to bed and collapsed. I double-checked myself: a little achy, sore in places, my hair wavy and messed up. My panties were on the floor. His soft blue T-shirt was on my body. He'd been here, in my bedroom, last night, for real. Like, *for real* for real.

It could've been five minutes or five hours later when the phone suddenly rang. Since Libby didn't speak English and James had never called me ever, who did that leave?

Duh.

"Morgan, I'm a terrible person and I'm sorry for everything I've ever done or will ever to do you, forever." I sighed. "Okay, dude?"

"Okay . . . dude."

Oh.

"Nice apology, though."

Not Morgan.

"Sorry," I said. "You're still talking to me?"

"You got drunk and weird. It's not like you puked in my Camry."

"Right."

Then Whit was over it, launching into a hyper-posi rant about how cool it was that I came to the party and how cool Tori thought I was and how cool the earth-quake felt and how cool Jody Bennett was taking the whole postparty cleanup thing and how everything was just totally cool. He refrained from mentioning James's return and how uncool James was being about our decision to piss off the canyons' most Banana Republican killers, so I assumed the reunion hadn't happened yet.

Would Whit even care? Naomi would. She'd probably ride a horse over me.

"So . . . are you alone?" I asked, trying to sound normal.

"She didn't sleep over, you voyeur, but thanks for the vigilant suspicion."

"Ew, I don't care about that." Kind of a lie, but I actually hadn't thought about it since the car ride home. I'd had my own fireworks, thank you. Still a relief, though.

"Sure you don't. Who are you referring to then?"

"Naomi." It was at least partially true. I was fairly interested in Naomi's reaction to my latest move to get her killed.

"Yeah, she's here."

"So the two of you are alone then?"

"Are you trying to freak me out?"

"No."

He didn't know.

"Sorry," I said.

"I'm coming over in, like, twenty minutes. Are you dressed?"

"Wait, you're coming over? I don't want to hang out today." I wanted to see him, but everything was too crazy. James and I were leaving for Joshua Tree at sunset, so I didn't have my usual blank-slate day to run around wherever, doing nothing with Whit. Even though I liked running around wherever. Even though I loved doing nothing. With Whit.

"Nuh-uh. Not going to let you be weird about last night. You got jealous. Big deal. I'm really sexy, it's not your fault."

"Ugh, it's not that."

"Okay then, you're just depressed and wiggy. You know I have to look out for you."

"Not anymore," I interrupted.

"Why not? Did Stiles fall on the wrong end of a wooden stake?"

"I don't think that even works."

"Well, what do you mean, 'not anymore'?" he asked, bored of this, ready to prove that I was just being a brat.

Time to make stuff up. "Bonnie and Elliott want to bond, like have a family day or something. Attendance is mandatory. There's roll call."

Whit actually laughed at that, which I guess I would've done too if I wasn't trying so hard to be left alone. Then he said, "Whatever. I'll be there soon. Thank me later."

"Noooo . . . ," I moaned, but he'd already hung up.

I threw on whatever—makeup, chains, earrings, Converses, ripped stuff, my usual—and pondered the results of my nonchalance in the mirror. Not bad. But I had to admit that wanting to look good for Whit—despite the fact that James was back and Whit totally boned out on me last night to be with some fluffy redheaded piece of lint—was by far the most inane, stupid desire I'd had in at least twenty-four hours. When I moved some clothes on the floor, I saw them: the sad gray sweat shorts that had defined my meaningless existence for five straight days. A dark instinct called out to me to put them on. But I shut it out and threw the shorts into the back of the closet. I wasn't meaningless anymore.

I yelled downstairs to see if my parents were home, but there was no answer, like always, and I didn't bother wasting my time hunting through the house for Post-it Notes about lunch ideas or bedroom upkeep or Lexus maintenance or Morgan. I was blasting some Kill Rock Stars sampler—a not-so-good, too punkish one—in my bedroom when suddenly Whit tapped me on the shoulder. He'd knocked, waited, tried the door, walked into the house, up the stairs, and into my room without me hearing so much as a sound. So much for self-preservation. So much for staying on guard.

"Please stop acting cool," Whit screamed over the music.

"It's not acting," I screamed back, then turned the CD off. "I'm tired, Whit. I'm hungover. Can't we hang out tomorrow?"

"Sorry. Breakfast burritos at El Coyote. Next."

"Whiiiiiit," I whined. I tried to physically push him

out my door, but he was too strong and I was too sleepy. I gave up.

"You can't just sit around and feel sorry for yourself. I thought we were past all that."

I had no other choice. I had to let Whit stay my daytime babysitter until James decided to let them know he was back. This family was crazy. What else was new.

"Fine," I said, heading downstairs. "TV me."

Whit plopped down next to me on the couch and hooked his arm around my shoulder. We kicked our feet up on the coffee table, flipped around, laughed a lot, talked trash, almost forgot all the things there were to forget. Which was a lot.

But just after we'd locked into a serious cartoon block, the phone rang. It was Naomi.

"Give the phone to my brother. I know he's there," she said, on edge.

"Hi to you too." I handed the phone to Whit. "You're dead, dude," I whispered.

"I'm so scared," he whispered back, smiling, easy breezy. He took the phone, held it up to his ear, greeted his sister a little too cheerily, and then went silent, waiting through what I could only assume was a hostile tirade on the evils of being friends with me, hanging out with me, or doing anything at all that involved me.

I shrank back to the couch. I'd eavesdropped on this

kind of convo before. Wasn't interested in a self-esteem demolisher just now.

Then Whit said, "What note?" A pause. "When?" He glared at me. "Okay." Probably wasn't okay. "Yeah, I'm coming home right now. Stop crying. Just wait for me, I'm leaving." Then he hung up the phone, walked over to the television, and turned it off.

I tried to gauge his anger. A four maybe, out of ten.

"What's wrong with you?" he yelled.

Okay, okay, more like a four out of five.

"You knew he was here? Were you going to tell me or what?"

I stood up to face him. "Oh, like you told me when he called?"

"Whatever. That was different."

"Not even."

"Don't you think this matters to me and Naomi?" he spit at me.

"It's not my job to tell you. Why should I?" I spit back.

"Because we're, like, friends or something?"

"What are you so pissed about? Aren't you happy?"

"Happy?" he yelled, shocked. "Do you think I'm stupid? Do you think my sister's stupid?" He was genuinely mad, not cute mad, not sweet mad with hints of playful sarcasm, but, like, ready to be completely brutal mad.

"Whit, seriously, you're being a jerk."

"I know why he's back, because I know why he left. And he wasn't supposed to come back, because he told me it'd be too dangerous if he did." He punched the cushion at the end of the sofa. He wiped at his eyes beneath his glasses. "So no, I'm not happy."

"Fine," I barely said, hiding my eyes. "Don't be."

"And you shouldn't be happy either, because if he's back, that means we're all screwed." I didn't look up but I thought he was crying; his voice was doing that shaky thing that mine always did.

"We have a plan," I said.

"Yeah, well, I don't want to hear it."

I got up and grabbed his shirt and held on tight. I would beg, I would do anything; I couldn't watch another bridge burn. "Whit, you can't hate me. Everyone hates me."

He rolled his eyes, threw my hands off him, said, "Boo-hoo," and left me standing there. Alone with the Powerpuffs.

Obviously, Whit, I *can* just sit around and feel sorry for myself. If you need me, that's what I'll be doing all day until James shows up. And probably a little after that too.

When the sun set, my parents still didn't show up, but James did. And he didn't even seem mad at me anymore.

He fixed my window and listened to me whine about Whit and helped me write a note to my parents saying I'd be sleeping over at whoever's house. Plus, he brought me a Diet Coke—in a bottle, not a can, but still—and smilingly suffered through several outfit changes, a few micro-meltdowns, and a couple of self-pitying rants. And throughout it all James happily took the bait when I fished for compliments or sympathy and basically acted like a real boyfriend. And I guess I acted like a real girlfriend too: manic and nuts as hell.

Eventually I locked up the house and turned off the lights and we hit the road. Once we were on the highway to Joshua Tree, James let me lay my head in his lap and I drifted off. Sometimes I'd wake up from five minutes of sleep and feel him lightly stroking the side of my face. Or I'd come to on my back, looking up at him looking straight ahead into the night, the window cracked with the wind blowing in, like a man just taking his woman out to the desert for some romance.

Unfortunately, my chance for romance had cut off somewhere between five and five fifteen this morning. This wasn't even a business trip. This was like a shake-down-Libby-or-bust kind of thing. Blah-blah or die trying.

We were only a few exits from Aunt Lynn's when I roused myself, stretching my sore neck. I tried to remind myself why we were here.

"You know, Libby wasn't exactly easy to talk to even when she was normal," I said, searching under the car seat for my shoes.

"Don't worry."

"Well I'm, like, only *completely* worried."

"You said she was okay."

"I said 'sort of okay.'" That was still being generous. "What are you going to ask her?"

"I don't know yet."

"What if she won't talk to us? Or what if she sees you and has some insane post-torture flashback and starts screaming or crying or something?"

"Why would I mean anything to her? She's barely met me."

"Oh, you know you all look alike."

"That's prejudiced. That's like pulse profiling." He raised his eyebrows.

"And that's, like, a Whit joke."

I noticed James grip the steering wheel tighter, but he said nothing.

"What?" I asked.

"Nothing."

In some ways James was still a typical teenage dude. I sighed. "What, James?"

"Nothing." But he didn't mean nothing. "You and Whit really messed things up."

"But we were successful," I said. It seemed like an important detail to stress.

And finally we were there: the semicircle dirt driveway, the softly lit adobe house, the wide front porch with the potted cacti and wind chimes and bench-seat swing. The lonely dark desert, littered with crooked, creepy Joshua trees.

We got out and headed toward the front door.

Then James said, "What do you consider successful?"

I swallowed hard. Point taken. I'll let you know the answer to that one once I've reunited with my possibly comatose, most likely deranged, ex-best friend.

I hadn't called in advance—which I only thought of after we'd knocked on the door—but for some reason Aunt Lynn didn't seem remotely surprised to see us. She just bustled us in, offered us herbal tea, pomegranate seeds, edamame, hot wash towels. While we hovered in the living room she casually related the story of calling Stella, telling her sister that Libby had just come out for an impromptu desert relaxation retreat to help sprout alfalfa, make candles, and plant succulents. Then a gust of wind rattled the wind chimes, reminding me of why we were here: to scavenge the clangy, chimey recesses of Libby's mind.

"Is Libby awake?" I asked. It was only ten thirty p.m., but who knew?

"She is; she's reading out back. She'll be so happy you're here." Lynn didn't beam the same radiant light anymore. There was a slight sadness in her that I'd put there by dropping Libby in her lap. "You can go through the side gate next to the house."

We nodded, and she patted my hand and left to tend to the teapot, feed the cat.

Outside everything was quiet except for a faint breeze. There were a thousand stars. We walked around on a pebble pathway that led through a gate into the back. The sound of our feet on the gravel was too intense, too suspenseful. I tried to walk lighter, but James urged me forward.

Past the house was a small open cabana area with some tables and chairs under a trellis-style roof. Seated in one of the chairs, facing away into the desert, was the silhouette of a figure shaped like Libby, long and lean. As we got closer I squinted my eyes to see in the direction she was staring. There was nothing out there. Sand. Shrubs. Joshua trees.

When we were by Libby's table standing next to her, James gestured for me to speak, but I didn't have anything to say. How could I expect her to remember me when remembering her was this hard?

"Libs, hi," I said, sitting in the chair next to her.

She was Libby and she wasn't. Her face looked severe,

starved, like she hadn't eaten in a month. And the skin around her eyes was faded and gray, colorless. Someone who didn't know her that well might've thought she just looked tired. But that wasn't it. Libby looked tired after our five-day camping trip in the eighth grade. She looked tired in the morning after every really great party, after cramming for exams, after that week we thought we had mono but it was just food poisoning from some nasty sushi. This was something more, worse, different. I didn't know what this was.

She was barefoot, in a pair of Lynn's jeans that were dated and too baggy, wearing an oversize tie-dyed T-shirt, and in her right hand she loosely held a book—*Stranger in a Strange Land*, obviously Lynn's, Libby hated sci-fi—the pages turning in the wind. She didn't break her gaze into the black, silent distance.

"Hey, it's Quinn," I said. "I came to visit." I touched her shoulder.

"Oh." Her voice was an alien thing.

"How are you?"

Then for the first time she looked me in the eyes. Hers were glassy, fogged over. She gripped the hand I'd put on her shoulder and held it in her lap. She rubbed along the inside of my wrist. "Why did you come?" she said.

"I wanted to see you. See how you were doing."

She stroked my skin. My veins? I felt James move in

closer toward us. "That's cool of you," she said slowly.

I needed to make this moment saner. I needed to get to my point and get my hand back and get the hell out of here. "Libby, I need to ask about some stuff, but I don't want to upset you."

She didn't react. Then James sat down in the chair next to me, and Libby's eyes locked on him, her nails digging into my hand. "Who's that?"

I wrenched my hand free and rubbed at where she'd scraped the skin.

"You remember James," I said.

James stiffened. "Hello," he said. No handshake.

"No," Libby said, eyes still locked on James. "Who are you?"

"He's Naomi's brother," I said. "Remember Naomi Sheets? From school?"

"Hello," he said again.

"Hi." Finally she looked back to me. "Ask about what stuff?" she said, without any expression.

"Listen—," I started.

But James interrupted, "We need to ask about Stiles. He wants to kill us. Do you know why?"

Her eyes scanned every inch of James, searching for something. Then she said, "I think so. It's because I'm here."

James nodded.

"It's not that big a deal, though," she said, looking back to the desert. "He's not like that. He's just . . . possessive."

My mouth fell open. Like in a cartoon. "Possessive? That's a joke."

But she wasn't joking. Her face was cold and dazed, an empty skull with two hazy eyeballs looking out of it. "He's just really into me."

I felt that getting-up-too-fast feeling, blood rushing in the wrong direction, then spiraling away in a whirlpool. I was lost: Libby never knew Stiles wasn't human. Even though he bit her. Even though he sucked her blood. She must've thought he was just kinky or weird or a little too intense. I could've felt relieved that Libby was so oblivious, since that made James's secret safer, but I didn't. I felt sucker punched. If anything, the idea made me lonelier. Libby and I couldn't share our shared fate. We weren't both in love with forever twentysomethings. In her mind she was just in love with an average post-high-school, food-eating, James-Spader-looking jerk. I was flipping out.

I turned to James, hyperventilating. Libby couldn't help us with anything if she didn't understand anything.

"Okay, so maybe he won't kill us," James said, going along with Libby's cluelessness. "But he wants to hurt us. He's angry. We need to avoid him."

Libby nodded vacantly.

"Where does he usually hang out?"

"I don't know. He leaves after I'm already asleep."

"Doesn't he go out to eat?" James asked.

"I don't think so." She hesitated, her eyes drifting. "But he drinks a lot. There's nothing ever in the fridge but bottles of wine."

James said, "Thanks, Libby."

"That's it?" I whispered.

He shushed me.

She said, "Okay," and let her eyelids slide closed. She sat frozen in the dark.

"We're gonna go now," James said, standing up.

"We're leaving?" I said.

He nodded. "Bye, Libby."

She opened her eyes and looked at us. She beckoned with her hand to come nearer.

I didn't want to, but we both stepped closer.

"Don't hurt Stiles," she said. She was dead serious; becoming dead to me. "I love him."

I couldn't deal. I snapped. I put my hand on her cheek and shoved her face away, hard. She barely blinked. I turned and stormed back toward the side gate.

All of this, this whole visit, the hand-holding and the looking-in-the-eyes, it all meant nothing. Less even than the last time I'd been here. We'd known each other since forever, but it meant nothing now. It was as empty as the desert. I heard James call my name, but I shut it out like everything else.

I pushed open the gate and got into the car and slammed the door. No one was getting a good-bye. Tears wanted to come, but I didn't listen to what tears wanted anymore.

James scrambled out from the backyard and walked fast to the car and got into the driver's side. "Why'd you do that?"

"Who cares?"

"She has no idea."

"I don't care." I turned away from him, because he was part of this and I wanted no part of any of this.

"That's not true."

"Drive."

"Okay." But he sat still, waiting, the keys dangling from the ignition.

"Just drive, James."

Finally he turned on the car and pulled out of the driveway. Minutes later we were getting on the highway, leaving it all behind.

"You should know," he said suddenly. "If it's just a little bit at a time, it isn't that painful. The feeling can be pretty . . . subtle."

I didn't want to hear it.

"They sometimes don't even realize what's happening. They're too in the moment."

I remembered my fantasies of James's bite, the way my imaginary body melted into his bloody kiss. Libby had actually felt that. She'd felt it and she liked it. But she didn't even know the kiss wasn't a kiss, that Stiles was drinking her, taking her life.

I shook my head. "Whatever, that isn't even Libby."

"Of course it isn't."

"Doesn't matter now, though."

He rubbed my shoulder. "It still matters."

But I didn't know if it did.

"She's becoming one."

He said, "She *was*," and looked right at me.

So Libby was something in between.

We rode for a while without talking. The radio was on low. There were other voices. Outside it was a black blur.

I tried to picture the future: senior year, rushing home every day right at dusk, avoiding the big game, homecoming, tech rehearsals for the fall musical, anything that met at night, avoiding Naomi, Morgan, my parents. And in this vision of daytime yearbook staffs and study groups, Libby was just a mysterious dropout, another high school casualty to gossip about.

I glared at James. "So what now?"

He looked at me, saw the pain on my face, but didn't answer.

"Why did we even come here?"

"I know what we're going to do," he said.

"What?"

"We're going to poison them."

What? "How?"

"Before I got sick from that girl's blood, I didn't know anything like that could happen. I'd never been wrecked like that. But that was just accidental, some pills, drugs or something."

"Okay."

"So we could fill Stiles's bottles with something way harsher. Something chemical, completely toxic."

"Do you mean, like, laundry detergent or paint thinner?" What were we supposed to look for, warning stickers with a skull and crossbones? I didn't know where to get poison.

"Maybe. I'm not sure."

I wasn't too numb to feel his hand squeezing mine.

"It might work."

I nodded.

"Remember how bad I was?"

I nodded more.

"That was just traces. This could be brutal."

"But if it doesn't kill them, will they at least be

screwed up enough for us to finish them off?" I couldn't believe I lived a life where I could seriously say sentences like this. It was Valley girl/scary movie/action flick stuff.

"They'll definitely be screwed up."

"So . . . this is going to work?"

"Yeah, I think so." He paused, thinking. "Totally."

I looked outside, at the Inland Empire racing by, at my city sleeping, lonely truckers headed nowhere. I looked back at James. It felt like he was all I had left, and I tried not to think he might leave again.

"I believe you."

"Then come closer."

I leaned closer.

He kissed me on the lips.

"Can I come home with you?" I asked.

He said, "Whit and Naomi are there." But it wasn't a no.

"So?"

He paused then said, "So. Come home with me."

I could've cried. And this time I'd let the tears have their way.

17.

KITTEN

Back before I had someone to wake up next to, I used to daydream about waking up next to someone. Now that the fantasy was finally possible for me, it was impossible with James.

You can't share a magic morning moment in a pitch-black closet. Can't do anything really but inch your body like a worm down in the direction of the exit. Because lingering in there doesn't mean gazing into your sleeping lover's face, watching his chest rise and fall, tracing the contours of whatever with the tips of your fingers. It only means staring into so much darkness your eyes start to cross.

Lying there like a blind person, I tried to imagine James next to me, looking beautiful, tender, dream-ing of our future together. But the longer I imagined it, the lonelier and lamer everything got. When our future seemed as black and bleak as the stupid closet, I peaced out of that hotbox.

And into another hotbox. James's room was stuffy, dusty, and dim. I stumbled across the carpet and stepped outside the door. The day—what day was it anyway? Monday?—felt especially sweltering, a numb blanket of light, the sky bleached white with smog. The air buzzed with the distant drone of a thousand air conditioners blasting at full power. Out of it, I wandered down the stairs to the garden, where everything was either limp and browning or dry and dying. Charlotte Sheets's basil plants in particular were scorched, the color of mud, the smell of a plate of pasta sitting way too long under the heat lamps at Olive Garden. I tore off a leaf from a honeysuckle bush, and it disintegrated against my fingers. I stared at the ashy bits, letting them blow away into the warm wind, and thought, *This could be Stiles*. Then, *James*.

"So now you're torturing our plants?" Whit asked, walking toward me in only a pair of plaid boxers, his hand over his forehead to shield his eyes from the sun.

"Whatever, already dead, see?" I picked a dead leaf up off the ground and crumpled it into dust.

"Yeah, I see." His voice was sarcastic but tired. "But isn't it dead enough without your help?"

I didn't answer, just picked dead leaf fragments off my hands.

"What are you even doing here?"

"I slept over."

"I mean in the garden."

"Just looking at the plants."

"They were a lot more to look at when they were alive."

"Whit," I said. It was too hot for this.

"'Whit,' what?" He said it like a challenge. "Nice outfit too, by the way."

I glanced down: I had on only a T-shirt and underwear, and my feet were dirty from walking in the garden. Whit still shielded his eyes from the sun, unamused. He didn't shield his eyes from my naked legs, but it didn't matter. His face already looked different. Like he'd convinced himself not to forgive what I'd done. Like he'd convinced himself to move on. I pulled the T-shirt down as low as it'd go.

"You should go home. He won't be up for hours. And Naomi gets back from the stables at three. Probably shouldn't be sunbathing in your panties then." He turned to leave.

I rushed out, "Hey, what are you doing?"

He paused, looked confused.

"I mean, like . . . today."

He stared at my face for a few seconds, squinting in the harsh light. The sun was bleaching us out, erasing us. Whit was disappearing—and not just to his room.

"I'm hanging out," he said. "Alone."

"Why are you so mad at me?"

"Don't ask questions you know the answers to," he said sharply. "It makes you sound stupid." Then he turned around again, held up three fingers to remind me of Naomi's return time, and went inside.

I was alone with all the dead stuff again. I wandered through the garden, feeling sweat on my face but not caring. There was another bed of herbs behind the honeysuckle I hadn't seen, so I plopped down next to them and stuck my hands in the dirt, stretching my fingers into the warm, dry texture.

A couple of feet away toward the house I noticed a half-rusted tin watering can lying on its side. I reached over and grabbed it. There was still a decent puddle of old water left in it, so I found the only plant with some green leaves left—some mint or cilantro or something—and gently poured the contents of the can down over it like a hot, short rain. It still looked pretty dead. Too little too late.

I let my body fall forward, my chest against my knees, my head on the ground, and let my eyes get blurry. Sunshine soaked my skin, scalding, numbing me. Every bridge was burned or burning.

I needed to run away, but James had driven and he wouldn't be getting up till later, and I couldn't justify stealing his car since he was the only person I still knew who didn't hate me. I thought about walking, I thought about the line in that song: "Only a nobody walks in L.A." Leaning against the house was Whit's black Schwinn ten-speed, but I'd never learned past training wheels. Triple stranded. No choice but to go back upstairs and flip through old magazines and think about all the movies where someone dies from being poisoned.

An hour later, in James's room, still in my panties, hot as hell, woozy, sweating, trying to remember if anyone actually died in that poisoned goblet scene in *The Princess Bride*, I had a brief but important reality check: my parents. What day of the week was it? When had I promised them I'd be home next? When was the last time I'd gotten a note stuck to my cheek? I had answers for none of these. I had to at least call. But James had no phone, only the main house did. This day just kept sucking.

I hunted around for my clothes, but when I found my skirt I remembered why I wasn't wearing it: James had accidentally ripped a huge tear down the middle of it last night. Hot and heavy then, stupid and annoying now. I glanced around the room for something to cover myself with, but he wore the same clothes every day, he owned nothing. Folded neatly in a corner I found a faded, threadbare quilt and wrapped it around my body like some toga-dress thing. It'd have to do. I slipped on my high-tops and headed for the front door.

Knocking would only bring someone who didn't want me around, so I tried the knob first and it opened. I tiptoed through the living room, maneuvering for the phone next to some hand-carved African lamp. Then I heard a spoon against a bowl and Whit's voice: "Breaking and entering?"

He was in the doorway to the kitchen, eating a bowl of cereal, staring at me.

"I just needed to call home real fast, sorry."

"I don't care, go ahead," he said, going back into the kitchen. I heard him drop his bowl into the sink and then pad down the stairs.

I dialed, waited through three rings, then left a message: doing fine, be home soon, no big thing. As vague as possible. Obviously I was—as my mother would say—cruisin' for a serious bruisin' in the grounding department. Somehow not the top worry on my list.

Now what?

The question echoed in my head. James was in a coma till dusk. Naomi's arrival was impending. Whit wanted nothing to do with me. I was still half-naked. I felt pathetic, depressed, a wreck. No pants, no car, no training wheels.

I collapsed at the top of the stairs and sat on the first step. In my head I saw Libby floating in the desert, Morgan scowling by the pool, Naomi screaming, Whit frowning. Then suddenly I saw Whit—in reality, at the bottom of the stairs—not frowning, just looking at me, a slight smirk around his mouth, one hand on the banister. Something had thawed.

"The song remains the same with you, huh, Lacey?"

I dropped my head—it was all so seriously ridiculous—and then Whit was there, putting an arm around my shoulder, leading me to his room.

With Whit not hating me, I saw it all again like I did the first time: William Claxton, Woody Allen, Edward Hopper, Groucho Marx, Arthur Miller. Plays, records, drawings, photos. Whit was the coolest. He slouched against his pillows, and I sat on the edge of the bed.

"So," he said. "How'd everything go last night?"

I dragged out a long sigh.

"That awesome, huh?"

"I'm over it."

He sat up next to me. "You're never over anything."

"Can't help Libby, and she can't help us."

"What did James say?"

"Nothing."

Then Whit said nothing. He opened his mouth but just to breathe through it. When he lifted his hands, I thought they were coming for me, to touch my face or stroke my hair, but Whit only took off his glasses for a second and rubbed his eyes. "So is there a plan?"

"Sort of. I don't really understand it."

"It'll be okay, Quinn."

"I guess."

Life was a Malibu wave, surf it or sink. Or stay out of the water. But it was too late for that.

Eventually we relaxed. I curved my body like a C around Whit. The room felt safe and sound. The night felt far away. At some point I sank into sleep.

And when, sometime later, Whit roused me awake, the room was much darker.

"Naomi's in her room," he said.

"I better go."

"Don't forget the, uh"—Whit pointed to my bare legs—"thing."

"Thanks." I ruffled the hair on the top of his head, grabbed the quilt, and hobbled my way out his door and up the stairs, still yawning.

I was a couple of steps into the kitchen when my heart seized and I froze: A stranger in an old sweatshirt with his back to me was rummaging through the cabinet beneath the sink. I started to back away but bumped against a picture frame, making a noise, and he spun around.

"There you are." James had his hood up, and he looked tired.

"Wait, what time is it? What are you doing up?" I rushed to his side and took off the quilt, holding it up to shield him from the wide beam of low purplish light coming through the kitchen window. The sun was setting, but it wasn't gone.

"It's okay, it's not direct," he said. "I'm fine." He kept digging around under the sink. "There it is."

I looked inside the cabinet to see what he'd found. In his hands was an economy-size jug of liquid Drano.

"What's that for?"

"You know what it's for. Will you go wait in the living room?"

"Why?"

"I need to talk to all of you."

"What do you mean 'all of us?'"

He gave me a look. It was a "Get with the program" look.

"What? Why?"

Three of us in the same room was bad news. Four of us would be war.

"Please just do it."

"You're going to use Drano? Will that even work? I thought you were going to get, like, arsenic or rat poison or something." I tried to remember *Heathers*. Her lips turned blue and she smashed right through a coffee table.

I heard footsteps, and Whit came up the stairs, nodded at me, and passed into the living room. I followed him and found Naomi already there, leaning against a windowsill, twisting a piece of hair, staring into space. Whit perched on the edge of the couch and tapped his fingers nervously on some ashtray lying on the mantel.

"Would it kill you to put some clothes on?" Naomi asked, snapping her head toward me, her eyes ice.

"I . . . don't have any," I said, then shrugged, then looked to Whit. He shrugged back.

"Naomi, just give her something," James said as he came into the living room, a small black plastic bag in one hand, the top of the Drano bottle sticking out. He put an arm around my shoulder, obviously making things worse.

"It's fine, I'm cool like this," I said.

"Not really," Naomi mumbled under her breath.

Whit sighed and snapped his fingers twice. "Let's just get on with it."

James gestured to the mudcloth couch Whit was on, but Naomi didn't move, so I didn't either. "I need you all to stay here while I'm gone tonight."

"Done," Naomi interrupted.

"Yep," Whit seconded.

"No," I said. "I'm coming with you."

"Not for this." There was no debate. "I have to leave now while there's still a little light, before they wake up." James pulled his hood forward and looked me in the eyes. "Stay with Whit, promise?"

"I promise."

"I'll be back. Don't worry. No one needs to worry."

But I was already worrying. And I was already preparing to break my promise. I couldn't risk James alone against the twins, armed only with a bottle of drain cleaner and a hoodie. Things could go wrong. They always did.

James hugged Whit, who hugged him back, and then Naomi, who kept her arms straight at her sides but nuzzled her head into his neck, and then me. I squeezed him with all my strength. Then I kissed him on the lips, right in front of everyone. This was where we were, and I was done pretending we were somewhere else.

Finally he stepped back, his eyes moving across us. I didn't understand the silence, but then I realized: He was hesitating. He was scared.

"What's in the bag?" Naomi asked.

"Drano," James said back.

"What for?"

Whit shook his head. "Don't say it."

"Say it."

I looked to James. "Is it a secret?"

Whit interrupted, "It's *all* a secret. Just go."

"Tell me," Naomi said.

"Chill out," I said.

She opened her mouth, maybe to scream, but Whit shoved a finger in her face. He also pointed a finger at me.

"Both of you shut up."

Naomi stared at the ground. I stared at the ceiling.

"Please," James said, and then he turned and went out the door.

No one did anything for a second. I looked down at my naked legs, over at a family portrait, around the room, anywhere.

Naomi stared at me. "What's he going to do to Stiles?"

I had nothing to say. The truth was retarded, ridiculous. A lie seemed even more so. "Poison him."

"He's not going to drink that stuff."

"But if he did . . . ," I said. "You remember that night."

"What about it?"

"James was screwed up."

"You bitch."

"Naomi!" Whit yelled. "Just go get her something to wear."

Naomi sharpened her stare, knifed me with it. "You made your coffin, now lie in it." Then to Whit, a little disgusted, "You're smarter than this." Then she left.

Whit shrugged, gave me a sweet look. "Whatever. Guess I'm not."

A second later Naomi flung some balled-up black dress up the stairs. "Here."

Whit picked it up and handed it to me. Then he went downstairs, leaving me alone in the living room to change.

I tried to shimmy into the thing, but it was supertight around the waist, so I had to stretch it and keep wiggling my hips to get in. I tried to scope my reflection in the big bay window. The dress was a Kelly Bundy cut, not my thing at all. And it also wasn't much longer than the T-shirt I'd been wearing. I looked kind of slutty actually. Naomi, you suck.

I had to get back to my house, and I only knew the phone number of one free taxi service in the city: Morgan. It was pathetic, weird, low, rude, evil, all those things, but I had no choice. I grabbed the phone, dialed, and mercifully he let us skip past the lameness, the silences, the tense sarcasm. He could tell from my hello that I wasn't so whatever tonight.

"I need a ride home."

"Okay, from where?"

"I'm at Naomi Sheets's house."

"Why?"

"Morgan."

"Sorry, I don't get it. Naomi has a car, right?"

"Please," I said.

There was nothing on the other end. I thought he'd hung up.

"I can't leave Olivia here," he said finally.

"Oh."

"Never mind. I'll bring her. What's the address?"

I gave it to him. He was thirteen minutes away, maybe less.

"I owe you. Again."

"Just be outside."

This was working. Confidence was creeping back in. All I needed now were shoes.

I hunted around the living room for a minute and then remembered that I'd left my Converses in Whit's room. I dashed down the stairs and threw open his door, which slammed right into his shoulder.

"Hey, watch it!" he yelled.

"Why were you standing right there?"

"I was coming to get you." He stopped, looked at me, and held back a laugh. "Where's the rest of that dress?"

"Very funny. She hates me. Old news." I grabbed my shoes and sat on his bed, starting to tie the laces. "Morgan's picking me up."

"You know I can't let you go. You heard James."

"Look, it's chill, I just have to remind my parents I'm alive. It won't take long." One shoe done, on to the next.

"And I've got to relax. I'm going to have a nervous breakdown if I stay in this house."

Whit shook his head. "He told us to stay together."

"I'll be safe at home." Second shoe done.

"You're safe here."

"No one's safe anywhere."

Whit moved the hair out of my eyes, tucked it behind my ear.

"I'll just run in, say hey, get the Lexus, and come right back." I was handing out empty promises like boxes of kittens today.

"Just . . . don't let anything happen to you. James would kill me." He tried to smile.

We hugged, and I was out the door. The house was darker, the sun was basically down. How much had I already missed? James was probably there by now, maybe even inside. The plan was so flawed, so random, I could only doubt it.

I sprinted up the stairs, through the living room, out the front door, up the driveway to the street. The light was fading, the horizon a dim crimson line. One minute later a car horn honked and Morgan pulled around the corner, his sister Olivia sitting in the front, waving at me. I hopped into the backseat, and we were off.

Olivia had a ton to say. Morgan, not so much. So we let her ramble on about Nickelodeon, Judy Blume, shiny stickers, fuzzy stickers, swimming, whatever. Now this was a sister I could get into. This sister loved me.

When Morgan finally parked in front of my house, I felt the strangest sensation. It was either like I never expected to see the place again or like I'd forgotten it still existed at all. I turned to Morgan, who hadn't given me crap for the stupid short dress, hadn't grilled me about Naomi or the rest of her family, hadn't made me apologize profusely or thank him incessantly, who'd only let me be, in peace.

"Morgan, you amaze me," I said. I meant it. Maybe everyone hated me, but I loved them all. They were all amazing.

"My parents are still in Maui. You could come over if you—" But Morgan knew me so well, knew I wouldn't go back to his house with him, that he actually stopped himself midsentence.

My heart hurt. How could it be so unconditional, so endless? I'd done nothing, literally nothing, to deserve this. I was just a flip-flopping flake. "No, I'm cool."

"Got it."

"I wish I could tell you this was the last time I'll need something like this."

"I know."

"How about we say one more time and then I'll promise to stop, like, ruining your entire life?"

Free kittens, anyone?

Morgan stared at me, amused.

"Right, okay." I laughed. "Going now."

I high-fived Olivia, squeezed Morgan's hand—transmitting all my psychic unspoken love—shut the car door, and watched them drive away. The Lexus was in its usual spot. Inside, the keys were on the kitchen counter. On the fridge, the sweetest note yet:

> *Quinn, got your message. No phone number where we could reach you, cause for some alarm. But we know you're fine and we're trying not to "spaz," as you would say. Reminding you to eat, sleep, wash yourself, come home every so often. Please do all those things. Love, Mom*

I grabbed a pen and scribbled on the same sheet of paper:

> *Mom and Dad, doing awesome. Sleeping at Naomi's again tonight, but I promise I'll come home after that and stay for a while. Because I miss you guys. Taking the Lex, hope that's cool. Quinlan*

Oh, I was getting grounded for sure. Whatever. The Diet Cokes were gone. So was the sun.

I ran through stop signs and ignored speed limits and got to the twins' place in about six minutes. There was no light left, streetlamps had turned on, prime-time sitcoms were about to start; it was officially night. I squinted in the shadows and got nervous and decided to park a couple of blocks away just to be safe.

The streets were empty. I spied in some front windows and saw families walking around, TV sets on, dinner tables cleared. Life was normal everywhere except in my tiny microcosm, where life was totally psychotic. My boyfriend was lugging around a jug of Drano, I was stalking through strangers' front yards like a homeless weirdo, my parents were nowhere, and my friends were all pissed or perma-fried.

Finally I got back to the twins' property. I ducked down low and creeped alongside a row of cacti running parallel to the driveway. I snuck past the main house, past the short brick wall dividing the main house from the guesthouse, and as I entered the backyard I froze—I could just make out a hooded figure crouched in some bushes in front of the window.

I took a deep breath and made a break for it, dashing straight across the lawn to the bushy shrubs James was hidden inside. As I got closer I saw he had one hand on the edge of the windowsill and was trying to peer in, but the curtains were closed. When he heard me approaching he whipped around, his eyes panicked.

Then the color in his eyes drained. The gray went

grayer, if it was possible. He looked destroyed. Like I'd died. Like I'd chosen to die.

I ran to him anyway and hugged him, careful not to make a noise.

"Are you crazy?" he whispered.

I nodded because, yes, I was crazy, and there wasn't a better way to explain it.

He just stared at me, broken. I waited for him to say something, but he didn't.

"It's okay, I'll help you," I whispered.

"No, you won't." He turned and stared back at the window in silence.

"Did you go inside?"

James nodded but wouldn't open his mouth, his face still hard. Seeing him this worried worried me. Over his shoulder, shoved deeper inside the hedge, I noticed the bottle of Drano, empty and without its cap.

I trembled and gripped his hand. "What do we do now?"

"Just wait. Wait for them to drink." He stared ahead, so bleak. "Pray to God."

So we waited. James and I sat like that forever, camouflaged in the bushes, deep in the leaves. Time passes strangely when you're doing nothing and saying nothing yet terrified out of your mind. Maybe we waited thirty minutes, maybe three hours. Gnats buzzed in our ears.

Ants crawled on my shoes. We were in the trenches.

I'd almost started to meditate when a sudden sound broke our trance: a car driving up the alley on the other side of the guesthouse. Doors swung open, loud music blaring from a stereo, then the car turned off, doors slammed, and footsteps clicked against concrete, coming closer.

Then there was the sound of a door opening on the far side of the house. Apparently there was another entrance facing the alley. And apparently people were coming over. They'd come in. Stiles and Sanders had guests. No, no, no, no, no.

We heard voices in the living room, muffled but recognizable. Dewey. Cooper. The gang was all here. James looked at me and mouthed the word *Who*. I shook my head sadly and mouthed back, *Two more*. This was going to get so much worse.

Footsteps came closer, and James yanked me facedown into the foliage just as Dewey's hand snatched the curtains open. Neither of us moved a muscle. More muffled voices. The footsteps went away.

Every nerve in my body was pulsing, a blur of electricity. My lips were pressed against dirt and leaves, my hair tangled in branches, my mind in fragments.

I tried to get a grip. I slowly sat up and peeked through the bushes, through the window. Dewey was on the couch, legs crossed, talking to Cooper, who was over by the kitchen. I tried to concentrate on their words, but I couldn't make out any of the conversation. I closed my eyes to focus on the syllables, but then James tapped me and pointed, his eyes wide with shock. I looked up.

Cooper was in front of the fridge, one hand on the door, the other tilting back a tinted glass bottle. He was drinking.

James didn't breathe and neither did I. We watched, frozen, so frozen it felt like my heart had stopped. I was like James.

Cooper finished the bottle and set it on the counter. Dewey kept talking, gesturing with his hands. We kept waiting. Then the wait was over.

Suddenly Cooper dropped to his knees and clutched a hand to his throat, coughing violently. Dewey leapt off the couch, shouting. Cooper's face turned more blue than pale, and then he fell to all fours, hacking, losing control. For a moment he thrashed back upward, his face lit up for us to see. It was all there: dread, chaos, pain, death. Cooper was dying. Again. This time for good.

But before we could celebrate, Stiles was there, bent over Cooper's body, screaming at Dewey. He grabbed the empty bottle off the floor and sniffed it. Sanders was there now too, crossing the room, yelling something at both of them. Then Stiles snapped his fingers at Dewey, who was grabbing bottles from the fridge and putting them on the counter while Sanders started pouring them down the drain. There were dozens of them.

Then Stiles crouched back down by Cooper, who was still twitching slightly, and stared at his body.

I tried not to. I did anyway.

He was dead. Realizations floated up like fog from somewhere deep inside me. *This is what death looks like. Is supposed to look like.*

Then James was shaking me. "Get in your car!" he scream-whispered. "Go, drive to your house!"

But it felt like nothing. My body was just a shell, just a guesthouse. Sometimes people lived there and sometimes no one did. It felt empty now, and one day it'd be empty forever.

"Come on, get up!" James was pulling at my arm. I let it happen.

Then I was up, on my feet, watching James's face, animated, panicked. His mouth made the strangest shapes.

"Do you understand me?" I heard James asking.

I tried to nod but looked back inside instead and saw Sanders walking toward the front door, yelling something at Stiles. Then he opened the door and slammed it shut behind him.

"Wait, where will you be?" a weird voice asked from my throat.

"I'll follow you." James's hand around mine, dragging me across the grass.

"Why?" Night air, my feet breaking into a run.

"Don't talk, just go, now!"

Everything was a tunnel—we were hurtling along the only path, one destination. We were past the brick wall, past the main house, onto the street. A man walking his dog stopped and waved, but I didn't understand what he was doing in this reality so I didn't wave back.

James shoved me toward my car, shouted one last "Go!"

I came to. I was here. A thousand things were happening.

Now I was the helpless kitten, hoping someone would take me home.

18.

GANG

I don't know what I thought about during the drive to my house. Maybe James, maybe dying, maybe nothing. I have no memory of it. There was a blur of streets and signs and stoplights and the feeling that everything in my life was accelerating to some fatal crash. But suddenly I was parking in my driveway, James right behind me, and my hands were shaking. I looked through the windshield at my house, and the realization hit me hard: This place was no longer safe. Nowhere was, not anymore.

A flashback of Stiles shaking Cooper, sniffing the bottle, outraged, calculating. Something in his black eyes said it: He knew I was the one responsible. I didn't know what to do tonight. I had no idea how to make it to tomorrow morning.

And instead of focusing on that, instead of figuring

out a way to help all of us, a different, darker thought floated up in my mind. Maybe Stiles had never wanted to kill Libby. Maybe he'd just wanted to turn her into one of them. Maybe he had, and Libby wasn't human, and our rescue was for nothing. I couldn't swallow. I'd started all this, and I didn't have the power to end it.

Then there was a knock on the glass and James was at my window, mouthing the words, *Quinn, there's no time.* I dropped my head in my hands and stared at the floor. I wanted to cry and cry and not stop until the car was full of tears and I drowned. But that'd take forever, and I didn't have forever. Like James said, there wasn't any time.

"Fine," I said through the glass, then took a deep breath, flung open the door, and walked up the stone steps toward my house.

When I got to my front door, I turned around to take James's hand, but he wasn't beside me. He was back by the Lexus, leaning against it. He wasn't coming in.

I shouted, "James," desperately.

"I'll wait out here. Just grab some clothes. Hurry."

I stared at him, then nodded. This was only our first stop tonight.

Inside all the lights were on. Even weirder, my parents were home. A new panic set in. Any interaction with my mother and father required a minimum of half an hour, which was half an hour more than I had to burn tonight.

I sprinted upstairs to my bedroom and emptied my LeSportsac of all the stupid crap I carried: papers, pens, notebooks, an extra bra, socks, sunglasses, mascara, lanyard string, locker key, glitter nail polish. I surveyed the rest of my room for stuff to pack. I grabbed a pair of Docs, some cutoff shorts, a Nirvana shirt, my dad's cardigan, and that was it. I had no idea if that was enough, because I had no idea when I'd be back.

Racing down the stairs, I remembered to smile. My parents loved when I smiled.

"Quinn, is that you?" my mother called from the kitchen.

"Yeah, I was just grabbing some stuff."

In the kitchen my mother and father were dancing happily around each other, working in separate stations— Mom on dishwasher, Dad on Tupperware—listening to some funky Stevie Wonder song on the radio. Look at them. More amazing people I loved, more amazing people I'd let down.

"Got your note. Or whatever you'd call this." My mother held up the paper, stained with some sort of sauce, and waved it like a piece of evidence.

"So you know I'm sleeping over at Naomi's tonight. Good," I said, super casual, perching on a stool and setting down the keys to the Lexus. I only needed to hold this act together another five minutes and then I could bounce.

"No way, José. You've been out two nights in a row," my dad said, looking over from his saucepan. "I think that's enough."

My father's logic. Still lost on me.

"But Dad, I slept at home the night before last. So . . . technically this would only be the second night out, and *that* would be enough. Then tomorrow night I'll sleep at home." My own logic. Equally lost on them.

"Uh-uh, I don't think so," Mom said. "Movie night at home with us. You can call Naomi and invite her to sleep here."

"Compromise," Dad said, very pleased.

I considered a new counterattack. The smell of whatever they'd cooked was making me dizzy. And hungry. But James's words echoed: *There's no time.*

"Sorry, can't do it," I said. "I promised Naomi I'd sleep over. Her parents are out of town and she's watching the house, so she needs company. She gets scared at night." Then I pushed it even further: "I'm just trying to be a good friend."

Was anyone buying this? Somewhere Naomi was laughing her ass off. I hoisted my bag over my shoulder to indicate that I was leaving, that our conversation was wrapping up.

"You know, you can't just write a note saying you're taking the car. That doesn't count as asking for permission," my mother said. "And what dress are you wearing?"

"Focus, Mom. Morgan had a flat tire, he was stranded. It was an emergency."

Shameful.

But the very sound of his name instantly softened her scowl, and she reached and gave me a tender rub on the hand. If I'd just bring Morgan over for dinner one night a week every other week, I could probably do whatever I wanted forever. Knowing that made me want to smash something.

"That was nice of you. But you're not roadside service. Next time ask. You may now go to your friend's house." My mother put her arm around me. She squeezed me. Suddenly I wished I wasn't in such a rush.

"Thanks, Mom." I wrapped my arms around her waist and hugged her middle like a teddy bear. "But I gotta motor. Morgan's outside waiting." I excused myself from the embrace. As long as they went on just like that—dancing, cooking, smiling, eating, expecting very little out of a totally impossible teenage girl—everything would be okay. My smile, in that moment, short but sweet, was totally real.

"Can't promise we'll save your leftovers," my father warned, with his head in the fridge.

"That's okay. I don't eat vegetables."

That made both of them laugh. It was good to see.

I'd done it. In and out and in seconds flat. I skipped down the steps, relieved to be free, happy to be alive, about to sing out for James, when suddenly I saw them. James. With Sanders. In front of my house. Talking. My heart felt like it puked in my chest. Sanders was on my front lawn. He could kill my parents. He could kill me. I froze in place, staring at the vampires.

They exchanged some final words and shook hands. Then Sanders turned his head, caught my eye, flashed a grin, and walked away, down the street, into the night. I wanted to scream until I lost my voice. I dropped down to the grass instead.

I heard James approaching. He bent down next to me and asked, "You ready?"

My mind was cracking, the pieces shipping off to every character and every scene in my life. Of course Stiles and Sanders had been here before—at least one of them had—but they'd never let themselves be seen. Even after we stole Libby and they had every reason for revenge, they still never crossed that line. Now that line was just chalk, blow on it and it blows away.

"Come on, we have to get back." James's hands guided me to the car.

"What was he doing here?"

"He wanted to talk."

"About what?"

"Fixing this."

"Why was he at my house, James?"

"I'm working it out."

"We can't leave my parents here."

"They'll be fine. They're safe," he said, opening the door and pushing me into the passenger seat. Once inside he started the engine and was instantly speeding, going almost fifty, weaving through the winding canyon roads.

I clenched my fists, gripped the leather of the seat.

James looked over at me. "Sanders and I are going to make a deal."

"You can't trust that piece of—"

"It's done," he interrupted, sterner.

"It's a trick. Whatever he's saying, it's a lie." The twins didn't play nice, and they certainly didn't play fair.

"No. He doesn't want to fight. He's sick of all this." We were all over the road, going way too fast.

"Spare me. He's lying. He's evil." The worst. The second worst.

"Quinn, I'm asking you to trust me."

"Does he know we killed Cooper?"

James met my eyes, then looked back to the road and ignored me.

"Does he know it was us?" I yelled.

"He knows, but it doesn't matter. They don't care about Cooper any more than we do."

"But . . . it wasn't meant for Cooper. Do they know that?"

James nodded.

"So we're dead," I said. I couldn't process another tragedy. One per day was my max.

"No, we're fine. I just have to make sure."

"Make sure how?"

He paused. "We're meeting later."

James was meeting Sanders later.

"Are you stupid? That doesn't make any sense. Stiles will be there and they'll kill you and I'll never see you again!" My voice was a wail. I punched the car door.

"I obviously wouldn't go if I thought that was true."

"Please don't go. Stay with me."

"I'm making it easier to stay with you. I swear. Whatever I have to trade with him, I'll do it."

"What is there to trade? Except me?"

"Something else that Sanders wants."

Then we were there, cruising down the Sheetses' driveway, parking, sitting in silence. I turned to look at James, and he leaned in and kissed me, hard. When I kissed him back, he pulled me over the seat divider onto his lap and we locked lips, the steering wheel jamming into my spine, my knee banging the seatbelt buckle, my elbow the window, my head the sunroof. We breathed in each other's mouths and eyes and ears. He slipped a hand up my thigh, under Naomi's dress. I grabbed his face.

"Please don't go," I whispered.

"I'm not leaving for hours. I'll be with you all night, until you're asleep."

"I won't fall asleep. How could I?" But I was exhausted. I could already feel my body aching for bed.

"Come inside."

My stomach groaned. Loudly.

"I'll feed you."

"You're trying to sedate me."

Then he leaned forward, pushed me closer to the steering wheel. "Let's go."

"To your room?"

"No, the main house."

"They don't want me in there."

"I don't care what they want," he said. "I need you all together tonight. Can you understand that?"

I could. I wanted to be together with everyone too. James, Whit, Mom, Dad, Morgan, Libby, even Naomi. Stella Block. Jody Bennett. Tori, for heaven's sake. I wanted everyone to be together and make it through tonight together.

We started walking toward the front door, holding on to each other tightly. I thanked God for this closeness, anything we could share now that wasn't tears or shouts or freak-outs. And I thanked God we were close because when we got about twenty feet from the door I spied it lying there, white with blue-red lips, contorted, gross, deader than dead.

Cooper's body.

James froze and held up an arm to stop me from getting closer. As if I wanted to. I stared at it, hypnotized. I waited for it to disintegrate, turn into ash, disappear. I waited for it to catch fire, dissolve, explode. I waited for the supernatural. But Cooper's dead body was like a regular dead body. Aside from the bluish lips and glassy eyes, he looked pretty much the same as he did the last time I saw him, at Libby's party, in the kitchen. I tried to remember him like he used to be, when he was just a jock I saw around school sometimes, pre-bloodsucker, the salad days. But the memory was too faded. All I could see was his body in front me, dead for the second time.

My emotions cycled through a Ferris wheel of changes, from terrified to disgusted to sad to okay to completely psyched. I crested on the last one. One of the four was gone, hallelujah. No one would miss him.

"Go back to the car!" James shouted at me. He didn't want me to look at it.

But I'd already soaked in the sight. Actually seeing

one of them dead was like a revelation: It could totally be done.

"Did you hear what I said?" James was still shouting, more frantic.

I pretended to walk away.

Then I heard him run to the house, open the door, and start calling out for Whit and Naomi. Once he was gone, I turned back around and stared some more at Cooper. I thought of all the horror movie endings where the villain jumps back up, not dead, for some maniacal final fight. I stepped slowly toward his body and, when I got close enough, kicked it. It felt like nothing. Double dead.

Then a voice said, "What are you doing?"

I looked up.

Whit was in the doorway, watching me nudge a corpse with the tip of my Converse. He looked haggard and crazed, like he'd been ripping his hair out. "Will you just get inside, please?"

"James told me to go back to the car."

"So he didn't tell you to play with the body?"

I shook my head no.

"Get in here."

I walked around Cooper to Whit, who put his arm around my shoulder in an exhausted way and led me through the door and into the living room, where Naomi was balled up on the couch, crying into James's lap. His hands stroked her hair and rubbed her back, alternating. It'd only been a couple of hours, but somehow it seemed like days since I was last here. So much had happened.

"How long has he been out there?" James asked Whit.

Whit shrugged. "Ten or fifteen minutes maybe."

"What happened?"

Whit pushed his glasses up on his nose. He was stiff, sweating. "We heard a car pull up and thought it was you. Then the porch light turned on. Naomi went to the door and it was just lying there."

Naomi broke into a fresh set of sobs.

"Then we heard a car start and they drove off. We couldn't see who it was."

"Stiles." James didn't ask.

"That's what Naomi said, but I don't know. It was dark, could've been his twin."

"No." James met my eyes. "Not Sanders."

Naomi lifted her wet, red, splotchy face and said to all of us, "It was Stiles."

"Who's the body? Did you know him?" Whit asked.

"A friend of the twins," James said. "He used to go to school with Quinn and Naomi."

Whit looked at me.

"One of the Spaders." I shrugged. "Taste-tester."

James glared at me. Whatever. They had a right to know why Stiles was dropping bodies on their doorstep.

353

"The poison wasn't for him," James explained. "It was for the twins. He drank it accidentally."

"What?" Whit was pissed. "You killed the wrong one?"

"There is no wrong one," Naomi said. "Kill all of them."

"Well, I'm sure they'll be very understanding about this." Whit was near violent, lashing out. "Could you please have better aim next time? If they don't murder us first?"

James looked crushed. I felt it too. His plan could've been good and it could've saved us. It just didn't.

He looked at Whit, then at the ground. "There won't be a next time. It's over."

Naomi stared from James to me and back again. "How? How is it over? This is a threat. It's not even close to over. They're sadists," she cried. She closed her eyes. "I know what Stiles is like. He's not finished with us."

"He will be after tonight. James is going to fix it," I said.

Whit pointed toward the door. "Well, can he fix the situation on the porch too?"

"I'll figure it out," James said. He propped Naomi up against the couch cushions, then stood up.

"No, not yet," I said, grabbing his arm. He promised he'd be with me until I fell asleep. It was nine, maybe nine thirty. My stomach rumbled again. "What about dinner?"

"Whit will give you some food." James rubbed my shoulder. "Fifteen minutes. Less."

"We keep splitting up. That doesn't seem smart."

"What if he brings another body when you're gone?" Naomi whispered.

"There are no more bodies," James said.

"That *you've* killed," she said.

He sighed. "That's not going to happen."

"Will you two please just let him get that corpse out of here?" Whit screamed. He turned to James and said, "Go figure it out."

Naomi and I stopped talking and James walked past us, out the door. We didn't hear him heave the body off the ground. We only heard him drive away.

No one said anything for a minute or two. Then I wondered out loud, "Where'd he go, do you think?"

"I don't know. He has to burn the thing," Whit said.

"Where do you go to burn a body?"

"I said I don't know."

I nodded, bit my tongue.

"Are you hungry, or what?"

I nodded again.

"Naomi?"

She shook her head no.

"Fine," Whit said. "I'll be in the kitchen." Then he turned and left.

Once Naomi and I were alone, the living room felt

twice as massive, like it could fit fifty people. I sat on a footstool carved into the shape of a zebra. She stayed huddled up on the couch, her head buried in her knees.

Then she spoke. "I can't believe you're going to eat."

"I know."

"Last supper."

It was a joke, so I tried to smile.

"Your friend, Libby. That could've been me." She looked up from behind her knees into my eyes. "Whit told me what she was like."

I sighed, remembering the desert, everything. "No way, you were too smart, you knew when to get away. She fell for it."

"So did you."

"I know."

She rested her head on her knees, looked at the ground. "You know, Stiles was a lot different . . . before."

"Just a regular jerk?"

"Yeah." She almost laughed, but couldn't. "I didn't know when to get away, though. He dumped me."

"He sucks, Naomi. Stinks, whatever."

"Yeah."

Her face looked pained, haunted by whatever had happened between her and Stiles. Almost like a part of her still cared about him. Or at least like she had at one time, when he was human. But *that* Stiles barely even existed anymore. Whatever he'd done in his old life no longer counted. Not to me. To Naomi, though, it seemed like it lingered on.

I said, "Remember when you asked me if I was afraid to die?"

"Yeah."

"Well, I am now. But I believe James. He's going to work it out with Sanders. He's going to make things okay." Saying it out loud helped make it real.

She just stared at me, icy, said, "You are so delusional," and rolled her eyes.

So I walked away.

Whit was sitting at the kitchen counter eating couscous and chickpeas with hot sauce, and there was a second bowl made up the same way. He slid everything across the counter to me.

I held a bite up to my lips, blew on it. "She hates me."

"Jesus, Quinn, who cares? You're obsessed."

"So?"

"So don't be."

"Too late." I ate the bite.

He set down his fork and looked at me. "Why do you think Naomi doesn't have any friends? Why do you think I moved across the country for college and didn't want to come back?" He didn't wait for a response. "We like our secrets secret. We're not into bonding over it either. Get it?"

I got it. But if James could really convince Sanders to back off and get his psycho brother to do the same, then nothing would have to be like this. Whit would want me around again. James would be closer to me than ever. Even Naomi might loosen up. I had to believe. It was still the summer, glorious and hot and open. It was L.A. We were young. Some of us wouldn't be that way forever, but we could have fun together for now. We could be happy. We could at least try.

I reached for Whit's hand. "You're my best, best friend."

"Quinn," he said, sighing, "this isn't a gang you can join."

I nodded, tried to see past his words. "But you love me. In your way."

Whit just stared at me. He sighed again. But it wasn't a no.

Suddenly we heard the front door open, footsteps, and James came into the kitchen. He looked unbelievable. He looked like he always did, classic James—greasy, grungy, beautiful. I could play it down to Whit, but I couldn't lie to myself: I *was* obsessed.

"Okay, it's done," James said.

"Good." Whit nodded, stood up straight. "We can't stay here, though."

I frowned. "Why not?"

"Stiles was here."

"So? He won't come back. Right?" I looked to James. Whit looked at him too. "Right?"

"Right." James nodded.

"Naomi isn't staying here," Whit said. "That's not happening."

"Well, where do you want to go?" James asked.

"A motel?"

"None of us is twenty-one. They won't rent us a room."

"Your house?" Whit looked at me.

I shook my head. "The twins know where I live too."

"We can still stay here." James put his hands over both of ours.

"No," Whit said, severe, pulling his hand away.

No one was budging. The night was deepening.

Only one option rose in my mind. I was *actually* considering it. I was *actually* going to go through with it. I stared at the phone. It looked so harmless. Whatever. Not anymore.

"I know a place. It's safe for the night for sure."

"Quinn," James started.

"Just round up the gang," I said to Whit. Then I did what had to be done.

19.

BURN

We were a motley crew.

Morgan had answered when I called, had acted normal when I invited myself and the entire Sheets family over for the night, and was now at his front door, scanning our faces, wondering what the hell he'd gotten himself into.

"Um, come in."

I hugged him as I entered. "Owe you. Again."

Naturally Morgan asked what the police had said when we called to report the break-in—my pathetic cover story as to why the Sheets siblings didn't feel comfortable staying at their own house tonight—but James smoothed it all out. He said he'd be going down to the station in a couple of hours to file a full report. All that was missing was an old gold necklace and some cash from a drawer. It looked like they'd tried to take the TV but couldn't carry it. Probably some kids messing around but, you know, better to stay away for the night, just to be on the safe side.

In this improvised fairy-tale version of reality, my mother and father were having a dinner party tonight, hence my place was off-limits; Naomi had no other friends; Whit and James were visiting from East Coast schools and didn't know anyone in the city anymore.

Morgan reacted with "Uh-huh, uh-huh," over and over. Like he didn't believe us. Or like he did. But overall it didn't seem to matter to him too much why we were there, just that we were there, hanging out with him, allowing him into the fold, into our shady gang of runaways. He listened to our description of unbelievable events and took it all at face value. He opened his arms to me without hesitation, for the eightieth time, and to the three aliens I swore were the Sheets family. He dumped his sister at her friend's for the night, showed us how to fold out the couch into a bed, and offered us beverages and snacks plus bonus accommodations like extra towels for the shower and socks in case the air-conditioning made our feet cold at night. And I let him do all of this— let him invite a make-believe creature into his house, let him harbor the wanted and hunted, put him in potentially mortal danger—all to save my ass. Somewhere a scoreboard clicked over. Morgan moved high into the double digits, while my numbers dropped fast into the negative.

For some reason James was being talkative, which was strange. Of course, watching James interact with other humans was strange in general. He seemed somehow unreal, slightly off. I kept glancing at Morgan to see if his suspicion or survival instincts might kick in, but they never did. James's voice was too hypnotizing. Morgan just stared and listened, his mouth half-open, transfixed. Libby and I weren't just loopy, duped Canyon girls. The seduction worked on everyone. Almost everyone.

Whit and Naomi were warier. The more captivating and soothing James became, the more detached and guarded they got. Already Whit was doing his barely there thing, withdrawing, space cadet–style. Naomi resisted the opposite way, by freezing over, cold and critical. She was leaned up against the couch, staring at James, her blue eyes burning with a weird secret resolve, like she had a purpose. Like she was on a mission. If I didn't know better I would've thought she was two seconds away from blowing our cover. Her eyes were pitiless.

Eventually the small talk ran dry, the chips were just crumbs, the house tours and bathroom breaks had ended, and all the cops-and-robbers lies had been used up. It was late at night, which meant it was time to worry about

James's journey. A flash of Sanders grinning at me from my front lawn. Mashed teeth. If there was anything in this world that the twins wanted more than revenge, I prayed James could offer it to them.

The grandfather clock in the dining room rang once. One a.m. Naomi yawned and stretched out her arms. Morgan cleared some plates and cups. I tried to feel positive, remind myself we were safe, no one could track us here, we weren't being stalked.

But there was still an undercurrent of dread. Now the feud had a body count. And tonight would determine tomorrow. Tonight could determine forever. James kissed me on the top of my head.

Then Naomi yawned again, stood up. "Good night," she mumbled.

James went to her and held her, whispering something in her ear. Then he stepped back and let her go, down the hallway to Olivia's room, to the bunk bed we'd be sharing tonight.

Morgan was next, back from the kitchen. I thanked him too many times, couldn't thank him enough, tried to gush out all my gratitude, appreciation, and indistinct waves of love. I allowed Morgan to save me, yet again, and I didn't promise him it would ever be any other way.

When he turned to say his third good night before leaving the room, he caught a glimpse of me sandwiched between Whit and James on the couch, and something in his face told me he knew. I didn't know what; it was vaguer than that. Like maybe some realization about us, and me, and the way things were. And maybe he was okay with that. I thought I felt him release me in some way. It was hard to say for sure, though. It was a long walk down a long hallway to his bedroom. It was a long time until we heard Morgan open and shut the door.

Then there were three. The night had peaked, and now it was winding down. It was already technically morning but not real morning. I gripped both of their hands even though Whit wouldn't curl his fingers around mine. He was still in a daze, unfocused, off somewhere I hoped was a vacation from this.

Suddenly James squeezed my hand and stood up to go. He said good-bye to Whit, rubbed his shoulder. It struck me as sad in that moment: blood brothers drained of such a bond. The older would soon become the younger and only ever be the younger, forever. It was the age of backward.

I followed James from the couch to the front door. During the brief walk I noticed I didn't feel restless and stressed. It wasn't a matter of believing James; I believed *in* James. To believe in the undead, to believe that they were real and in your life and loved you, made it slightly easier to believe that enemies could be turned. Not turned into allies but turned away, to other interests. I realized too that Stiles and Sanders might not even consider me an enemy. I was just a small, silly speck, an annoying human nuisance. I was a blip on the radar. Someone who'd live less than a century during their eternity.

Then I looked up at James, my James. Here it was again: this effortless, simple beauty that folded my insides up like tiny pieces of origami.

I smiled at him.

He smiled back.

Then James lifted me, held me up, kissed me. In my head music swelled, cymbals crashed. But it wasn't the longest kiss, because it wasn't the last. If a heart could beat just for someone else, mine would for him. If a heart could start to beat after years of silence, maybe his did, for me.

"Try not to worry too much," James whispered.

"I'll try."

"I'll be at home, in my room, when you wake up. Come find me."

"But you'll be asleep."

"So wake me up."

"Okay." I kissed him again, then thought of something. "Make them promise they can't hurt Libby either."

"I know, Quinn."

I sighed. "So I'm going to see you tomorrow?"

"Of course." He moved his hand to the doorknob, then paused. "It's already tomorrow." James pushed my bangs to the side. He touched my cheeks. They were dry.

I closed my eyes. "See you soon."

"See you so soon."

I kept my eyes shut until he was gone and the door had closed. I leaned there for a few seconds before turning around and going back to the living room. Whit was still on the couch. The loneliness didn't have to creep in just yet. I had Whit. I had a little while.

I snuggled in beside him but he was somewhere else, zoned out. I lifted his arm off the cushion and draped it around my shoulder like a scarf.

Slowly he noticed me and took his arm back. "Don't do that."

"Sorry." I sunk down. "So what are you going to have for breakfast?"

"What?"

"I want bacon and an omelet and French toast. With cranberry juice, Diet Coke, and water."

"What?"

"For our celebration breakfast."

"I'm not celebrating the fact that we're alive. We *should* be alive." His face was unamused.

"I know."

"So it doesn't matter what I'm eating for breakfast."

"What about a milkshake?" I patted his stomach. "Mmmmm."

Whit stood up. He wasn't on vacation anymore. He was right here, with me, and unhappy about it. "Can you please stop pretending things are normal?"

"Okay."

"You saw a dead body tonight. Don't you care?"

"Yeah." Of course I cared. I was psyched as hell.

"That was a dead boy."

"A dead vampire."

He fixed me with his eyes. "James is a vampire."

"Not like that."

"Yes, Quinn, just like that, and some boyfriends don't leave a trail of dead bodies." He faced away from me and said into the wall, "But you're not interested."

"Interested in what?" I stood up.

He waved his hand at me like he was batting away a bug. "Nothing. Never mind."

"You knew I was in love with him. I don't know what you want from me."

He rolled his eyes. "Are you done being the center of the universe now?"

I lowered my eyes to the ground. "I love you, Whit."

"You love too many people."

"That's a stupid thing to say."

He covered his eyes with his hands. "I'm tired."

"I'm sorry."

"It's fine."

I looked down the hall and saw no one. "Can I kiss you good night?"

"Quinn." He sighed. I made everyone sigh.

"Please?" I said, already walking toward him. He didn't move or react as I touched my lips softly to his, just for a second, then backed away.

"What was that for?" he asked, slightly bored.

"It was for tomorrow morning, when everything's going to be okay, and for tomorrow night, when we'll all be hanging out together."

He just stared at me blankly.

I melted into a hug, but he didn't really hug back. "Whit, you're my best friend."

"You don't need to keep saying that."

"I know." But I felt like I did. I felt like I had to get best friend key chains, lockets, charm bracelets, anything. I had to bind us together officially somehow. "I just like to."

He yawned. "Can I go to bed now?"

"If you want."

Whit started pulling the fold-out couch into a bed. I hovered behind him, not wanting to leave. He put blankets on the mattress, grabbed a pillow, and undressed down to his boxers. I still stayed.

"Whit, you're not going anywhere, are you?"

He reached and turned off the lamp next to him. "When?"

"In general."

"Don't have any plans to." He laid his head down. "Good night, Quinn."

"Good night." I turned off the other lamp and headed down the hall.

I had done everything in this house that I could to make everyone happy or at least happier. I was the last one up. I thought about James, wherever he was: some empty Hollywood freeway, some bar, some parking lot. I couldn't picture it, but I prayed his plan would work, was working, had worked.

Thankfully, the doorknob to Olivia's room twisted silently, so I tiptoed in, trying not to make a sound. Naomi was in the top bunk, on her side, facing the wall. Finally I slipped out of the skanky short black dress and crawled onto the bottom mattress.

In my underwear, in an eleven-year-old's bed, I tried to remember all the words to "Give It Away Now." I picked out toppings for my celebration breakfast omelet, for some future pizza with Whit, for some glorious baked potato I'd eat soon. I thought about how prom took place at night, how the drive-in movie theater was open at night, how the stars came out at night. And there were concerts, night school classes, art walks downtown, even Disneyland was open extra late a few times a year. James and I would have no shortage of things to do. There was a lot of stuff—a bunch of rad stuff—for us to do.

"Wake up." Naomi shook me kind of hard and said again, inches from my face, "Wake up."

"What time is it?" my voice rasped. I was covered in sweat. I kicked the blankets down to my feet.

"Eight."

I rubbed my eyes, adjusting to the light, the day—hell yeah, the day!—but couldn't quite focus on her face. Probably pissed about something.

"I need to talk to you."

"Can't we do this later?"

"No. Now, before Whit gets up."

"Fine, what?" I finally opened both my eyes.

She pulled the chair closer to the bed and put her hands in her lap. "I want you to understand something."

I sat up. I blinked the rest of the sleep out of my eyes. And then I saw Naomi clearer. Pissed wasn't the right word at all. Severe. Steely. And surprisingly put-together for so early in the morning.

"Listen."

"Okay."

"Stiles is the way he is because of me."

"He's the way he is because he's a jerk, that's all."

She shook her head. "No. It's because I told him about James."

I tensed. "What do you mean?"

"We'd been together, like, a couple months or something. And we finally did it." She looked at me, almost demurely. "You know?"

"Yeah."

She hesitated, then, "It was my first time."

"Okay."

"I told him about James. I'd never told anyone. Besides Stiles, I've still never told anyone."

My first reaction was, *So what?* None of it seemed like a big deal. At eight in the morning it only felt like the recounting of a dream right after you have it, so you don't forget the details.

"But then Stiles kept asking me about it, every kind of question. He wanted to know where the bar was, if I knew who changed James. He even asked me how to tell what one looked like.

"But I only knew what James looked like. Like how he's pale but not really. How his lips are kind of purple. I told him don't look for fangs. Don't look for black clothes or whatever." She rubbed her forehead. "I wasn't even thinking. . . ." Then she hit her forehead, looked down at my bare feet on the carpet. "Anyway."

I just stared at her, waiting.

"And when I tried to describe the club, the show that night, everything James had told me, it wasn't enough. He was totally fixated. If there was a vampire anywhere near that bar, anywhere in the city, Stiles was going to find him. He even wanted me to take him there." She paused at that, stared straight in my eyes. It was like her eyes were telling me, not her voice. Then she finished, "I told him no, never."

"Right after that he stopped calling me. We never even, like, broke up, he just ignored me at school and told everyone I was a prude and that was it."

I shook my head.

"Then like a month later I saw him, and I could tell he wasn't Stiles anymore." Naomi wasn't being wistful, she wasn't lost in some reverie.

"How'd he do it?"

She said, "How have we avoided it?" but didn't wait for an answer. "*We* didn't ask for it. He did. You look hard enough, you'll find anything."

"Freak," I whispered.

"Most people didn't even notice. Even when it happened to Sanders. Then their friends."

My mouth was hanging open.

This was all happening. At my boring high school.

"So . . . Stiles changed all three of them?"

"Probably."

"Did you tell James about it?"

"No." She eyed me tiredly, like she knew I'd bring things back to James. "But when he came back this summer, I really wanted to. I was following him that night at your video store."

I froze, caught off guard. That was like ancient history. Multiple lifetimes ago.

"He'd been home a few days, sulking. We barely talked anymore. I just wanted to see what it was like. I wanted to see where he was always disappearing to." She shrugged like this was the most obvious desire, not the sickest one. "He stopped outside your video store. Then a lady came out and he pulled her off the road, somewhere, I don't know."

My mind rewound itself, first in fast motion, then slow-mo.

Pause: the action buff.

"He was just . . . drinking her blood. Feeding. Whatever." She breathed slowly, like she was trying to think straight. "I thought I could watch, but I started screaming. I went crazy. I tried to shake her awake, but she was already dead. That was her blood."

"On your hands."

"Yeah."

"Oh my God."

"James was mad I'd followed him, but I didn't care." Then she looked up at me, serious. "It was the worst thing ever. I hope you never have to see that. But maybe you should see it. Because then you wouldn't forgive him, like I don't."

"I'm sorry." I reached a hand out to touch her knee, but she pushed it away.

"Don't be. That's not why I'm telling you any of this."

My heart sank, every nerve on edge.

"You can't forget what it means to be like them. Like James. Stiles. You have to understand how it works."

"I do."

"You and James killed one of them. Now they'll kill one of you. One of us."

"They made a truce."

"Don't be such a baby. You can't reason with them, they're not people. You can't make a truce with instincts. Or thirst."

"James ended it. It's over."

"Until they're dead, they'll never stop."

Last night's optimism was gone. Her words made me ill. James. "No, it can be different. It doesn't have to be so vicious."

"Quinn. I know you love him." She looked dead into me. "But that's only possible because he still acts so human. Way more than Stiles or any of the others."

I closed my eyes.

"And those parts of him that you love—the weak, nice human parts—are the exact reasons we can't trust him to save us from all this." She put her hand on my knee, lowered her voice. "You're only here right now because James wants to be like a human, and wants to love other humans. *None* of the others want that."

My eyes still closed, I shook my head. Not to say no, just to get the words out of my ears.

"They know he's weak too. Whatever Sanders told him isn't true. There's no peace, no secret handshake or anything." The scorn in her voice was rising.

My head was starting to pound. I opened my eyes. "You're acting like you think all of them should die."

"And you're acting like they'd all make good boyfriends."

"No. Just one of them."

Would no one in this family stick up for James? When he'd offered Sanders God knows what for all of our safety in return?

"Naomi, I'm sorry. I just think we should leave it up to James."

Naomi grabbed both my knees and dug her fingers in. "Do. You. Want. Him?" she asked. "Because if you do, your only fear should be losing him. I'm trying to make that not happen. So help me do what he won't."

"Help do what?"

She didn't flinch. "Burn whatever life is left out of them."

"We're already breaking the truce?" I had to repeat the word. I clung to its meaning.

"You're not understanding," Naomi said. "If Stiles and Sanders are gone, the truce won't matter. There are no consequences if there's no one left to be betrayed."

"But we're betraying James. He'll never forgive us."

She sat back, blew air out of her mouth. "Don't be stupid. He forgave you and Whit for pulling that stunt that got us here in the first place. He even forgave you for sleeping with Whit."

I narrowed my eyes. "I never slept with Whit."

"Whatever."

"Whatever, I didn't."

"Well, he'll forgive you when you do."

I was fuming now. "Last night you were out of your mind when you saw Cooper's body. I saw you, you lost it. What's changed? You want to kill someone now?"

She got excited, leaned in toward me. "I did lose it. But then I saw you."

I *had* been into it. I still was. But that didn't mean what Naomi wanted it to mean.

"This would be just like that. More of them dead. That's what you want, right?"

"I guess," I said.

"You know I'm right about Stiles and Sanders."

Maybe I did.

"You know they're the worst."

They were.

"And they're not finished with this family. Or you."

Maybe they weren't.

I couldn't believe I was saying it even as the words were leaving my mouth. "Fine. What do we do?"

Naomi placed my LeSportsac on the bed next to me. "How long do you need?"

"Two minutes." Less. I wasn't even considering brushing my teeth or hair; I hadn't even packed a toothbrush or a comb.

"I'll be in the living room. Come the second you're ready."

"What are we going to do, though?" I asked, rummaging through the bag for my shorts, shaking it to find my eyeliner.

"There's a can of gasoline in Morgan's garage," Naomi said plainly. "I found it earlier while you were asleep."

No way. Too insane. And yet too totally sane.

Then she said, "Two minutes," and walked out the door.

I had everything on in one. Cutoffs, Nirvana shirt, Docs, eyeliner—the contents of my bag, minus one cardigan. I dressed with purpose. My hands were steady. If I wouldn't be scared tomorrow, then why be scared now? I did want those Spaders to burn. Couldn't deny that anymore.

Naomi was staring out a window at the pool in the backyard. Somewhere in that blue mass of water, a soggy promise letter might still be floating. James had come back. But not to fight. I'd do him one better then. I didn't need his strength during the day. During the day I could fight for him.

"I have to say good-bye to Morgan real quick."

"We'll be back in less than an hour. He won't even know we left."

"But what if he wakes up and we're gone?"

"Okay go, hurry." She shooed me off.

Down the hall I opened the door to Morgan's bedroom and slipped in. He was lying on his back, spread out like a starfish. So that's how he slept. Just like me. I perched at the foot of his bed and shook his ankle, then said his name once, twice, three times, until he opened his eyes.

"Are you okay?" he asked, confused.

"Yeah, no, I'm great," I said softly. "Naomi and I just woke up a little early. We're going to get doughnuts. Want one?" It was a bad lie. Now we'd have to burn down a guesthouse and then stop for breakfast.

"Uh"—his eyes were barely open, his voice barely there—"no thanks."

Lucky break.

"Okay, going now." I got off the bed.

"Hey." He sat up on his elbows. "Naomi's kind of hot."

"I told you."

"Did you?" He grinned, blinked his eyes, pretending not to remember.

"It's cool beans, Morgan," I said, threw up a peace sign, opened the door, and shut it behind me.

Naomi was already by the front door. She had a can of gasoline in one hand, only it wasn't really a can. It was more like a giant jug, and by the way it swung when she walked, I could tell it was heavy and full. It stank, too.

"Whoa," I said. "Are we going to burn down the whole neighborhood?"

"Whatever. There's a brush fire in the canyon, like, every week. It's fine."

Apparently Naomi and I were the new natural disaster.

"Okay, let me just say bye to Whit now." I started to walk to his room, but she grabbed my arm.

"No. He doesn't trust you. Leave him alone."

"I'll tell him we're getting bagels."

She stared at me like I was crazy. "Are you crazy?"

"Fine." *Bye, Whit*, I thought, as she yanked me

through the door, into the bright sunlight of a summer morning. *I'll buy you a milkshake if we make it through this.*

As we walked out toward the driveway, my eyes drifted across the lawn, the stupid antique wheelbarrow, the driveway, and it hit me: no car. Of course. James had taken it last night. I wanted to throw a rock through a window. Our plan aborted before it was even begun. It wasn't fair. I looked to Naomi.

"Calm down. We'll take that." She pointed to a sun-bleached white beach cruiser leaning against the side of the garage.

"I can't ride a bike."

"Just get on and hold this, okay?" She handed me the jug, wheeled the bike into the driveway, and swung a leg over the seat.

"Are you kidding?"

But she was not kidding. Not even a little. Not at all.

The ride felt longer than it actually was, longer than it would've felt even if you thought about how long it felt to ride a bicycle three miles in the sun, up the canyons, while sharing about two inches of a banana seat with someone who didn't like you very much.

But the roads were mainly empty, a light wind blew through my hair, and the stench of gasoline was making me high in a semi-psychedelic, chill way. Nothing seemed that dangerous in the sunshine. Nothing seemed ominous at eight thirty in the morning.

Then we were there, slowing to a stop, Naomi sticking out her legs to keep us balanced. I got off, and she wheeled the bike to some dense bushes in the front yard of the neighbor's house and stashed it there. I glanced up and down the street, scanning for movement. But no one was really around. One dad-looking guy a few houses down came out and picked up his *L.A. Times*, but that was it.

We stood at the top of the driveway, staring down toward the guesthouse. I noticed in the morning light that most of the grass and plants around the house were tan or brownish, scorched by the deep summer and no rain. Everything was dry. I wished the place were burning already. Everything looked flammable.

We took off at a brisk pace down the driveway. I held the jug. When we got about ten feet from the front door, Naomi pulled a crappy blue 7-Eleven cigarette lighter with a yin-yang on it from her pocket.

"You ready?" She sounded keyed up.

"Do we have to go inside? I don't want to," I whispered.

"Too bad." She squinted up at the roof. "We can't do real damage unless we're inside. But the wood on the roof looks old. It's gonna come right down."

It was time.

We crept up to the door and tried the doorknob. Locked. Naomi's eyes scanned: no welcome mat, no rocks, no plants, no porch furniture. Then she reached up and slid her hand along the top of the door frame until something shiny fell to the ground with a *ding*. Stupid, obvious, suburban Spaders.

Naomi turned the key and cracked the door an inch and peered inside, waiting for a second, then swung it open all the way, and we stepped quietly in. A bad wave of déjà vu flooded through me. The place was the same. Still. Silent. Strangely cold. The same thick, heavy curtains covered the windows, the same minimal furniture and generic decorations. No one with a soul lived here. Real people had real stuff. This was just some dark, empty crash pad for burnouts with nothing to live for. I felt myself getting pissed. It felt awesome.

I twisted the cap off the gasoline jug and poured a little on the couch cushions. It splashed out and soaked in.

"More," Naomi whispered.

So I tilted the jug at a steeper angle and liquid came gushing out, all over the couch and carpet. I walked around pouring more on the coffee table, the walls, the curtains. Naomi pointed to the ceiling, where two wood beams crossed with two others.

"How?" I asked.

She grabbed the jug from my hands and climbed up on the kitchen counter so she was higher, then started dousing the old wooden crossbeams. Gas was dripping from the ceiling now, making puddles on the kitchen floor, a weird gasoline rain. The fumes were thickening, the smell was overwhelming. I was huffing chemicals, staggering around, hallucinating. I felt like laughing. Screw these jerks. Screw their empty truce. I gave the thumbs-up to Naomi, who shot me back a loopy, drugged smile. She wobbled across the kitchen counter, draining the jug all over everything, the fridge, the stove, more chairs, until the flow dribbled to a stop. It was empty. She shook it dry, then tossed it in the middle of the floor and laughed out loud.

Then I heard my own voice: "Do it."

And I heard my own thought: *Burn it down.*

Naomi hopped off the counter onto the carpet, which was like a sponge now, soggy with gasoline, and we both stumbled toward the front door. The room reeked. I felt brain cells dying. I felt happy.

Then Naomi reached her lighter out toward the curtains and, with a flick of her thumb, sparked it.

Then we were outside, the fresh air in my lungs like a splash of cold water to the face. We slowly backed away, sobering up, watching the walls flame up, watching the curtains sizzle with pale blue fire. At first it was almost delicate the way the flames crawled and spread across the house, little tendrils of orange and yellow slipping through the paneling on the roof. Smoke began gently spewing into the sky.

I wondered how long we should wait before leaving. Until the entire house was roaring maybe? Longer? At some point soon, neighbors would notice, 911 would be dialed, fire trucks would arrive. I knew we needed to be gone by then. But Naomi was spellbound, engrossed in what we had created. What we were destroying. She never took her eyes off the fire, not even for a second. Not even to share a surreal high five, a humble victory dance, some small moment of bonding. She was rooted to the ground, her face lit up, drinking it in. It was sort of like we were watching *Jurassic Park* again, only way weirder and more illegal. I stared at her staring at the fire, trying to remind myself that it was really, truly over. Then Naomi's face went white, her eyes went wide, she said, "Oh my God," and stumbled back a few feet.

I turned toward the house and saw what she saw. Stiles. Standing in the living room. Looking like he always looked: shiny black hair, cold gray eyes, purplish lips. Seething with hate. His eyes pierced directly into mine, never blinking. Then he moved toward the window and reached his right hand out, pressing it against the glass, his five fingers a pentagram of pale skin. Stiles was dying again, and he knew it. He just stood there glaring at us, his face occasionally obscured by black plumes of smoke. Then he walked away, back into the house, out of sight.

I grabbed Naomi's hand, and she clasped fingers with me. We took another step back together. The fire roared.

Naomi's other hand was over her mouth. She made noises, not words.

"Did you see Sanders in there?" I asked, frantic.

"What?" Her face was still blank, her gaze still frozen on the spot where Stiles had stood, where his hand had left no mark on the glass.

"Sanders. Did you see him with Stiles?"

"What? I—I don't think so."

"Is he in there? He's in there, right?"

"Where else could he be? Of course he is." Naomi nodded. She kept nodding and nodding. "He's in there."

I was about to turn and drag Naomi down the driveway, but suddenly there was a loud banging sound. Stiles had slammed open the door and was standing in the doorway, smoke streaming out, staring at us. For once his clothes were actually messed up, dirty from the smoke and soot, and his hair was out of place, sticking up, not plastered and perfect. The mask was off. This was what he was. Mouth half-open, eyes lifeless and bitter, head slightly lowered like an angry animal. Just some predator.

The fire was raging all around him, but he didn't move. It was a duel without weapons. A silent showdown. We were only fifteen feet away, but the sun was out so he was stuck, stranded in the doorway, inferno on one side and sunshine on the other. We were burning. He was burning. And in the bedroom, still asleep or passed out or hopefully already dead, Sanders was burning too. He just had to be.

The smoke grew denser, billowing out into the California air, adding to the smog. The flames crackled and popped as they consumed the roof and the walls. A window somewhere shattered from the heat. Naomi squeezed my hand. And a single low guttural growl ripped through Stiles's mean teeth. He felt it for real. He was mortal again.

Then, strangely, he seemed to calm down. His lips curled into a small, knowing smile. It was the freakiest thing I'd ever seen. He held the expression for a minute and then turned and slammed the door.

Neither of us spoke. The whole house was dissolving in a web of red and orange and yellow flames, the sky darkening with huge clouds of choking smoke. This was the end.

"We should go," I said.

Naomi pulled her hand from mine and slipped it into the pocket of her sunflower print dress. "Yeah."

It was hard to take our eyes off the blaze, but finally we did. We walked side by side up the driveway toward the street, saying nothing.

Then out of nowhere Naomi said, "I know what James would've given up. I mean, I could guess."

"What?"

"His spot at the school."

Then James could stay. He wouldn't have to go back east.

Naomi looked at me out of the corner of her eye, and my face must've looked too blissed, too blessed. "Now he doesn't have to give it up, though. That place is the best thing for him, for all of us."

Maybe.

"Have you ever thought about the future?" Naomi asked.

James. Whit. James. "Sure."

"Like how this will all end for you?"

"What do you mean?"

She caught my eyes. "Are you going to become one too?"

"I hadn't really thought about it." It was sort of true. I sort of hadn't.

"Better start," she said.

"Yeah."

Naomi was done here. The gasoline was gone. The

lighter was in her pocket. She was walking away from it all, at the end of the driveway, already climbing on the bike, ready to go home.

But I wasn't quite ready yet. I wasn't bored with this yet. Whatever. Okay.

ACKNOWLEDGMENTS

For their editorial insights, professional support, and superb guidance, thanks to Ann Behar and Tara Weikum. For inspiration, motivation, and the endlessly useful phrase "rookie mistakes," thanks to Jennifer Cacicio. For believing in me since literally day one, thanks to my mother. And, lastly, I'm grateful to my best friend and beyond, Benjamin Shearn, without whom the film of this book would not already be cast.

JOIN
THE COMMUNITY AT

Epic Reads
Your World. Your Books.

FIND
the latest
books

DISCUSS
what's on
your reading
wish list

CREATE
your own book
news and
activities to share
with friends

ACCESS
exclusive
contests and
videos

Don't miss out on any upcoming EPIC READS!

Visit the site and browse the categories to find out more.

www.epicreads.com

HARPER TEEN
An Imprint of HarperCollinsPublishers